# NOTHING HAPPENS BY CHANCE

## VANESSA LAFLEUR

North Carolina

Published in the United States by BQB Publishing
(an imprint of Boutique of Quality Books Publishing, Inc.)
www.bqbpublishing.com

979-8-88633-011-3 (p)
979-8-88633-012-0 (e)

Library of Congress Control Number: 2023941839

Book design by Robin Krauss, www.bookformatters.com
Cover design by Rebecca Lown, www.rebeccalowndesigns.com

First editor: Andrea Vande Vorde
Second editor: Allison Itterly

For my dad, who taught me to love stories and write for fun.

PART 1

# LIFE AWAY FROM HOME

# CHAPTER 1

# ROCHELLE

*March 28, 2091*

F eet sliding over a thick mat of damp leaves, I raced down a narrow trail surrounded by bare trees. Glancing over my shoulder, I expected to see at least two people catching up, but I was alone in a world of silent gray mist. To my left, the abandoned hospital building appeared in a clearing. Evie said that it had once been a place of comfort for patients with terminal illnesses, but it closed fifty years ago due to financial problems. Everyone at the Advanced Education Institute said it was haunted, but it didn't look scary to me. Just lonely and lost in the woods.

Slowing to a jog, I pressed my hand to the left side of my head. "Max? Any advice?"

The little speaker I clipped over my ear to communicate with Max during our practice missions had been the subject of my most recent letter to Todd. Todd wasn't surprised Max and I could communicate effectively—all three of us had been best friends since kindergarten—but he did think it was a bad idea to put Max's crazy ideas in my head, to make every moment an adventure. He decided not to warn the TCI though. According to Todd, if the Threat Collection Initiative found out what trouble Max and I could cause, they would send us home for sure. Despite writing to Todd every day, I missed hearing his voice and the comfort of holding his hand.

"You're almost to your retrieval point and way ahead of everyone else according to their coordinates," Max said, his voice echoing in my ear. I imagined him sitting at his computer, watching twelve dots slide across the screen. "Stay on course, and if you're willing to take a detour, we'll get an A for sure."

"I'm in." I glanced down at my khaki uniform pants, already splattered with mud. Although Max's detours were always messy, he knew what he was talking about, and my aunt Audrie and her work partner, Sid Dotson, were proud of us every time we succeeded at our skills training test. They led our skills training every afternoon.

"Take a left in three, two, now."

Following Max's directions, I veered off the trail and picked up speed despite the slick leaves beneath my running shoes. Eleven of my classmates had left from the same starting point, taking directions from a partner to retrieve their colored ribbon and return to the starting point as quickly as possible. It was a test of endurance, communication, and cooperation.

"There's a clearing ahead. Two of the others are close to their retrieval points, but you'll get to ours first." Max's voice kept me focused as I plunged forward, ignoring the icy burn of late-winter air in my lungs. The trees gave way to the gray sky above, and I spotted my green ribbon hanging overhead at the end of a sturdy branch.

I couldn't jump high enough to reach the branch because the trunk was too thick to shimmy up, and there were no lower branches to boost myself up.

"Why did you stop?" Max's voice startled me.

"I can't reach it."

"There's no problem we can't solve." Max's confidence had become an unstoppable force. "What do you have that you can use?"

"I have an idea." Pulling off my jacket, I swung one sleeve over the branch and caught the other one as it came over the side. Gripping the sleeves, I pulled myself up, wrapped my legs around the branch, then my arms, and grabbed the ribbon.

"Got it!" I dropped from the tree, pulled on my jacket, and dashed back into the blur of trees.

"You're more than halfway through the mission now," Max encouraged. "Stay on course until you see a culvert. Climbing the hill to the road will add at least a minute to your time, so I recommend going under it."

"Is an extra minute really going to kill us?" My eyes watered from the cold wind, but I could still see the thick slush in the ditch ahead. "Didn't you say we're ahead of the others?"

"Forget about the others. We're in a race with ourselves, and we're about to beat our record time."

"Fine. But you owe me." I shoved the ribbon into my pocket, then dropped to the ground and used my elbows to propel myself forward through the drainage tunnel. Seconds of icy misery brought me to the other side. Recognizing the gravel road that would lead me back to my starting point, I sprinted for the finish line.

"Almost there," Max cheered. "A few more feet. You're doing great."

Through the hazy mist, I could make out the shape of the picnic shelter, scattered with tables where Max and our classmates sat in front of computers, guiding their partners through the mission we'd been assigned. I raised the ribbon into the air and jogged between a trash can and folding chair, our makeshift finish line.

Max scrambled to his feet, hands in the air, and ran toward me, abandoning the laptop in front of him. "That was amazing. You beat our old time by a minute and nine seconds. Rochelle Aumont and Max Delgado. The best future spies the TCI has ever trained."

I pressed my hands to the top of my head, elbows pointed out, and took deep gulps of cold air. The unrelenting winter wind sliced through my wet clothes, and I shivered.

"Great work, guys." Audrie jogged over from the shelter where the others were still focused on their task. "You two are officially the most successful partnership I've ever coached."

"We've had years of practice." Max flung his arm around me, and I was grateful for the warmth that radiated from him. "The neat gadgets are helpful too."

Audrie smiled. "If I remember correctly, I owe you a happy birthday, Rochelle. We'll celebrate this weekend when you come to stay with me." My aunt sometimes took me off campus to stay with her for the weekend.

I looked at Max. Even though he'd made more friends here than I had, I still felt bad about leaving him all weekend again.

"Don't worry about me, Rochelle." Max gave a thumbs-up to some of his friends who were just crossing the finish line. "Just bring me a cupcake or three."

Audrie laughed. "After church on Sunday, the three of us will go out for brunch and stop at my favorite bakery. You guys can pick out whatever you want."

Max grinned. "Sounds good to me."

"Nice job, guys," Audrie shouted over her shoulder as a pack of teenagers carrying an assortment of colored ribbons jogged across the finish line, panting and coughing. "Get a drink, and we'll critique your performances inside." She turned back to us. "You two are dismissed for the day. I have no critiques. Good luck with the rest of your midterms." She smiled as she headed back toward the picnic shelter.

Some of the others gave Max and me dirty looks as they passed us to get to their water bottles. Most of them didn't like us because they thought we got special treatment. They weren't wrong.

While all the other kids had to pass rigorous tests to get into the Advanced Education Institute, Audrie had pulled some strings to get us admitted.

"Let's get out of here." Max slung his bag over one shoulder and mine over the other, and then we fell into step together as we made our way across campus to the dormitories.

It was hard to believe we'd already been at the AEI for three months. While we were only juniors in high school, the advanced classes made it feel more like college. We stopped at the big mailbox in front of the library. I pulled out my daily letter to Todd from my bookbag and dropped it into the slot, listening to it flutter against the other mail inside.

"Don't you ever run out of things to write to him?" Max readjusted the bags. "I can barely come up with enough to tell my family during my Sunday phone call. All we do here is study."

"I tell him about what we're learning in class, what we eat for lunch, what all of the buildings look like." I shrugged. "He doesn't think it's boring."

I felt bad for writing to Todd every day and my cousin, Kinley, only twice a week, but I always saved my Sunday phone call for her. I worried about Kinley being alone in Maibe, and hearing her voice always made me feel better. Todd gave me updates on what he heard from his sister Emma, Kinley's best friend. From Todd's letters, I concluded that Kinley was working too much.

"Three months ago, I thought spy school would be all about going on undercover missions. You know, exciting stuff," Max said as we continued down the sidewalk. "But I guess this isn't so bad."

"I've already failed my mission." I lowered my voice despite the deserted sidewalks. "Even with Audrie's help, I haven't been able to figure out the passcodes."

My aunt's main reason for bringing me to New York was to find the three words my dad had chosen to use as passcodes to access important research. Sometimes I wondered how things would have turned out if my dad had never gotten mixed up in his best friend's scientific experiment. Eric Bennett and the five other scientists had been conducting research to create a vaccine that would protect the world against all viruses, but in the process discovered a way to increase the severity of common viruses. If they all had known how to handle the research, maybe none of us would have been involved in this pendant business and maybe my dad would still be alive.

"I don't know why they're so worried about the passcodes anyway," Max said. "The passcodes don't even matter until the TCI has all eight pendants to make the key. No one even knows where the research is yet. Right?"

"Probably. I'm just tired of Molly always being one step ahead of everyone. And it's even worse now that she's with the Defiance." My stomach twisted into a knot. Molly Bennett. Last year, our friendship changed forever when she told me about our dads' involvement with the pendants. I'd refused to join the Defiance with her, and now she was hurting my friends and family to get to me.

"The TCI won't let the Defiance win the race to the research." Max turned to me and winked. "Plus, Keppler is probably sabotaging the Defiance from the inside right now."

My thoughts drifted to our friend. At first we were frustrated that he didn't tell us about signing an agreement with Audrie to go back to the Defiance working undercover. But there were bigger things to worry about. I wanted to believe he could handle himself with the ruthless gang that was waging war across the country. He wasn't like them, and I didn't know how long he could pretend.

"I just hope he's safe," I said. "I'm sure he has everything under control." Max laughed. "He probably misses us so much he'll let us call him by his first name when he gets out of the Defiance again."

"I don't know." I laughed. "It would be weird to call him Charlie. It would be weird if he called me Rochelle instead of Aumont."

"That's what's happening in another dimension right now." Max raised his eyebrows and twisted his mouth into an expression of awe that made me laugh.

We reached my building. I stopped right inside the door and unlocked my mail compartment. I pulled out a manilla envelope from Todd, a regular envelope from Kinley, and another from Emma and Todd's other sister, Lily. My hand reached all the way to the back of the little square space, but it was empty.

"Still nothing from Kat? Even on your birthday?" Max handed me my bag. "That's pretty rotten of her. Just wait until the next time I see her."

"I guess she's still mad." I looked at the letters in my hand. "I'll just keep writing to her until she forgives me." I'd promised my sister I would never go with Audrie. Now I was in New York and Kat was in Omaha, and our family had been torn apart. It had all gotten out of my control.

"You shouldn't be worrying about any of this on your birthday." Max grinned. "If the dining hall doesn't have tomato soup and grilled cheese sandwiches, I have a toaster and a hot plate in my room."

I smiled and shook my head. "You know you're not allowed to have either of those things."

Max looped his arm through mine and guided me down the hallway toward the stairwell. "None of it is mine. My former roommates left it behind, so I can't throw it away." He'd had three roommates in the last three months. Two of them couldn't take the pressure and quit, and one got kicked out for not following the rules. "After that, I can sneak off campus and get us some ice cream."

"We can't leave," I yanked Max to a stop. "They can track your phone." Our flip phones issued to us by the TCI were only used to contact our teachers and classmates on campus. They also used our devices to track us and make sure we didn't leave when we weren't supposed to.

"They can't track mine." Max laughed. "They brought me here because I know how to make trackers, and they don't think I can disable their tracking on my phone? This is spy school. They expect us to do things like that."

I sighed. "All I want for my birthday is to hang out like we used to." Aside from our morning three-mile run and our history class, I barely saw Max. He was usually playing Ping-Pong with his friends from Sid's workshop. "I could really use some help with my precalculus homework. Can't we just get something to eat and then go to the library?"

"It's your birthday." Max shrugged. "If you want to study, I'll help you."

"Thank you." I swung my bag over my shoulder. "But first I need to shower. I'll call you when I'm ready."

"Are you sure you don't want me to walk you all the way?" He shoved his hands into his pockets. "Your bag is pretty heavy."

"I'll be fine." I sighed. "And I'm sure Evie is still in class." My roommate was the only person I'd ever met who was as smart as Max, and they had most of their classes together.

He blushed and looked down at his shoes. "Right. Maybe you should invite her to study with us later. You know, because it's the polite thing to do. And she's so smart and pretty."

"I'll ask her." I patted Max's shoulder.

"Great." Max forced a smile. "I'll see you later."

We parted ways at the end of the hall, with Max turning back to the front entrance and me ascending the stairs to the third floor. The locked door indicated, as I had expected, that Evie hadn't returned from her midterm yet. She was a great roommate and the only friend I'd made since Audrie moved me to New York, but I was thankful for a few minutes alone.

Inside, I removed my muddy shoes at the door and tossed my mail onto the desk by the window before peeling off my filthy windbreaker. I threw it in the bathroom hamper along with my wet and dirty clothes, took a quick shower, and dressed in my warmest pair of sweatpants and my favorite sweatshirt from home. I unzipped the front pocket of my bookbag and pulled out the hummingbird charm bracelet I'd placed there before skills class. It was the last gift my dad had ever given me. It brought me the comfort I needed while living away from home. It had been almost two years since he died.

I fastened the bracelet around my left wrist, sat down at my desk, and opened my mail.

The first card was from Todd's sisters, Emma and Lily. They wished me a happy birthday, told me they missed me, and said they always looked forward to my letters. Kinley's card said she couldn't believe I had turned seventeen, that she missed me more than she could explain in writing, and she would buy me any present I wanted when I came home. She was really busy with her classes and had taken on extra hours working at the hospital.

Todd wrote a long letter about the snowfall in Maibe, working with his dad, his college calculus and drawing classes, and his excitement for spring weather. He'd sent me a sketch of my house surrounded by snowy scenery, and a necklace with a green gem on a gold chain.

Taking a deep breath to fight back a wave of homesickness, I walked to the mirror and clipped the necklace around my neck. It sparkled in the light, the same shade of green as my eyes. The same

color as my dad's, and Kinley's, and Audrie's. My brown hair, still
wet, hung over my shoulders. It was longer than I usually wore it,
but I didn't have time for a haircut. The baggy clothes I'd chosen
hid my slender figure, which was a family trait as strong as the
green eyes. For a moment, I was overcome with a surreal disbelief
that I could look so much like myself so far away from the people
and the place that made me who I was. As much as I wanted to
believe life at the AEI was an adventure and the key to my future,
I missed Todd, I missed my family, and I wanted to go home.

# CHAPTER 2
# CHARLIE

*March 30, 2091*

T he sidewalks between the Defiance building and my usual coffee shop bustled with people on their way to work. I walked carefully over the slushy sidewalks, pulling my hood up against the giant snowflakes that melted as they fell. It was just before eight in the morning and everyone was in a hurry, but when they saw the black *D* on the sleeve of my gray jacket, they slowed down and stepped aside to avoid brushing shoulders with me. Griff Spencer considered it an act of respect, but I knew they feared the consequences of catching one of us in a bad mood.

I didn't like having the *D* branded on my arm. After all, it almost got me reported to the authorities. Instead Audrie made me sign the agreement to work undercover. At least now that I was on the inside, I could make sure the Defiance stayed away from Rochelle, Kat, and Kinley.

I crossed the street and darted under the awning of the nearest coffee shop. The bell on the door dinged as I entered the warmth of the little room. Customers occupied every one of the few tables inside. They diverted their eyes but watched me through their peripheral vision. I pretended not to notice.

For a second, I closed my eyes and let the comfort of warmth and aroma of coffee carry me back to the Aumonts' kitchen. Usually, I tried to push Maibe out of my mind, but sometimes, on a bad day, I let myself remember home for just a minute. Although

Kansas City was only three hours away from Maibe, Nebraska, I might as well have been on another planet. But if I ever went back, it wouldn't be the same. After the Aumonts saw me working with Molly three months ago, they probably thought I was a traitor.

I stepped up to the counter and showed the barista the *D* on my jacket. It was how members of the Defiance got out of paying.

"What can I get for you, Mr. Keppler?" asked Bridget, the girl with long blonde hair who always took my order.

"The usual times two."

Every morning, I ordered a large coffee and a doughnut. But it was Friday, the day of our weekly strategy planning meetings, so I ordered the same for Griff. He wasn't good with mornings.

"Here you go, Mr. Keppler." Bridget slid my order across the counter. "Have a good day."

"Thank you." I picked up the coffee tray and made my way to the door.

The customers watched me with the usual mix of fear and curiosity. They knew that as long as they didn't break the rules, they were safe. They weren't affected by the rationing of food or shortages of medical supplies like everyone outside Defiance territory. It had been like this since January, when the war began. Ten years ago, no one would have predicted a disgruntled group of teenagers could wage a war against the country, and succeed. The treatment of orphaned and abandoned children had already been a problem, but the fever had made it worse. It killed half of the adult population, and it was still ongoing. Now the streets were full of orphaned and abandoned kids.

Hurrying back through the slushy rain, I entered the main Defiance building and jogged down the hall to Griff's office. The door was open and, to my surprise, he was sitting at his desk. He had showered and changed, but he sat with his eyes closed and forehead in his hand.

I cleared my throat as I entered, and he slowly lifted his face. "And I thought I'd have to drag you out of bed." I placed breakfast on his desk and pulled up a chair.

"I'm surprised I woke up in my bed." Squinting, he picked up his coffee and took a sip.

"You're lucky I came looking for you," I said. "Otherwise, you would have woken up in an alley with frostbite. Maybe you should cut back on the drinking for a while."

Despite everything, I still felt loyal to Griff. We were practically brothers. After all, he'd been the only one who helped me when I was just a kid trying to survive the streets. He promised the Defiance would create a brighter future for the generation of children the world had left behind. At least, that's what I told myself, and potential recruits who read my newsletters. It was easier to believe the civilians of our territories were grateful for our presence than to see myself as one of the monsters taking their freedom.

"Come on, Charlie," Griff said. "We deserve to have some fun. This is a high-pressure job." He slammed his coffee down on the desk. "Lighten up. You even spent your birthday alone in a room, typing."

"I'm trying to help people. Quality newsletters mean kids like us know they have options."

I held the warm coffee in my hands. "You know I don't drink, and I don't care about my birthday."

"It's never too late to start." He took a bite of his doughnut. "Having a little fun isn't going to turn you into your dad."

"I'm sure he never thought a little fun would turn him into an abusive alcoholic either."

I stood and caught a glimpse of my reflection in the glass of Griff's display case. My dark hair was long enough to curl over my ears and cover half my forehead. My Defiance jacket hung from my shoulders since they weren't broad enough to fill it out. Despite my glasses, I still looked more like my dad than I wanted to, but his weaknesses would never be mine.

"Plus one of us has to be coherent enough to keep things running and keep you from freezing to death because you couldn't make it home," I added. "Isn't that why you brought me back here?"

"I brought you back here because I missed my brother, and you leaving was a mistake in the first place," Griff said.

I winced at the memory. Before I found safety with the Aumonts, I'd taken one of Griff's pendants. He caught me and beat me for it. "A mistake?" I said. "You would have killed me if I hadn't gotten away."

"We've talked about this. When I found the pendant in your room last year, I jumped to unfair conclusions." Griff said. "I should have known right away someone had framed you. That's why I came looking for you. To bring you home. You're the only guy in the Defiance I consider family."

I walked to the window and watched snowflakes melt on the glass. *Family.* I hadn't known anything about family until I arrived in Maibe. Even though I was a stranger, Kinley treated my injuries the night she met me. A few weeks later, Kinley and her boyfriend, Alexander, cosigned guardianship papers so I wouldn't be sent to a home for children. They were only nineteen. Even while Alexander was struggling as the youngest mayor of the town and Kinley was trying to raise Rochelle and Kat, they still found time for me. The year I lived in Maibe was the first time in sixteen years people actually cared about me.

"Charlie, I mean it." Griff shoved his breakfast aside. "You're my right-hand guy. The only person I can trust completely."

I turned away from the window. "What's Molly then?"

"Molly's my girlfriend. You're my brother. There's a difference." He leaned back in his chair and closed his eyes. "Now give me a minute to pull myself together before the meeting. Since you're here early, you can get everything ready."

"Whatever." At least it would give me something to do. It was easier to stay busy than to sit around and think about what I was doing, and what the Aumonts would think about it.

After finishing my breakfast, I set up for the meeting by laying out our maps on the card tables in the corner that served as our conference area. I found the copies of the minutes I'd typed from last week's meeting strewn on Griff's file cabinet and placed one in front of each seat at the table.

"Griff, do you have Charlie doing your work for you again?" Molly's heels clicked across the floor. "I thought you were going to get things ready last night."

He lifted his head and ran a hand over his hair. "Something came up."

"I see." Molly strode over to the table and took her usual seat.

"What is that supposed to mean?" Griff stood and shielded his eyes from the sun streaming through the blinds.

"First of all, you look awful." She folded her hands on the table. "If you insist on living your life this way, you should at least give me a little more power to make decisions. In case you weren't here in an emergency. You trust me, don't you?"

"Of course I trust you." He smiled. "You look especially pretty today. Is that a new dress?"

Ignoring them, I pulled the notepad and pen from the inside pocket of my jacket. As always, Griff would sidestep Molly's prompting to give her more power by complimenting her. Molly would roll her eyes and complain that he didn't treat her like a true partner.

The first of Griff's regional representatives showed up and, predictably, Molly and Griff stopped arguing. Once all five representatives had arrived, I listened to reports of our successes in pushing our borders deeper into the southeast, and north into the Midwest. I provided a synopsis of the information in my most recent newsletter, as well as my plans for upcoming issues.

I took notes just like I used to do at the town council meetings in Maibe. Working for Griff was different from working with Alexander. While they both wanted to make the world better, Griff believed true change couldn't come in a peaceful way whereas Alexander envisioned change through cooperation. I wanted Alexander to be right, but I couldn't deny that we street kids would never have a place in the world if we didn't make it our own.

After an hour, the representatives left one by one until only Griff, Molly, and I remained.

Griff surveyed the dots we'd stuck to the maps. "Can you believe it, Charlie? We have control of Louisiana, Mississippi, Arkansas, Tennessee, and Kentucky. The states around them are going to fall like dominoes in a matter of weeks, and once we cut off the east from the west and fully disrupt the supply chain, all the rest will fold. Even a year ago it never seemed possible. I should have had you writing your newsletters from the start."

I nodded. All I'd ever wanted was for my writing to be recognized, but the thought that it was fueling a war kept me up at night.

Griff clapped my shoulder. "Now that the truth precedes us, we'll win this war by the end of the year."

"We could win it sooner if we could just find the rest of the pendants and get that research." Molly sighed and shook her head. "That's our guarantee. Not Charlie's writing."

"I'm working on that." Griff walked to his desk. "I have some leads on the whereabouts of Brandon Davis."

Brandon Davis was the only scientist on the research team who was still alive. That meant he was Griff's best hope for getting his hands on another pendant. Each pendant was printed with a different word: *Spero. Optimus. Instruo. Pessimus. Tomorrow. Will. Be. Better.* The pendants had been divided among the six scientists, plus Rochelle's dad, although it wasn't clear which pendant belonged to which person.

"You're not working fast enough," Molly snapped. "I only brought you my dad's pendant because we agreed on what we should use them for."

Griff nodded. "Use them to unlock the research, develop a vaccine for anyone on our side, and unleash a super virus on everyone else. That's still the plan, but we only have four of the pendants."

Molly glared at Griff. "Then do something about it."

"I will. I will. Once my leads come together, Charlie and I will take a road trip to follow up," Griff continued. "With any luck, we'll have some good news on the pendant front soon."

"Until then, I have my own leads to follow up on." Molly stood and flipped her long blonde hair over her shoulder. I knew she had learned Rochelle wasn't in Maibe anymore and wanted to find out where she went. I pretended to know nothing about the Aumonts, which wasn't far from the truth. "I'll see you guys for lunch."

Griff confirmed our lunch plans with Molly while I rolled the maps and slid them into cardboard tubes.

"Let's go to the gym," he suggested after Molly left. "I need to get out of this place. Get my mind off this war."

"Last year I couldn't get you to stop working." I turned to Griff. "Now an hour a day is too much. What's going on with you?" Part of me hoped the war and senseless loss of life was getting to him. I wanted him to show me he was human for just a minute.

He rubbed his hands over his face and looked at me as if he were a little boy lost in the park. "What if I can't find the rest of the pendants? What if I never get the research?"

If I accomplished my mission, that was exactly what would happen. "What do you need it for? The Defiance is taking over the country without any of that anyway."

"For now, kid. For now, everyone is so desperate for a change they'll listen to my promises of hope. Everyone is so afraid of the unknown, so they fear the Defiance. But the day will come when I'll have to make good on that promise of hope, and I'll have to keep raising the bar to scare those who oppose us. I need the research, a vaccine for our followers, and a virus for our enemies."

I walked over to him. "You created the Defiance before you knew anything about the pendants. The only promise of hope any of us ever needed was to have a family. And the only thing we need to be afraid of is what the world will do to us if we don't have one." I'd been writing plenty of terrifying stories about the street kids' experiences that made me question how I'd survived before Griff pulled me into the Defiance.

"That's not how it works in the history books." He shook his head. "Just when a guy has everything going for him, it all turns the other way."

"History books?" I sat down across from his desk. "Since when do you read history books?"

He shrugged. "Molly says we don't live long enough to learn from our own lives, so the only way to succeed is to learn from the past."

I didn't want to encourage Griff, but I also couldn't stand to see Molly succeed at manipulating him. Before she showed up, he had been the one assuring me that he had a solution for every problem. But after three months with Molly, he was second-guessing everything he'd ever done.

"What does Molly know? She's been here a few months. We've been here since the beginning, and we're accomplishing your goal. Thousands of kids are joining us every week."

"What would I do without you?" Griff punched my arm so hard it hurt. "Go get ready for the gym. One of these days, you'll get some muscle on you."

I left the room, remembering my initial warning to Griff about Molly. *She'll stab you in the back.* He couldn't see her manipulation, but I could. What I didn't know was exactly what she planned to accomplish.

# CHAPTER 3

# ROCHELLE

*March 30, 2091*

"They could keep it down over there." Evie slid her physics book closer to herself. "Everyone knows you're supposed to be quiet in a library."

"Who?" I looked up from the equation I'd been staring at, realized I'd been fidgeting with my new necklace, and let it fall against my sweater. My mind had been flitting between missing home and the birthday weekend I would spend with Audrie. She was coming to pick me up as soon as she finished her meeting in the administration building.

Evie pointed over the half-height bookshelves to the line of tables on the other side of the big room where Max and his friends laughed and tossed a baseball from one end of the table to the other. She shook her bangs out of her eyes and pulled her long black hair into a ponytail. "What makes them think they can do whatever they want?"

Thunder rumbled outside and rain pelted the row of windows near our table. The weather had driven more people than usual to our quiet study space.

"I can go tell Max to keep it down." The last thing I needed was for him to get into trouble. I didn't want him to be sent to the reform school. But Max was Max.

"Don't bother," Evie sighed. "He shouldn't be your responsibility."

Evie had been the top student at the AEI until we arrived. Now Max was her competition for the top spot. When she talked about him, she used words like "annoying," "self-absorbed," "show-off," and "overconfident." Although I didn't like the way he acted around his new friends, I wished she could see the Max I knew. He was the only thing that made living away from home bearable.

"Why can't he just study like the rest of us?" Evie laid her book flat on the table, her usually wide brown eyes narrowing in frustration.

I slid my notebook aside. "I've known Max most of my life, and I've never seen him study for anything."

"Right. Because he's a genius." Evie rolled her eyes. "That's why he's six months away from discovering the secret to time travel." She stood and smoothed her orange hoodie. "I'll handle this."

I watched her weave through the bookcases toward Max when Henry Davis slid into the seat she had just left.

"Hey, Rochelle. Do you want to hang out this weekend?" He patted his perfectly gelled blond hair and flashed a smile that lit up his blue-green eyes. Henry was the most popular guy at the AEI, and most of the girls had a crush on him. His insistence on paying attention to me wasn't helping me make friends with them.

My hand automatically reached for my necklace. "I can't. I'm visiting my aunt." At least I didn't have to make up an excuse.

"You're always visiting your aunt." He folded his arms on the table and leaned toward me. "We should get to know each other. We already have a lot in common."

"You mean the pendants? The one thing we were told not to talk about." I sat back in my chair. Henry's dad, Brandon Davis, was one of the scientists involved with the research. He had made a deal to turn over his pendant to the TCI in exchange for his son's safety. So, Henry used the fact that we were both "pendant kids" to make conversation with me.

"We're not supposed to talk about them with the others," Henry whispered. "It's okay for us to talk about them with each other."

A baseball bounced on the table between us and rolled off the other side.

"Is he bothering you?" Max appeared next to me and didn't wait for me to answer. "Henry, how many times do I have to tell you that Rochelle has a boyfriend at home?"

I looked down at my notes to avoid Henry's eyes. Max knew Todd and I still weren't official.

"I'll bet she does." Henry stood and faced Max. He towered over my friend by a head. "Just like you have a brother in the Defiance."

Max laughed. "It's true."

It wasn't true. While we both thought of Keppler like a brother, neither of us were actually related to him. "Max, that's enough."

Ignoring me, Max stood up straight and puffed out his chest. At just over five foot six and 120 pounds, Max wasn't any bigger than me and didn't look even slightly intimidating. "He taught me how to fight and everything."

"I threaten to personally disprove all of your physics theories if you keep distracting me, so you decide to move closer to my table?" Evie said as she approached us.

Henry looked from Evie to Max to me and shook his head. "Enough of this. See you around, Rochelle."

Max opened his mouth to say something, but I caught his hand and pulled him into the chair next to me. "What are you doing?"

"Protecting you. That guy's a bully." Max started to stand, but I held him in place until Henry was out of sight.

"I can handle him. What's all that about Keppler teaching you to fight?"

The excitement drained from Max's face. "Knowing someone

in the Defiance gives me the credibility I need so Henry will think twice about starting a fight with me."

"There's no reason for you to fight anyone here." I gripped his shoulders. "You're here because you got in trouble for building trackers. What do you think will happen if you get in trouble here?"

"You're right. I'm sorry." He looked down at my notebook. "I remember teaching myself this stuff in middle school."

"Can you help me solve this one?" Grateful for the opportunity to focus his energy on something productive, I pointed to the first equation.

"Yeah. Easy." He picked up my pencil. "You just have to move this over here and subtract to get this to the other side . . ."

"Don't show her the hard way." Evie stood behind us, baseball in one hand. She snatched the pencil from Max and scrawled a bunch of numbers and letters under the equation. "See. Much easier."

"Or . . ." Max took the pencil and added two lines next to hers. "The way that most closely matches the way Rochelle's brain processes numbers."

As I looked at the solution in my notebook, I wondered whether my brain was capable of processing numbers at all. "Thanks, guys. Can you help me with another one, but this time take it step by step?"

Max glanced out the window. "I would, but Audrie just walked into the building." He looked up at the clock. "And we have workshop with Sid in ten minutes. Do you want to walk with me, Evie? I have an umbrella."

"Fine." She smiled. "You carry my bag and I'll carry the umbrella."

"Deal. I'll be right back." Max stood halfway before I pulled him down again.

"Promise you'll stay out of trouble?" I wrapped one arm around him.

He hugged me back. "I promise. I'll see you on Sunday." He slid away from me and darted across the room for his umbrella.

"Don't worry. I'll make sure he gets to workshop without any incidents." Evie closed her books and slid them into her bag. "He'll spend all day tomorrow working on his 3D printing thing with Sid anyway."

I nodded. His mind would be busy with developing new TCI gadgets, so that would keep him out of trouble. Plus, he was always on his best behavior around Sid, who was practically his idol. Before we could say anything else, Audrie walked up to our table, wearing high-heeled boots despite the deluge outside, heavy bag slung over her shoulder, umbrella dripping on the floor. My aunt was thin, but she wore the right clothes to look fashionable. Her brown hair, a little wet from the rain, brushed the top of her coat, but her green eyes sparkled when she smiled.

"Hey, guys. Are you studying on a Friday night?"

"Hi, Agent Aumont." Evie handed her bag to Max, who had reappeared at her side and held out her hand for the umbrella. "We're here to learn. It would be irresponsible to waste time."

"Who needs to study what they already know?" Max surrendered his folded umbrella.

"We have to get to workshop." Evie poked him with the umbrella until he started moving. "See you Sunday, Rochelle."

Audrie watched them walk away, eyebrows raised. "Are you ready to go?"

"Yeah." I grabbed my bag that was hanging over the back of my chair and shoved my notebook inside. "Do you know anything about precalculus?"

"I might remember a little if you show me your notes," Audrie said. "My car is on the other side of campus. We'll have to make a run for it."

"That's okay." I slung my bag over my shoulder and fell into step with Audrie as we made our way to the front doors of the library.

Outside the door, under the overhang, Audrie opened her umbrella. "Ready?"

We each put one hand on the umbrella's handle and rushed across campus, feet sloshing through puddles, drenching rain pelting our faces. When we reached the parking lot, we made a dash for her car, dove inside, and pulled the doors shut, laughing from the rush and relief.

"I thought for your birthday we could go shopping for new clothes and try that fancy restaurant for dinner." Audrie placed her bag and umbrella on the floor of the back seat. "Then we can buy a bunch of snacks and stay up late watching movies."

"Sounds great." I brushed my damp hair behind my ears and imagined how ecstatic Kat would be if given the same opportunity.

Rain thundered on the hood of the car, and Audrie let her hand drop instead of starting the engine. "We can do something else if you want. It's your birthday."

"It's not that. It's just . . . Kat always begged Kinley to take us to fancy restaurants in Omaha so she could plan what her future restaurant would look like." I turned to my aunt, already regretting my gloomy reaction to her plans.

Audrie sighed. "You still haven't heard from her?"

I shook my head. "She said if I left, she would never speak to me again, and I guess she meant it."

"Don't worry, Rochelle. Siblings fight. It's normal. I fought with my brothers all the time." Audrie was the youngest of the three, and she was lucky to have my dad and Kinley's dad as older brothers. "One time when I was still in high school and your dad was in college, we got into an argument over Christmas break. Auggie went back to college, and we didn't speak again for months."

I slumped in my seat. "What were you arguing about?"

Audrie started the car. "I wanted him to cover for me while I went out with friends, but he wouldn't do it. He hated lying to our parents."

"And he wouldn't speak to you at all?" It was hard to imagine my easygoing dad holding a grudge against anyone.

"Actually, I wouldn't speak to him." Audrie flipped on the windshield wipers. "I was Kat and he was you in this story."

"So, what changed your mind? Why did you start talking to him again?"

My aunt made a face but didn't look at me. "I snuck out and went to a party in another town with friends. It didn't take long for things to get out of hand, but when I wanted to get out of there, my friends didn't want to leave. So, I walked to the nearest convenience store and called Auggie. He drove from college to get me, snuck me back into the house, and told our parents he was there for a surprise weekend visit."

"That'll never work for me," I said. "I'm the only one who sneaks out, but never to go to parties," I added after a stern look from my aunt. "I only snuck out when I wanted to run for town council, and sometimes to talk to Todd on the roof."

"And to meet up with Molly," my aunt added. It was still a touchy subject we didn't discuss often. She was still angry that Kinley and I went to rescue Kat from Molly without telling her. Three months ago, the day before we left for New York, Audrie had forced Kinley to surrender her guardianship.

"I had to save my sister." I sat up to face Audrie. "Just like Dad came to save you."

"What you did was far more dangerous, and you know it." She shook her head. "I had a plan in place so you would have time to say goodbye to Kat and Kinley, but you ran right into danger without talking to me. I had to get you out of there before Molly and her Defiance henchmen showed up again and hurt you, Kat, or Kinley."

"Nothing bad would have happened if I'd spent one more day in Maibe." I turned to the window. "You're the one who panicked." I rarely argued with my aunt, but today I couldn't hold back my frustration. "If you hadn't made me leave so fast, I could have made Kat understand why I decided to go with you, and we would still be speaking right now."

Audrie sighed and shifted the car into drive. "Let's talk about something else. We're celebrating your birthday, remember? What would you like to do?"

"Can I call Kinley?" I already knew the answer, but I had to try.

"You know the rules. Only on Sunday." My aunt maneuvered the car out of the parking lot. "How about we go to a movie?"

"I don't want to waste time." I watched trees and houses blur by against the gloom outside. "I want to do more memory-recall exercises so I can figure out the passcodes and go home." It was how we usually spent our weekends anyway.

"Forget about the passcodes." Audrie slowed the car for a stop sign. "You clearly don't know them anyway."

"Then why are you keeping me here?" Her sharp admission of defeat sliced deep. "Why don't you just send me home?"

"Because I love you and I'm trying to keep you safe." She turned the car onto the highway.

"That's not what you said in Maibe. You said I was going to help you save the world." I shoved my bag to the side so I could stretch my legs. "Which one is true?"

"It's all true, Rochelle." She held the car steady as a truck splashed water over the windshield. "Now, I don't want to argue with you. I want to celebrate your birthday. What should we do?"

"You decide." Frustrated by her inability to give me complete answers, I crossed my arms over my chest and turned away from her. "You make all my decisions for me anyway."

I had once accused Alexander and Kinley of treating me like a child, but I was wrong. Alexander had let me run for the town council. He had trusted my opinions even though I was just sixteen at the time. Kinley had given me the freedom to hang out with my friends whenever I wanted as long as I was home before dark. They only wanted to protect me.

Kinley would have tried to talk through our differences, but Audrie just turned on the radio and continued driving. I rested my head against the window, wishing I had stayed at the AEI with Max and Evie.

# CHAPTER 4

# ROCHELLE

*March 31, 2091*

I sat on Audrie's couch, wrapped in a blanket, analyzing a photograph in one of her old photo albums. It had been my birthday. Three-year-old me, cheeks puffed out and ready to blow out the candles, crouched on a chair between my dad and six-year-old Kinley. Audrie stood behind me, holding my hair back so it wouldn't get too close to the three sparkler candles. She looked like the perfect protective aunt.

It was hard to believe that only a few months after this photograph was taken, she had walked away from my family. She was never back in my life until last July. Ever since, I'd been trying to figure out if she really wanted to be a family again or if she was just using me to get to the pendants. After our conversation, I was questioning her motives again.

It was three in the morning, and the apartment was silent except for the refrigerator running in the little kitchen. The rain pelting my window had woken me up, and my guilt after our argument had prevented me from falling back to sleep.

A door creaked and a light came on in the hallway. My aunt's apartment was small. It had a kitchen that opened to a living room. A hallway led to the two bedrooms with a bathroom in between. There weren't any pictures hanging on the walls, or any decorations. Her furnishings were a couch and an end table, a card table with two folding chairs, a bed and dresser for each bedroom, a few lamps, and two secondhand armchairs that didn't match.

"Rochelle?" Audrie shuffled down the hall, rubbing her eyes. "What are you doing up?"

"I couldn't sleep." Sighing, I looked down at the photograph again. "I don't remember this." It was upsetting that there were moments with my dad that I didn't remember. I couldn't bear the thought of forgetting one minute of my time with him during the fifteen years of my life he'd been alive.

Audrie approached and looked over my shoulder from behind the couch. "Oh, your third birthday. I remember that one." She laughed. "You wanted a cake with pink, orange, and yellow frosting. It took your grandma and me an hour to figure out how we wanted to incorporate all those colors. Your dad went to five stores to find this little kit of play-doctor stuff you wanted because you knew Kinley would like it."

I smiled. "We were still playing with that when I was ten." It wasn't surprising that three years later, at the age of sixteen, she would be accepted early to a medical training program in Omaha.

Audrie walked around the couch and sat down next to me. "The whole family came over, and we had dinner and sang Happy Birthday, and ate cake with ice cream. Then you opened presents, and your dad and I played with you and Kinley for the rest of the afternoon. We had a lot of fun."

"It was the last time you ever celebrated my birthday with me." I closed the album and slid it to the empty cushion beside me.

Audrie nodded. "You're right, and I'm sorry about that. I wish I had been there for every birthday, and I especially wish I had planned better for last night."

"I'm sorry about the things I said in the car. I just miss everyone at home." My hand reached for the charm bracelet on my left wrist.

"I know it's hard." She nodded toward the album. "When I first left Maibe for TCI training, I would look at those pictures every night and cry because I was so homesick."

"Then why didn't you ever come visit?" I didn't want to start another argument, but I wanted real answers from my aunt.

Audrie sank back into the cushions. "My mom was upset when I left home for TCI training, and my brothers tried to talk me out of going. I thought they were trying to control my life, which made me want to join the TCI that much more just to prove I was right. By the time I reached out to say, 'I told you so,' my mom and your uncle Arthur thought I would be a bad influence on you, Kat, and Kinley. Auggie offered a few times to sneak the three of you away to meet me, but I knew it would be too hard to say goodbye, so I told him I was too busy."

"Oh." I wanted her to have a better reason for not visiting, but at least she was being honest. "So, your job was more important?"

"Not more important, but still important. It challenges me, and I get to travel all over the country and protect people from threats they don't always know exist." She watched me from the corner of her eye. "In high school, I decided I wanted to do something that had a big impact on the world. My dad was a high school teacher, and my mom was the director of the home for children in Maibe. If I followed in either of their footsteps, I wouldn't have even half the opportunities to change the world that the TCI has given me."

I leaned back into the cushions and forced myself to remain quiet even though I disagreed with most of what Audrie had said.

"But I have let my job get in the way of more important things. I regret losing touch with my family. If I could go back, I would have apologized and spent every birthday and holiday with you guys. I never got to say goodbye to my mom or brothers, and I'll never forgive myself for that. Even worse, I wasn't there for you three when you were dealing with the fever, and you needed me."

I sighed and shook my head. "It's good that you weren't there. Otherwise, you would have gotten sick too, and you'd be gone like Grandma, Uncle Arthur, and Aunt Grace."

"Or maybe not." My aunt slid her head to the side so it touched mine. "I've been all over the country and I haven't caught it yet. Maybe I'm immune."

"You should be more careful." Just thinking about how sick I'd been and how much I'd lost because of the fever brought tears to my eyes. "I don't want you to get sick." Nothing happened by chance. My aunt abandoning our family had saved her life so she could be here for me now, and I didn't want to lose her too.

"I'll be careful. I promise." She patted my hand. "My point is, I'm sorry I wasn't there for you."

"Maybe it was for the best." I used the blanket to dry stubborn tears. "I needed Kinley to take care of me and help me recover. I would never have made it through that and the funerals if I knew I would have to move away from her." Kinley had taken care of me when Dad and Grandma weren't home. She had helped me with homework. Most of all, she had comforted me through all the loss we had experienced. Sometimes I forgot she was only three years older than me.

"No, Rochelle. I didn't mean I would have taken you away from home." Audrie sat up and looked at me huddled in the blanket. "I know Kinley loves you and Kat more than anything in this world, and I'm sorry I took you away from home."

It was the apology I didn't realize I needed. Although I loved my aunt, I didn't like the way she'd spoken to Kinley as if she hadn't been a good guardian for more than a year without any help. "Was that possible? That I could have stayed?"

"I don't know." Audrie ran her fingers through her hair to fluff it in front. "I don't even want to admit this to myself, but when I first reached out to you, it was just part of an assignment from the

TCI. I had no intention of sticking around or being a part of your lives. Just get in, get the pendant, and get out. But once I met all of you, I realized what I'd missed over the past fourteen years, and I wanted my family back."

Pushing the blanket aside, I stood. "Then why didn't you offer to bring Kinley and Kat here too?"

"I knew Kinley couldn't leave in the middle of her medical program. I wanted to bring Kat along, but my boss said he could only make one exception for admission to the AEI. To him, none of this was about family, so he told me to choose who would know the most between the two of you. You're the oldest, and I wanted to get you far away from Molly. So, I chose you."

"Maybe I was the wrong choice," I said. "Maybe Kat's the one who knows everything." How could she claim to love all of us and then choose me over Kat? How could she let her boss tear my family apart without even explaining why she had been forced to make that decision?

"Rochelle, I'm sorry." She stood and took my hands. "I was heartbroken when I found out I would have to make that choice. But I was supposed to be investigating the pendants, and it was dangerous for everyone if you stayed."

I tried to pull away from her, but she held my hands. "You should have at least put up a fight and told your boss you had better ideas."

"You're right," she relented. "I should have handled a lot of things differently, but I messed up, and this is where we're at. You three are my nieces and the only family I have left. I wish we could all be together, but we can't right now. So, I've chosen to be thankful that at least you can be here with me."

Watching my aunt blink back tears knocked all the anger and frustration out of me. "It's not all your fault." If anyone were to blame, it was me. "I didn't tell you I had a pendant. I didn't tell you about Molly. But I'm going to fix it and figure out the passcodes. I promise I'll figure it out."

Audrie shook her head. "Rochelle, it's okay."

Ignoring her, I continued. "And when this is all over and we can go home, Kat and Kinley will forgive you. We'll tell them everything you just told me, and they'll understand. You already talk to Kinley once a week. That's a good start."

"You're all we have in common to talk about." Audrie forced a smile. "We were really close when she was little, but I guess neither of you are little kids anymore."

I hugged my aunt. "You just got off to a bad start with her. We can fix it."

"We'll see." My aunt held me in a tight hug. "It's kind of cold in here. Do you want some hot chocolate?"

I laughed. "It's three thirty in the morning."

"Didn't anyone ever tell you that's the best time for hot chocolate?" Audrie let go of me and walked to the kitchen.

Following her, I hoisted myself onto the counter and watched her pour ingredients into a pot on the stove. "Audrie, how close is the TCI to finding all the pendants? When can I go home?"

"I wish I had a good answer for that, but I don't know." She shoved the milk back into the refrigerator. "What I am sure of now is that your dad didn't want you involved in any of this. You found his pendant by accident, and that's it."

"That's not true." I slid off the counter. "If I don't know the passcodes, the TCI can't get the research and I can never go home."

"No, Rochelle." Audrie wrapped her arm around me. "I don't want you to feel responsible for this. All the TCI has to do is secure as many pendants as possible so we can make sure no one can access the research, not even the Defiance. You've done your part. Now let the TCI do the rest, and once things calm down and Molly realizes she'll never get to the research, you can go home."

"But I'm supposed to be helping you. At orientation, Head Agent MacCormack said he expected me to contribute everything I know about the pendants and passcodes. He said if I'm not useful, I don't belong here." Head Agent MacCormack was intimidating. Even Audrie was tense around her boss. During my brief orientation meeting, he hadn't smiled once and said he doubted I could keep up with the course work. He had made an exception due to the circumstances, but that wouldn't happen a second time.

"Don't worry about MacCormack. Your midterm grades were impressive." Audrie stirred the hot chocolate. "You've proven that you belong here. And we've spent months talking through your memories. You've contributed plenty of your time to help us."

I pulled two mismatched mugs out of the cupboard, not wanting to admit how long I had to study to earn an A average. "But I still want to help. My dad was part of this, and I feel responsible."

Audrie nodded. "I know, but I don't want you to put any more pressure on yourself. From now on, spend time with friends and focus on your studies. If you happen to think of anything we missed, let me know."

"Are you sure you won't get in trouble if I don't figure it out?" I wrapped my arms around myself, feeling the chill Audrie had mentioned earlier. From that one meeting with MacCormack, I had gotten the impression that Audrie had promised we would be able to provide the TCI with the passcodes.

"I'm not going to get in trouble." Audrie smiled. "And I'm sorry I lost my patience with you last night. I've never raised a teenager before, but I promise I can do better."

"It's okay." I slid the mugs to the stove so Audrie could fill them. "I can do better too."

I had no intention of taking my aunt's advice. If she wouldn't help me sort through my memories, I would do it on my own until

I figured out the passcodes. Although the pendants had thrown my life into chaos, I now knew my aunt would never have walked back into my life without them. Whether she believed it or not, she was supposed to find her family, and I was supposed to make sure the research would end up in the right hands.

# CHAPTER 5

# CHARLIE

*April 2, 2091*

**T**ake these stories as a warning. Be suspicious of anyone offering a warm meal, a night of shelter, or a ride to the hospital. If you're lucky, they'll return you to the nearest home for children and you'll suffer the consequences of a runaway. More likely, you'll be given poisoned food or become a victim of medical experiments. The goal of our country's leaders is to eliminate as many undesirable street kids as possible by any means necessary. Anyone under the age of eighteen without parents is at risk of all these perils. If this describes you, we have a place for you in the Defiance. Join us and, rest assured, you will always have safe food and shelter, the best medical care, and, most importantly, a family to watch your back.

I typed the words clumsily on the laptop Griff had given me. As usual, my newsletter was filled with true stories about corrupt doctors and cynical adults who were cleaning up the streets by any means necessary. They came from interviews with fellow Defiance members who joined after narrow escapes and near-death experiences. Sometimes I embellished the details for more exciting reading, but I didn't have to make up the horrors the street kids had been experiencing for years.

The stories I'd been writing weren't so different from the whispered warnings I'd heard years earlier. *Don't go near a hospital. Stay in a home for children long enough and they'll sell you into a life of labor. Trust any adult to help you and you'll regret it forever.*

That was why the Defiance grew by hundreds every week. My newsletters documented the greatest fears of every street kid, and thousands of copies were distributed once a week beyond our borders in the areas Griff planned to invade next. Who would turn down the security we could offer in an uncertain world?

I tried not to think about the consequences of my work. By following Griff's orders, I was the only respected journalist in Defiance territory. Millions of people were reading what I wrote, and I didn't want that to end. After returning to the Defiance and getting the dose of reality I had avoided in Maibe, even I knew my generation's best chance at a better life was the Defiance. The world needed to change, but it would come at the price, as it always did, of lives and destruction. My writing could fuel that, but more importantly, if Griff continued to succeed in his takeover without the pendants, he would leave the Aumonts alone and there would be no need to unlock the research.

The blinking cursor at the end of my last sentence dared me to add my usual call to action. *Everyone remember, adults are out to get us. Avoid them, don't cooperate with their requests, and help the Defiance defeat them.*

Squeezing my eyes shut, I pulled my hand back. What would Kinley think of me if she knew I was discouraging kids from seeking medical attention? What would Alexander say about my encouraging chaos and lack of cooperation? I couldn't imagine either of them hurting anyone.

Did most adults really want to eliminate us? How many people would rather help if we gave them a chance?

I opened my eyes to the fear-mongering stories on my screen. Nothing inspired action like fear. People would believe the craziest theories if they were scary enough, if they were what they wanted to hear. Did that apply to me too? Was I letting fear blind me from the stories of people helping street kids like I'd experienced in Maibe? My finger moved toward the delete button, then stopped. There weren't enough Kinleys or Alexanders to fix the world. The Defiance was the best promise I could make.

Tired of trying to sort fact from fiction in my own writing and my own life, I closed my laptop. The fluorescent light over the workbench buzzed. I slid to the front of my folding chair hidden among cases of oil and crates of spare parts, and glanced up at the clock. Five minutes to eleven.

The back room of the garage that housed our Defiance vehicles was the best place to make private phone calls. It didn't even look suspicious for me to be in the garage late at night because I was the head of our vehicle maintenance department and preferred to do most of the work myself.

No one else knew about my Monday-night phone calls with Lareina. We'd been in touch since I'd left Maibe, and if there was one thing we agreed on, it was that we wanted neither the Defiance nor the TCI to get their hands on the research. When Lareina heard I was going back to the Defiance undercover, she gave me her Spero pendant to earn Griff's trust. We agreed that if I collected the three remaining pendants, she would come in with the final pendant, Optimus, that she had hidden in Maibe. And then we would unlock and destroy the research together. The problem was that the TCI had some of the pendants and no one had figured out the passcodes yet. Still, I held on to this plan as proof that I was still good. Plus, since Lareina was in Maibe, she was my only link to the people I cared about the most.

Taking a deep breath, I dialed Lareina's number and listened to the hollow ringing on the other end of the line.

"Maibe Home For Children." I recognized Lareina's voice immediately.

"Hey, it's me." I squeezed my eyes shut and rubbed the bridge of my nose.

"How many more pendants did you find?" It was always her first question.

"None." From experience, I knew it wasn't the answer she wanted. "But Griff has a new lead on that scientist, Brandon Davis."

"I expected the Defiance to be better at this. You made it sound like Griff had a good handle on the situation."

"He's handling it fine," I snapped. "We have more important problems like helping kids who don't have families to look out for them." As far as I was concerned, the best plan was to keep Lareina's Optimus pendant hidden to prevent anyone from ever accessing the research.

"Are you listening to yourself?" she snapped back. "You've been doing that for weeks. Making comments that paint the Defiance as the good guys. They don't help kids. They brainwash them, and they're clearly getting to you too."

"We give them the food, shelter, and family the rest of the world won't." I gripped the phone so tight my hand hurt. "They would have welcomed you with open arms, and you could have avoided that whole ordeal you went through to get to Maibe." I was the only one who Lareina had trusted to write down her survival story, her journey on foot from San Antonio to Dallas with a detective trailing behind her all the while until she'd finally caught a train to Maibe.

"I'm sure they would have," Lareina said. "Especially when they found out I was hiding the Spero and Optimus pendants."

"It's not my problem that the adults who are supposed to help us are letting the world burn instead. It's not my fault the world is full of abandoned kids. They don't know that they have a better choice than joining the Defiance."

"They do have a better choice. You and I both know it." Lareina's voice softened. "We've both been through some tough stuff, but wasn't it worth it to get to Maibe? I'm sure the Defiance's definition of family is a lot different from what you experienced with the Aumonts."

"I wouldn't have ended up in Maibe without the Defiance. And we both know Maibe can't take every abandoned kid in the country."

"I get it. The Defiance was there when you needed help. But you can't believe they're the good guys, Charlie. There are other people like the Aumonts, and other places like Maibe."

"They're hard to find. I know from experience." If every kid knew someone like the Aumonts, the Defiance wouldn't exist at all.

Lareina sighed. "I wish you would have let me tell Rochelle about the Spero and Optimus pendants. She could be really helpful now that she's with the TCI."

My hand tightened around the phone. It wasn't the first time Lareina had mentioned Rochelle as a solution to our problems, but I wanted to keep her safe. "I'm sure it's hard enough for her being away from home, and this isn't something you can explain to her in a letter," I said. "Remember, you told me she can't receive phone calls."

"Hey, buddy. What's wrong?" Lareina's voice was gentle and far away. She wasn't talking to me anymore. "Come here. It was just a bad dream."

I imagined Lareina picking up a little boy and comforting him. A knot of homesickness tightened my throat. I wanted a hug from Kinley or a pat on the shoulder from Alexander. The comfort of human touch. Advice and understanding. I needed to talk to Rochelle. To hear her tell me everything would be okay, that there was a plan, that there was always hope, and tomorrow would be better.

"Charlie, are you still there?" Lareina's voice startled me.

"Yeah. I'm here." I rested my head back against the wall as the loneliness of my situation enveloped me.

"I have to go for now, but I'll talk to you next week." All the fight had drained from her voice. "You're still on board with our plan. Right?"

"Yes. I'll keep you posted on any pendant progress." I closed my eyes as exhaustion closed in on me.

"Take care of yourself. We'll talk soon." The phone clicked.

There was no right side, but I trusted Griff far more than I trusted Rochelle's aunt Audrie. The Defiance hurt people to accomplish their goals, but so did the TCI. Did my plan with Lareina mean I was disloyal to the Defiance? Did my loyalty to Griff keep me from being trustworthy to the TCI? The darkness I'd been running from all my life closed back in around me and there was no one to pull me out.

Sliding my computer into its bag, I turned off the lights and locked the door to the garage on my way out. I pulled up my hood against the cold and jogged across the street to the main Defiance building. All I had to do was find Griff, get him back to his room safely, and then I could go to bed. Sleep would clear my head, and everything would be better in the morning.

Deep in thought, I passed the door to Griff's room. Retracing my steps, I knocked, hoping for an answer but not expecting one.

"Come in," Griff shouted.

I pushed the door open and walked into the room. "Hey, I thought you'd still be out."

Griff sat at the table with a bottle of beer in his hand. The four pendants were laid out in front of him. "I was looking for you. Where've you been?"

"The garage. Time for oil changes. I just got in."

"Take a look at these. Tell me what you notice." He pointed the bottle at the pendants.

Unsure about the direction of the conversation, I set my laptop bag on the table and picked up one of the pendants. It was the usual black, shiny, plastic-like material shaped like a triangle. The word "Spero" was written across the bottom curve in white letters. I'd once lied to Griff and told him it was Auggie Aumont's pendant. As long as Griff believed me, he had no reason to search for a pendant in Maibe and hurt my friends.

"Nothing. What's wrong with them?"

"It's hard to tell, but they're fakes." Griff placed his bottle on the table. "Ever heard of 3D printing? I had some of our people make copies of the real ones just in case we have an opportunity to make a trade. These won't work as part of the key like the real ones, but if they tricked us maybe they'll trick those TCI agents. If it comes down to it, we'll let them think we're giving them what they want while we finish our mission."

Max had once told me it would be easy to print fake pendants, but I'd shot his idea down. More pendants, real or not, made me uneasy.

"It's just a backup plan if the TCI gets too close." Griff studied my expression. "I talked to my TCI guy. I got confirmation on Brandon Davis's last known address. The TCI hasn't come up with any new leads, but we have better methods. I have a meeting tomorrow afternoon, and then we'll leave for Colorado right after."

"Great. I'll finish my writing before we go." I turned to leave.

"Your name came up." Griff tossed the words out casually. "My inside guy seems to think you signed some kind of agreement with the TCI. Why would he say that?"

Forcing myself to breathe, I turned back to Griff. "After that meeting you and I had before Christmas, I went back to Maibe, and Agent Aumont was there visiting her family. She found out about the brand on my arm, and the only way I could stay out of trouble was to say I was on the TCI's side. I haven't thought about it since I got back."

Griff nodded. "So, you haven't reported anything to them?"

"To the TCI?" I laughed. "No." It wasn't technically a lie. I hadn't reported to Audrie even once since I'd been back with the Defiance.

"I'm glad you feel that way. There's an opportunity coming up where I can get your old friend Rochelle Aumont away from those scums." Griff stood. "I've decided to take it."

My heart pounded, but I kept my voice even. "That's a bad idea, Griff. If she's with the TCI, she's with her aunt, and the TCI thinks she knows valuable information. They won't just let us have her."

"From what I've heard, she hasn't helped them figure anything out. They basically think she's a fraud. We'd be rescuing her." He picked up his bottle and took a sip. "Unless you have some reason for wanting her to stay and help the TCI?"

All I cared about was protecting Rochelle, and now I didn't know whether she was safer with Audrie or with us. Some selfish part of me wanted to go along with Griff so I could see Rochelle every day. The rest of me feared what the Defiance would do to her.

"No, it's not that. It's just . . . everything's going so well, and I don't think we need to create any problems."

"Problems?" Griff punched my arm. "Molly will have her friend back, you can convince Rochelle to side with us and pull Molly with her, and if we're really lucky, Rochelle will be able to give us some guesses on those passcodes. And she escapes before the TCI turns on her. We all win."

"How can I argue with that?" I said. The only thing I'd done right was keep Griff and Molly away from Rochelle, and now I was about to fail at one of my only two responsibilities. How long before I failed to secure the research too? "When is she coming?"

"Depends how things play out this week. I'll keep you posted." He tossed his empty bottle in the trash. "That's my only one tonight. I'm going to be more responsible from now on. Just like you said." Griff held out his hand. "Brothers always."

I clasped his hand. "Brothers always."

I knew I was fully betraying the family I'd left behind by agreeing to Griff's plan, but if I didn't, he would think I was working for the TCI. It didn't matter which side I was on. There was nothing I could do without becoming an enemy of both sides.

# CHAPTER 6

# ROCHELLE

*April 3, 2091*

**M**y hand raced across my notebook as I tried to keep up with Mr. Hawley's history lecture. He only stopped talking when he noted important information on the dry-erase board at the front of the room. I'd learned that everything he said down to the smallest detail could, and often would, show up on the test.

"Rochelle," Max whispered from his desk next to me. "Do you have any more tissues?"

Still writing, I reached into my bag and pulled a few from the front pocket.

Mr. Hawley stopped talking to scrawl a list of dates on the board, and I turned to Max. He sniffled as he worked on a Rubik's Cube under his desk.

I poked his arm with my pencil and pointed to my notebook.

Max grinned and tapped the top of his head. "I've got it all up here," he whispered before sneezing into his sleeve. He had been fighting a cold for the past two days, but that wasn't enough to slow Max down. When I couldn't talk him into getting more sleep, I made sure to carry a pocketful of tissues when we went on our morning run and pack my bag full of them for the rest of the day.

A loud ding echoed through the room, and Mr. Hawley

glanced at his phone, then raised his eyebrows at us. "Max and Rochelle, Head Agent MacCormack wants to see you both in his office immediately."

I had never been called to Agent MacCormack's office before, and I'd been at the AEI long enough to know he only spoke to students who had done something wrong. At my orientation, he'd greeted me with, "As long as you stay out of trouble, I won't see you until graduation."

"Did he say why?" Max discreetly slipped his Rubik's Cube into his bag.

"No." Our teacher slid his phone back into his pocket. "You'd better hurry. He doesn't like to be kept waiting."

The rest of the class watched us, already whispering as we gathered our things. Max stumbled but caught himself as he passed Henry's desk, which led to muffled giggles.

"Are you all right?" I asked when we were safely in the hallway.

"Fine," Max grumbled. "Henry does annoying stuff like tripping me all the time, but I'm not giving him the satisfaction of a response. Just stay away from him. I don't like the way he talks about you."

"Don't worry about me." I fell into step beside my friend. "I just don't want you to get in trouble. Or more trouble than we're already in."

"Don't look so worried, Rochelle." Max linked his arm through mine. "Maybe MacCormack just wants to congratulate us on our good grades so far."

"We'd never be that lucky. We're in trouble for something." I shoved my hands into my pockets. "What if he found out you're tampering with the tracking on your phone?"

"Maybe he thinks I need a new challenge so he's going to

upgrade my phone, and then I'll have a touchscreen and internet access like Sid and Audrie." He sneezed into his sleeve and turned to me. "Either way, my phone has nothing to do with you."

"It doesn't matter. When you get in trouble, I get in trouble." I sighed. "Can you name one time when you were in the principal's office and I wasn't there with you?"

"A few, actually." He wiped his nose with a tissue. "But that was just school in Maibe. This place is different."

I cleared my throat and rubbed my eyes where anxious tears burned in the corners. "Getting in trouble here would be far worse. I've already caused so many problems for my family. I can't do this to Kinley. I can't disappoint her again."

"Rochelle, she's safe in Maibe." Max's grin vanished. "We're in charge of our own lives here. We're free. Even if we get in a little trouble, we'll handle it and move on. We won't get a lecture from Kinley, and I won't get grounded by my *tía*."

I shook my head. "Don't you miss home at all?"

Max shrugged. "I'm trying to focus on the positive. My classes are actually interesting, and the kids here want to learn. The food is pretty good. I can play Ping-Pong all night if I want to. And the AEI provides brand-new computers and lab equipment for me to use on whatever experiments I want. What's not to like?"

I walked silently beside him. I wished I could see life as an adventure. Maybe I would enjoy my time at the AEI as much as he did.

"I know you miss everyone. I do too." Max wrapped one arm around me as we approached the administration building. "I know it seems far away, but one day we'll be home working on the time machine, and this place will only be a memory. We might as well enjoy it while it lasts."

I couldn't hold back my smile. Max had always wanted to

grow up to be the greatest inventor of our time. "I'm so glad you're here. I don't know what I'd do without you."

Max sneezed twice. "You'd probably have more tissues."

Laughing, I pulled the last two from my coat pocket and handed them to him.

"What if they have news about Keppler?" He blew his nose. "Maybe he's done with his undercover work and they're sending him home. Or maybe he's coming here."

"Maybe," I agreed so I didn't have to dampen Max's hope with reality. We both missed Keppler and worried about him every day. Max once had the courage to ask Audrie for updates about him, but she told us she couldn't disclose that information. I wondered what would happen to Keppler if the day came when he could safely leave the Defiance. I wanted him to return to Maibe and resume life as normal, but Kinley had been so upset about the way he left that neither of us mentioned his name when we spoke on the phone.

Audrie waited for us in a chair outside the head agent's office. She jumped up when we came into view and stopped us a few feet from his open door.

"Before we go in, everything Head Agent MacCormack is about to ask is optional. Don't feel pressured to do anything you don't feel prepared for." She kept her voice low, and her constant glances at the door shattered her usually calm demeanor.

"Good, you're all here," MacCormack's booming voice interrupted my aunt. "Come on in."

"Yes, sir." Audrie placed a hand on each of our shoulders and steered us into the office.

MacCormack waited for us inside the door. He stood a foot taller than Audrie even though she wore high-heeled boots. He had broad shoulders and a barrel chest, and he was fit. The head agent walked to his desk and sat down. His blue suit was ironed to perfection, and his dark hair was neatly combed.

"Max. Rochelle. Have a seat." He gestured to the two chairs in front of his desk.

Audrie nudged us forward, and we each took a seat. My aunt remained standing behind us.

MacCormack leaned forward, elbows on his desk. "I've heard good things about both of you from several of your teachers. That's why I think you'll be perfect for an upcoming assignment."

Max slid to the front of his seat but remained uncharacteristically quiet.

"The Defiance is gaining ground faster than we expected," MacCormack continued. "And they're crediting new propaganda with their progress." He handed each of us a piece of paper with typed writing printed on the front and back. "I'd like to know if this is really what's drawing so many people in."

My eyes scanned the headlines: *Home for children profits from selling teens into life of labor. Never trust a doctor. Join the Defiance; lose the fear.* Charlie Keppler's byline appeared under each article.

"What can we do to help?" Max's serious tone indicated he felt the same betrayal I had. After months of believing Keppler was on our side, evidence of the opposite was in writing, right in front of us.

MacCormack smiled, blue eyes glittering with amusement. "I'm sure you understand our adult agents don't exactly fit the profile of the disgruntled teenagers who are joining the Defiance. We have intelligence about a recruitment meeting taking place in Pennsylvania tomorrow. All I need from you two is to attend and observe, then report back to me on what drives these kids, and what kind of information we could put out there to counter the Defiance and make their promises less attractive."

Max shot to his feet. "I'll do it. Count me in."

There was no stopping him, and I couldn't let him go alone. "I'll go too."

If Kinley knew I was leaving the state to walk into a Defiance rally, she would have a nervous breakdown. But helping the TCI would give me a chance to stop Molly and go home.

MacCormack stood, arms behind his back. "I appreciate your willingness and courage to assist in the fight for good. Report here after your last class, and we'll go over the details. You're all dismissed for now."

I returned the newsletter to the head agent's desk, then filed out of the room with Audrie and Max. We walked in silence to the front doors.

"Audrie, have you heard from Keppler at all?" Max stopped and turned to her. "Is he helping you, and that's how MacCormack got that newsletter?"

"He hasn't made contact yet." My aunt pulled a tissue from her own pocket and handed it to Max. "That doesn't mean he won't. Sometimes it isn't easy to find a secure location to call from."

Max nodded and blew his nose. His usual grin had vanished.

"Are you sure you're feeling up to undercover work tomorrow?" Audrie touched her hand to his forehead. "It's not too late to back out." She'd known us long enough to understand that I wouldn't let Max walk into something like this alone. The only way to talk me out of it was to talk him out of it.

"I'll be fine by tomorrow. This is important." He rubbed his nose and turned away from us to sneeze several times.

"We'll be okay as long as we're together," I assured my aunt. "Plus, I'm here to help you save the world, remember? This might be my only chance."

"Okay." Audrie hugged me. Considering our last conversation when she wanted me to forget about the pendants, I was surprised she was letting me go. Maybe we didn't really have a choice. "I have to get to my next class, but I'll see you for MacCormack's briefing."

I said goodbye to my aunt and walked over to Max, who sat in one of the lobby chairs analyzing the newsletter MacCormack had given us.

"You weren't supposed to keep that." I sat down next to him.

"He never asked for it back." Max held it between us so I could see it too. "It sounds like his writing style. Why would he help them? How could he write this stuff?"

"Let's not jump to conclusions." I lowered the paper from our line of sight. "He can't blow his cover. Maybe he didn't have a choice."

"How do you force someone to write something like this?" Max slumped in his chair. "He could have at least put some typos in there so we'd know he's working under duress. I think he switched sides."

"If we ever see him again, he'll be able to explain it all." I wanted to make Max feel better, but I wasn't so sure myself that we hadn't lost Keppler. He'd always said he belonged with the Defiance. Maybe returning had made him realize how true it was. "Let's focus on the positive. We're going on an undercover assignment to save the world." The excitement drowned out any nervousness.

Max perked up, his grin returning. "They picked us, out of everyone, when we've only been here for three months. We were born to be spies. Wait until I tell all my friends I'm going on an undercover mission. I'll be the coolest guy here." He folded the newsletter and shoved it into his coat pocket. "Who needs Keppler anyway? I have you and all my AEI friends who actually take my ideas and theories seriously."

"We should probably get to class." I didn't want Max to give up on Keppler, but I didn't know what I could say in his defense. Whatever choices he made with the Defiance, he would need his family eventually, but the longer he was away, the more of us he lost.

# CHAPTER 7

# CHARLIE

*April 4, 2091*

"Wake up, kid." Griff punched my arm twice.

I slid away from him until the car door impeded my escape, and I opened my eyes. Through my window, the storefronts of a small town passed by in slow motion as Griff pulled the car along the curb.

Antiques and Anachronisms sat peacefully in front of us. The adjacent buildings, a restaurant, and a shoe store were equally quiet.

"You'd better wake up." Griff threw the car into park and cut the engine. "It's time to confront Brandon Davis. We're getting our answers this time."

Based on our past experiences, I doubted it. I sat up, rolling my shoulders and rubbing a hand over my face. We'd been on the road for ten hours, only stopping a few times to eat and stretch. Griff refused to take the most direct route because he wanted to avoid areas with known outbreaks of the fever. Griff was so paranoid about the illness, he believed even driving through contaminated air would be enough to infect us. I didn't argue. The ones who recovered from the fever were immune, but neither of us had ever caught it, so I didn't want to take any unnecessary risks. According to the paper, the pandemic was slowing down, and I hoped it would fizzle out before I had to test my immune system.

"You really think he's going to be in there?" I rubbed my eyes. "He hasn't been anywhere else."

"The TCI had reports of him entering this building just last week. They think he was living in the upstairs area over the store. Someone here knows something." He opened the glove compartment and pulled out a gun. On several occasions he'd tried to convince me to carry one, but I knew what he would expect next, so I refused. I said I preferred to deal with traitors and snitches the old-fashioned, personal way.

"This time I plan to get our message across," Griff said. "If Davis isn't here, someone has to pay the price. Eventually, he'll hear about it."

My chest muscles went rigid. "I thought we were here to question Davis?"

"It's taking too long." He pushed his door open. "We need his pendant and the codes to the research now. I'm tired of playing games, and so is Molly."

I knew Griff didn't need Molly's motivation to use violence to get what he wanted, but she certainly wasn't helping to sway him in the other direction either.

Hoping we would find the antique store closed and locked, I got out of the car and followed Griff to the glass door. A red and blue Open sign blinked in the front window.

Griff's hand gripped the door handle, but he didn't open it. "Wipe that look off your face. We've both known all along we would have to sacrifice enemies to the Defiance to build a better world for everyone else. Unless you think the TCI has better methods." He hadn't let up on the TCI references since his informant had mentioned my name.

"You're right. You're always right." No words would change his mind, and the last thing I needed was to be the next traitor on his list.

"That's better." He pulled the door open, and I forced my feet to follow him inside.

The building was a never-ending collection of shelves containing old dishes, knickknacks, figurines, and toys that formed a maze stretching deep into the store. An older man with a receding hairline stood behind a cash register that sat on top of a glass display case filled with old jewelry.

"What can I help you with today?" The man smiled as we approached.

"We're looking for Brandon Davis." Griff stood with his hand poised over the side of his belt where the gun was hidden under his shirt.

"I'm sorry." The man took a step back, a smile frozen on his face. "There's no one by that name here."

"That's funny." Griff pulled out the gun. "According to my intel, he was spotted here as recently as the weekend."

"Whoa. Okay." The man held up his hands. "I found a guy trying to sleep in the alley a while back. I let him sleep inside for a couple of weeks, but he took off three or four days ago. Said he had to keep moving."

Griff raised the gun, aiming at the clerk. "And I'm just supposed to take your word for it?"

"It's the truth." He glanced toward the window and the quiet, empty street outside. "I swear it's the truth."

"Where did he go?" Griff shouted with his finger on the trigger.

"He didn't say. He barely spoke to me at all." The man took a shaky breath. "He was just—"

A loud crash from deep in the labyrinth of shelves froze us in place.

Griff lunged forward and slammed the man's head against the counter. "Go check that out, Charlie. Find the person who's hiding in back and get him out here. I'll finish the inter-rogation." He shoved the gun into my hands without looking at me.

"You've got it." I felt like a coward walking away, but there was nothing I could do to help the man. It was a relief that I wouldn't have to watch Griff beat him, but I didn't know what I would do if I actually did find Brandon Davis hiding in the store.

I swerved through shelves of old antiques in the direction of the sound until Griff's shouting and the clerk's pleading faded behind me. Anyone could easily be hiding among the shelves, but I didn't take the time to search too thoroughly. I believed the clerk when he said Davis had taken off. That was Davis's pattern. He knew he couldn't stay in one place long enough to be spotted by anyone who was out to get him, and he managed to keep ahead of us. If he'd heard about the tragedies that befell Rochelle's dad, Griff's dad, or the other scientists on his team, he had the motivation to stay hidden.

Griff shouted something, and the hollow ring of shattering glass gave way to muffled pleading as I approached the back of the store. A soft rustling drew me through a doorway into an office-like room complete with a rolltop desk, a typewriter, and shelves of old books. For a minute I got lost in dreaming about the books I could write in a room like that, but the rise and fall of shallow breathing pulled me back to reality.

Slowly, gun out in front of me, I approached the desk and lowered my head until I could see beneath. A boy, maybe seven years old, was huddled under the desk. We made eye contact, and he covered his head with his arms.

"It's okay," I whispered and shoved the gun into my belt. "I won't hurt you." My stomach rolled with the memory of hiding from my dad the way this boy was hiding from me.

"What about my grandpa?" He peeked through his arms but remained scrunched in the dark corner.

"My friend just has to ask him a few questions." I cleared my throat. "Is anyone else here? Your parents, maybe?"

The boy shook his head. "I don't have parents. Please don't hurt Grandpa."

Frustration burned in my chest. I'd had enough of playing along with the Defiance. Enough of following Griff's orders so he wouldn't doubt my loyalty. The Defiance and the TCI had torn me away from my family and pulled them away from each other. I hadn't been able to stop that, but I could stop Griff from doing the same to this little boy.

"Everything will be okay." I squatted so I was at eye level with him. "No matter what happens, no matter what you hear, stay right here until your grandpa comes to get you. Okay?"

The boy blinked back tears and nodded.

Slowly, I stood and turned to the doorway. I couldn't stop Griff by force, and he was in no mood to listen to logic. The only card I had left to play was to offer him reassurance that I was his loyal brother. Pulling the gun from my belt, I put a scowl on my face and strode to the front of the store.

"Tell. Me. Where. He. Went!" Griff emphasized each word as I swerved back through the shelves. There was no reply.

By the time I emerged from the winding maze, Griff stood, fists clenched, over the clerk, who lay on the floor groaning, his face bloody.

"Who's back there?" Griff didn't bother to look up at me.

The man tried to lift his head but couldn't find the strength.

"Just a cat. I told you Davis wouldn't be here." I stalked forward until my feet planted right in front of our victim's face. "You get any answers?"

"Nothing." He kicked the man in the ribs, prompting another groan. "Go start the car, and be ready to get out of here fast. I'll finish the job." He offered me the keys, holding out his other hand for the gun.

"You start the car." I gripped the gun at my side. "I'm tired of you questioning my loyalty to the Defiance."

Griff gripped the keys and looked at me for the first time since I'd returned to the room. "You're telling me you want to finish this guy off?"

I prodded the old man's arm with my shoe. "Yeah. And then you're going to stop with the TCI remarks. Do you have a problem with that?"

Griff laughed. "Just get to the car fast. If someone hears the shot, they'll be on our tail in seconds."

"I'll be quick." I extended the gun and took a few steps back.

Giving the man one last kick, Griff slapped my back and retreated through the door to start the getaway car.

"Please." The man coughed and moved his arm so I could see the terror on his face. "I don't know anything . . . I have a grandson . . . please."

"Shut up and listen." I lowered the gun to my side and stepped up next to him so he could hear my lowered voice. "Wait until the car drives away, and then get that kid from under your desk and run far away from here. If the Defiance finds out you're alive, we're both dead."

"What?" Rubbing the back of his head, he tried to sit up.

"Stay down." I lifted the gun, sending him back to the floor. "Don't get up until you hear the car drive away." Aiming at the floor a few feet away from his head, I fired twice.

The man cowered on the ground as I darted through the door and dove into the passenger seat of the car. Griff stomped on the pedal, and we squealed away from the curb and sped through the little town in minutes.

As we flew down the highway, he turned to me. "It's about time you get away from that computer. You haven't been acting like yourself since I gave you that thing."

I shoved the gun into the glove compartment, wondering whether I was acting like the Charlie I'd been in the Defiance, the one I'd been in Maibe, or someone in between. "What about you? Last time I checked, you didn't take orders from anyone, especially not from Molly."

"Give me a break, kid." He swerved to miss a branch on the road. "What do you know about relationships anyway?"

Kat's face drifted through my mind. Then I remembered how she'd looked at me when I locked her in that freezer. I shook my head to clear it. "You're my brother, and you never let anyone stand in your way."

"That's what you think about Molly?" He kept his eyes glued to the road as he slowed to the speed limit. "She's the best thing that has happened to the Defiance since I found you. And she's right. We need those codes, and Brandon Davis is a dead end. Whether Rochelle Aumont knows any of that or not, she'll be a good addition to our team."

Sighing, I leaned back in my seat. "For months you've been telling me the Aumonts are a dead end. You said Molly was wrong about Rochelle knowing anything."

He glanced in the rearview mirror and, satisfied that no one was following us, let off the accelerator as we approached another town. "I know, but I thought we would have made more progress by now. Plus, according to my informant, Rochelle is doing some undercover work at one of our rallies in Pennsylvania. We can't pass up that opportunity." He looked down at his watch. "She should be there just about now, and I have guys on the scene keeping a look out for her. Let's get back to Kansas City. I'll make a call and get an update, and if it's good news, we'll find a place to get something to eat and celebrate."

A hand squeezed my lungs. "I don't want her in Kansas City with us. I don't want any part of this."

"Too bad. If we get her, I need you to verify her identity. I wouldn't want to surprise Molly with the wrong girl. That would be embarrassing." He guided the car to an off-ramp and took the sharp curve too fast. "I thought you and Rochelle were friends. What's the problem?"

"You don't know what she's like." My heart slammed inside of my chest. Griff knew where Rochelle was. "I don't need her to come in and mess things up any worse than Molly already has."

Griff punched my shoulder hard. "Relax. You and I are in charge like we've always been. At the very least, Rochelle can keep Molly busy. They can do girl stuff while we take care of real Defiance business."

If I couldn't protect Rochelle from the Defiance, then what was the point of anything I'd done over the past three months? How could I pretend to be loyal to Griff with Rochelle around to remind me of who I wanted to be? I wanted out. I wanted to escape Defiance territory, get away from Griff, and go home. But that meant death if anyone discovered the *D* branded on my arm, and I knew they were checking at state borders. The only way to ensure my safety and protect the world from the pendants was to stick with the Defiance. Rochelle was on her own.

# CHAPTER 8
# ROCHELLE

*April 4, 2091*

"You'll have to walk down the road for about a mile, and you'll see the others gathering." Sid leaned against the side of the car he had driven from New York to Pennsylvania. "Remember, you aren't there to ask questions. Just listen and observe. Max?"

"Listen and observe." Max stood beside me, squirming with excitement. "Got it. Can't we at least take the earpieces we use in skills classes so we can stay in touch?"

Sid smiled. "You don't have the training to use those smoothly enough not to draw attention to yourselves. It's safer if there aren't any visible differences between you and the other kids."

"The road's still clear." Audrie walked down the narrow trail Sid had taken when he pulled off a gravel road. We were completely hidden by an area of thick trees and brush. "It's safe to say no one knows we're here."

"It's pretty remote out here," Sid said. "Probably only farm equipment using that road."

From what Sid had told us, the Defiance always chose locations where their recruiting would go unnoticed. They had an underground network to spread the word through fliers and by word of mouth. It was rare for even the TCI to intercept any intelligence to the point that he doubted the validity of this information. Maybe there wouldn't be a Defiance rally at all.

"Are you guys ready?" Audrie's forehead wrinkled with worry.

"More ready than I've ever been for anything in my life." Max bounced in place. "I was born to be a spy."

Audrie sighed and placed a hand on Max's shoulder. "Remember, you're just a kid learning about your options with the Defiance. It's a serious situation. Not exciting."

"You're right." Max took a deep breath and stood still. "I can take this seriously."

"Be safe." Audrie pulled me into a hug. I knew she didn't like me going anywhere without her. "You'd better let me hold on to your bracelet and necklace. You'll want to blend in."

Reluctantly, I unclipped the bracelet, then my necklace, and placed them in my aunt's hand. "Promise not to lose them?"

"They'll be right here when you get back." She hugged me one more time. "You're so brave. I'm proud of you."

Those words should have encouraged me, but I was only going along to keep Max out of trouble and to help clean up the pendant mess. My aunt and I had agreed not to tell Kinley about my undercover work because it would only cause her unnecessary worry. I had written to Todd about it, but he wouldn't get the letter until I was safely back at the AEI.

"We'll celebrate your first mission this weekend," Audrie said. "Sid and I will be here the whole time. Just be careful that no one follows you when you leave the meeting. Go out of your way and double back if you need to."

I nodded. Once we walked onto the road, we would be on our own. No way to communicate with Audrie or Sid if we got in over our heads.

"We'll be all right. It's only an hour or two." Max shrugged. "What could possibly go wrong?"

"That's exactly what you should anticipate." Sid gripped Max's shoulders. "You remember what we talked about?"

Max nodded. "I remember."

Audrie's directions and Sid's advice were only making me more nervous. I appreciated them caring about us, but their concern made me question my own ability to successfully complete the assignment. I was relieved when Sid announced it was time for us to go.

Max and I exited the trees and started down the gravel road in the direction Sid had indicated. After several minutes of silence, I turned to my friend.

"Is everything all right?"

"Yeah, just thinking. I asked Sid about Keppler's newsletter, and he said it didn't look good for Keppler." Max kicked at the gravel each time his foot swung forward. "He said they can't offer Keppler immunity if he can't prove he was gathering information for the TCI."

"What does that mean?" I knew being involved with the Defiance was a serious offense and the penalties were only becoming more severe, but Keppler wasn't even an adult, barely seventeen.

Max shook his head. "Anyone found with the Defiance symbol on their arm at a border crossing can be executed on the spot. At the very least, they'll be sent to prison for life without a trial."

My chest clenched. "But he signed that agreement with Audrie."

"And he hasn't honored it. He hasn't called once." Max jammed his hands into his pockets. "I knew he would have to do things to show his loyalty to the Defiance, but I read that newsletter, and he couldn't have written that stuff if he didn't believe it. And he writes it every week."

"You can't just give up on him." I said.

"I know. I'm not." Max stopped. "It's just hard that we can't talk to him and he can't talk to us."

"We don't know what's true. Why he's doing what he's doing." I continued.

Max nodded. "And he doesn't know why we're doing what we're doing. Like my 3D pendant-printing project with Sid. If he knew, he wouldn't like it."

I patted Max's shoulder. "You're really making fake pendants?"

His shoulders straightened. "They look like the real ones, but they don't work like the real ones. I can't even begin to replicate the computer chip inside without taking one apart, and that's not allowed for obvious reasons. Without that chip, they don't work as a key."

"But if someone could take it apart, would it be possible to replicate it?"

Max shrugged and continued walking. "It would take a lot of work. I just thought these would make a good decoy if we needed one. Maybe a good way to test Keppler and find out whose side he's on."

"He didn't switch sides." I said. "I'm sure he has a good explanation for that newsletter."

"We should probably focus on our assignment for now." Max turned away from me.

He walked faster, and we kept up that pace for less than five minutes before we met up with others at an intersection and followed them to a field that was already swarming with kids. Most of them were around our age, but some were much younger. Many of them clustered into groups, and I wondered if they had come together. Max gripped my arm tighter as we weaved our way through the crowd to blend into the middle of the gathering.

As we trudged through a tangle of weeds and grass, I noticed teenage boys wearing gray jackets with a black *D* embroidered on the sleeve. I moved closer to Max and took his hand.

Max turned to me. "What's wrong? You're going to break my hand if you squeeze it any tighter."

"They're everywhere," I whispered despite the loud conversations around us. One of the uniformed boys looked at something in his hand, then up at me.

"Shouldn't they be over there?" Max nodded toward a hayrack that appeared to be a makeshift stage. "To guard the speaker?"

The boy I'd been watching tipped his head toward me, and two more dressed just like him slipped through the crowd in our direction.

"Something's wrong." I turned, pulling Max with me only to encounter a fourth boy in a gray jacket approaching us.

"Just stay calm." Max squeezed my hand, then let go. "We haven't done anything wrong."

"You two," the nearest one barked. "We have a question."

Surrounded and outnumbered, we had no choice but to let them herd us away from the crowd and the road to a secluded field dotted with bales of hay.

"We're here for the rally." Max smiled politely. "Is there a problem?"

"That depends." Icy blue eyes burned into mine. "Are you Rochelle Aumont?"

My heart stopped beating. "What?"

"No, her name is Kate. She lives on a farm down the road." Max glanced around, but there was nowhere to run. "We just came from there. I can show you." We'd learned about cover stories in skills class, but not what to do when they didn't work.

The biggest guy gripped Max by the back of the neck and pulled him away from me as he fished a photograph from his pocket and shoved it in Max's face. "Either you're lying to me, or she's lying to you. She looks just like the Rochelle Aumont in the picture."

"Rochelle Aumont, you're wanted by the Defiance for failure

to cooperate with several requests for your assistance." The boy who had first spotted me reached for my arm, and I took a step back.

"Leave her alone. You have the wrong person." Max ripped himself free from the boy's grip, but before he could get to me, a fist to the abdomen doubled him over. Then a kick to the back of his legs dropped him to the ground.

"Is that you or not?" The boy with icy blue eyes gripped my wrist and held the black-and-white newsprint photo in front of me. It was an article from the Maibe newspaper announcing the newly elected members to the Maibe town council from last spring. I stood in the middle of the group with Molly on one side and Todd on the other.

"Don't answer their questions." Max curled his knees to his chest, attempting to protect himself from a boot that smashed into his face instead.

I tried to tear my arm from my captor, but he only laughed and pulled me closer. "What's wrong? Forget your name?"

The boy closest to Max removed the gun from his belt and aimed it at Max's head. "Answer the question or he's dead."

Max touched the back of his hand to his bleeding nose and squinted up at me in a daze. There was only one way I could help him. "I'm the girl in the picture. I'm Rochelle Aumont."

"That's better." The boy lowered his gun to his side. "You two, get him out of here. We won't kill him in front of Rochelle since she cooperated."

"No." I lunged for Max, but the boy yanked me back and caught my other wrist.

The biggest guy dragged Max away by his arm toward a cluster of trees. Another boy walked alongside them, gun in hand. Max's wide brown eyes locked with mine as his body bounced over the rough ground.

"Please. He has nothing to do with this. I just met him. I lied to him about my name and everything. Please." I blinked away tears so I wouldn't lose sight of my friend. What if it was the last time I ever saw him? What would I tell his family?

"Don't worry about him." The boy holding me in place turned me toward him and nodded at someone behind us. "You have enough problems of your own."

"But—" A sharp sting exploded in my neck, and blackness closed in on my vision until all I could see were cruel blue eyes fading into darkness.

# CHAPTER 9

# ROCHELLE

*April 7, 2091*

I lifted my head from the table and strained to hear the conversation in the hallway. The three distinct voices were muffled, so I couldn't distinguish the words, but any sound was welcome in comparison to the long hours of silence. Glancing around, I observed the morning sun seeping around the shades that covered the windows. Two of the walls contained dry-erase boards, and the back wall was a shelf of books. I imagined it had been a classroom, but the desks and chairs were gone. There was only a single table and chair where I sat with one ankle shackled to the floor.

The last thing I remembered before waking up in this room was watching the Defiance drag Max away and then the sharp pain like a bee sting to my neck. Three times a day, two boys wearing Defiance jackets came in and demanded my name. I asked for information about Max. I followed my TCI training and gave them my AEI student ID number. They denied any knowledge of Max or a rally at a field in Pennsylvania.

To my knowledge, I'd been here three days, but it was difficult to keep track of time. Every day, my captors brought me a glass of water and a slice of bread. Once a day, they freed me from my restraint and escorted me down the hall to the bathroom. They guarded the door from outside while I used the facilities and searched for a way to escape the tiny windowless room. My interrogators were focused on their job, but they were not cruel. I was hungry, the room was cold, and I was too uncomfortable to get any meaningful sleep. Even if I'd had a pillow and blanket, my worry about Max would have kept me awake. The interrogations were a welcome distraction. In the silence, I prayed that by some miracle he had gotten away.

"I told you she wasn't a prisoner." The voice was deep, authoritative, and right outside my door.

"She wouldn't cooperate enough to verify her name. The rally guards said she admitted it in Pennsylvania, but under the circumstances, they couldn't one hundred percent believe her," the familiar voice of one of my interrogators responded. "All we know for sure is that she was where she was supposed to be, and she looks like the girl in the picture."

I'd been waiting three days for a change, an opportunity to escape. Taking a deep breath, I ran through all of my TCI training. Stay calm, pay attention to the details, note all information, and most importantly, don't give away any information.

The door opened, and a big guy with short black hair stepped into the room. "Are you Rochelle Aumont?"

Closing my eyes, I clenched one hand in the other. "I'm a student of the TCI, identity number 40269."

"I understand why you wouldn't trust me." His voice was gruff but patient. "You were supposed to get better hospitality. Charlie, get in here."

My tired eyes snapped to the door in time to watch Keppler trudge into the room. His hair was a little longer and he wore a Defiance jacket, but otherwise he was physically unchanged.

"Unbelievable." Keppler shoved his hands into his pockets. "Griff, this is your worst idea yet."

"Is this her?" Griff didn't take his eyes off me. "Is this Rochelle Aumont?"

Keppler's unreadable eyes met mine for a second then flicked to the floor. "Yes. That's her."

A smile spread over Griff's face, and he closed the distance between us. He was a big guy, almost a foot taller than Keppler, and was built like a football player. His dark hair was cut close to his head, and his blue eyes scrutinized me.

"Rochelle, I've heard so much about you from Charlie and Molly. It's great to finally meet you in person." He extended his hand. "I'm Griff Spencer."

My eyes searched for Keppler, but he had already gone. "Where am I?"

"You're in St. Louis. It's standard for all prisoners to come through here for interrogation. Not that you're a prisoner." Griff dropped his hand to the table. "Molly and I have been looking for you. We think you can be helpful to the Defiance, and when I found out you were with the TCI, I knew I had to act fast."

"Why fast?" Evaluating Griff's posture, movements, and gestures, I searched for a sign of the violent, cruel Defiance leader Keppler had described. But the guy in front of me was calm, relaxed, and in control.

"The TCI is corrupt. They're only using you for information they think you have. They'll hurt you if you don't help them." He gave me a sympathetic look. "There's a lot to explain, and we'll have plenty of time for that. How about I get you something to eat, and you can get some rest in the car on the way back to Kansas City." He held up a key and walked around the table to free me from my restraint.

"Isn't that all *you* want? To use me for information?" Tired, frustrated, and overwhelmed, I lost focus on my training. "My aunt isn't corrupt."

"Don't put too much trust in your family, kid. That'll get you in trouble every time." He laughed. "I understand you don't know me yet. I don't blame you for not trusting me. But you know Charlie, and he'll be driving us back to Kansas City. You trust him, right?"

I always had. At least until I saw the newsletter, which had even made Max uncertain.

"You shouldn't be in this place." Griff stood in front of me, hand extended. "You've been misled, but you haven't done anything wrong. Come with us and you'll understand."

I didn't want to go anywhere with the Defiance, but I wanted to talk to Keppler. Whichever side he had chosen, I wanted to know he was okay. Beyond that, going back to the Defiance camp would be an incredible opportunity to gather information for the TCI. If Keppler wouldn't help me, then I would figure it out on my own.

I placed my hand in Griff's. "Can you tell me what happened to my friend Max? He was with me in Pennsylvania."

"Give me a few days and I'll find out." He pulled me to my feet. "Rest assured, the orders were to bring you to us peacefully."

---

After leaving the interrogation center, Griff, Keppler, and I stopped at a restaurant in St. Louis. Griff ordered more food than the three of us could eat. At first, he threw out random comments about the good driving weather, a baseball game he and Keppler had attended, and the best places to eat in Kansas City. Despite his attempts to get Keppler talking, my friend remained silent, eyes locked on the plate of food he barely touched. Eventually, Griff gave up on casual conversation and said he would tell me what the papers never published about the Defiance.

"I saw a problem in the world: kids abandoned or orphaned at higher rates than ever, and no one willing to step up to help them. My solution was the Defiance. It started with a few kids rummaging for food in an alley outside the abandoned building I lived in. We took care of each other, found others who had no family. I met Charlie in those early years." He nudged Keppler's arm with his elbow. "The Defiance and homes for children were built on the same concept. The difference is that the homes for children are funded by the government and only act as a holding place for kids and provides them no future. The Defiance, on the other hand, funds themselves and works to build a future tailored to the kids in our organization. We're going to make the world a better place. Everyone needs a family, and it's our mission to make sure every kid has one."

I nodded in response but focused on eating slowly so I wouldn't make myself sick after eating so little for three days. I couldn't argue that Griff had noble goals. It was his method of achieving them that created problems. Then again, what had the TCI, or any other organization, done to help kids who had been abandoned because their families didn't want them or couldn't afford to care for them? Or those orphaned due to the fever? If Kinley hadn't stepped in, Kat and I would have been in a home for children or on the street. Not even Audrie had come to save us.

When we were back in the car, I pretended to sleep in the back seat. Exhausted, I wanted to lose myself in real sleep, but this was an opportunity to eavesdrop on secret Defiance plans. To my disappointment, Griff and Keppler didn't speak much. Every time Griff tried to start a conversation, Keppler only gave short answers and said he was concentrating on driving. Maybe the two of them weren't getting along, or maybe Keppler knew I wasn't asleep.

Eventually, I must have started to doze for real when Griff's hand nudged my knee. "Wake up, Rochelle. We're here."

Sitting up, I rubbed my eyes to bring the world into clearer focus. The building Keppler had parked in front of stood eight floors tall and took up most of the block.

"I'll show you around and get you to your room. Charlie, you want to help with the tour?"

Keppler stared straight ahead. "I have to take the car back to the garage and check out the brakes. They didn't feel right the last few miles."

"Whatever you say, kid." Griff opened his door and got out of the car.

I wanted Keppler to say something. I needed to know whether I could trust him, and the only way to find out would be to talk to him without Griff around. My door opened, and Griff offered his hand to help me out of the car. I would get my answers in time, but I had to play along and be patient. Taking his hand, I got out of the car and walked away from the familiar comfort of an old friend.

"Don't worry about him." Griff ran a hand back and forth over his hair as Keppler drove away. "When I agree with Molly, Charlie's mad. When I agree with Charlie, Molly's mad. You know what I mean?"

I nodded. "They didn't get along very well in Maibe either."

Griff smiled. "I'm hoping you can help me with that. Maybe we can work together to help them compromise on some important matters."

I told myself I should feel uncomfortable or afraid around Griff. He was supposed to be the villain terrorizing the country, but he had been a gentleman from the moment I'd met him. It wasn't hard to believe good kids could be pulled into the Defiance before they knew what they were getting themselves into. After all, that had happened to Keppler—the first time, anyway. Maybe my choice to work with the TCI in exchange for food, shelter, and education wasn't so different from his choice to join the Defiance.

"Making the two of them compromise isn't easy," I said.

"So I've learned." He laughed. "I guess that's something the two of *us* have in common."

Griff walked me through the building. He showed me where his office was on the first floor, and as we climbed the stairs, he told me he and Keppler had rooms on the third floor. My room was at the end of the hall on the fifth floor, across from the communal bathroom. Molly's room was next to mine, but she didn't come to the door when he knocked.

"Make yourself at home. I'll find Molly and let her know you're in your room. She'll take you to get whatever you need to be comfortable here."

I nodded and walked into my room. It was about the same size as my dorm at the AEI. There was a bed with a green comforter, a dresser, and a card table with two folding chairs pushed underneath it. My single window looked down into an alley. I turned to ask Griff when Keppler would be back, but he was gone and the door was closed.

I wanted to confront Keppler, but I didn't know where he went. I needed to call Audrie and find out what happened to Max, but I had no idea where I could find a phone. How could I design an escape plan when I didn't know what would happen if I left the room, let alone the building? Lack of sleep scrambled my thoughts, and suddenly the events of the last few days jumbled together like one long nightmare. It had been a mistake to leave the AEI. Now I was in a hole so deep I couldn't escape without help, but the people who had always come to my rescue didn't even know where to find me.

# CHAPTER 10

# CHARLIE

*April 7, 2091*

"This wasn't supposed to happen. Now Rochelle is here, with the Defiance." I gripped the phone so tight my knuckles were numb.

"So?" Lareina's voice came through the line calm and clear. "This is the break we've been waiting for. Now you can tell her about our plan in person, and she can help you figure out a way to get the other pendants from the TCI."

"What do you think she's going to do? Go back to wherever she came from, walk in, and take them? She can't help us. It's not safe for her to be here."

"She can handle herself in tough situations, probably better than you. She'll be fine," Lareina insisted. "It's good she's there. You need someone to help you keep things in perspective, and Rochelle can do that."

"No. I don't want her involved in this. I need your help to get her out of here." I sank into the folding chair next to the workbench. The garage was quiet, but I listened, expecting someone to walk in for a vehicle any minute. It was early on a Saturday evening, which was well within business hours for the Defiance. "I can sneak her out, but I don't want to put her on a train by herself. All I need you to do is meet us at the train station."

Lareina sighed. "That would be a mistake. Our only chance to destroy the research is with Rochelle's help. If you don't want to tell her, have her call me and I'll explain everything."

"How about you explain it on the train ride back to Maibe. I'll send you a ticket if you'll just come and take her home." I had no idea how I would sneak Rochelle out of here or how I would get her away from Molly. But I would figure it out even if it got me killed. I couldn't stand the way Griff was already trying to manipulate her, and I didn't even want to think about what Molly would say.

"What about you?" Her voice faded to a whisper. "Wouldn't they figure out you helped her get away?"

It had been three days since I had pretended to kill the clerk at the antique store. How long did I have before Griff questioned my loyalty again? "Griff is starting to ask questions about my connection to the TCI. I'm doing my best to convince him I'm loyal, but I might have to get out of here."

"You can't do that." Her sudden burst of anger made me glad we weren't in the same room. "I gave you the Spero pendant so you could go back to the Defiance. I didn't want to, but it was a sacrifice I was willing to make if it meant we'd save the world from the super virus that will certainly happen if the Defiance gets what they want. Don't tell me you're running away before we've accomplished what we set out to do."

"I'm not running away. We're talking about Rochelle. She's your friend." My voice rose in frustration. "When you came back to Maibe, she took you in without question. The Aumonts would do anything to help you, and you don't even care what happens to her?"

"I want Rochelle home more than anyone. Don't you think I would love to have my friend back here?" She paused. "You and Rochelle are safer and smarter together, and I know she wants to be part of this fight."

Rubbing my tired eyes, I rested my forehead on the workbench in the cluttered back room. "She feels responsible because her dad was involved. That's not a good reason for her to be involved."

"Why not? I'm responsible because a girl I barely knew told me to protect the pendant with her dying breath."

I shivered. *Ava Welch.* The daughter of Adam Welch, one of the research scientists. I knew it haunted Lareina that she couldn't save her life. Maybe that's why Lareina was so obsessed with the pendants: she wanted to carry on the mission halted by the deaths of a girl and her father.

"You're responsible because Griff pulled you into this mess," Lareina said. "All three of us have a part to play."

How could I argue? We were all trying to clean up a mess that was created before we were old enough to understand its consequences.

"This is our one chance to save the world from another disaster." Lareina's voice roared through the phone resting next to my head.

"I'm only seventeen." I lifted my head, keeping the phone to my ear. "The only high school I've ever been to was at Rochelle's dining room table. No one can expect me, or any of us, to save the world."

"We're all they've got. What kind of world do you want to live in?" Lareina challenged. "If you want a future, we have to fix this because no one else will."

"I don't have a future anyway."

"I want a future, and my kids at the home for children deserve something better than what we had. Don't be selfish."

"I'm not being selfish. This is about Rochelle." I slammed my hand down on the workbench. "The Defiance will brand her arm and brainwash her just like they did to me."

"They failed with you." Lareina's voice was gentle. "You know what's right and so does Rochelle. We just have to get all the pendants together, and then we'll destroy the research, and this will all be over."

"How? The TCI has at least one of the pendants, and Brandon Davis is a ghost." My breath hitched when I thought about the antique store. What if Griff already knew I didn't kill the clerk? What if his informant told him he was alive and well? I wanted out for good. "We're at a standstill. There's nothing more I can do here."

"That's why we need Rochelle. I'll bet she has all kinds of inside information from the TCI. Don't make any reckless decisions until you know all the facts."

I held my tongue. It wasn't even a week ago when Lareina accused me of supporting Defiance ideas. She couldn't even see how her obsession with the pendants was changing her. But I could. Every time we spoke, she was more desperate for information on my progress.

"Please, Charlie. We have to fix this together, or neither of us will ever talk to the people we love again. Don't you want to come back to Maibe? To your family?"

I wanted that more than anything, but I didn't see how letting Rochelle spend her days with Molly would help me face Kinley. Then again, if Lareina and I could end the race for the research, Rochelle could go home and the Aumonts wouldn't have anything to fear. Maybe she could put in a good word for me with Kinley. At the very least, we would be in charge instead of letting the TCI tell us what to do.

"Okay. I'll try to include Rochelle in our plan," I relented.

"Thank you." Lareina's voice was a puff of relief. "I've never trusted anyone with something so important. Go visit Rochelle. It'll make you feel better, and then we'll talk again on Monday."

"Okay. Talk to you Monday." I hung up the phone and sat for a minute with my face in my hands. Lareina didn't care about anyone but herself. I needed to talk to someone who cared about Rochelle and me. Someone who would listen to my concerns instead of putting their own agenda first.

Pulling the phone back to my ear, I dialed Alexander's number. I pictured his phone on the kitchen counter ringing in an empty room. Maybe he wasn't home.

"Alexander Brewster." The familiar voice was a slap of homesickness. "Hello? Is anyone there?"

I opened my mouth, but no sound came out. Where would I even begin? I waited for the phone to click on the other end before I hung up on mine.

Pulling myself to my feet, I shut off the lights and locked up the garage. I had to check on Rochelle. She'd been out of my sight for too long. Jogging the short distance across the street, I entered the Defiance building. Realizing I hadn't even asked Griff where Rochelle's room was, I assumed it would be close to Molly's and took the stairs to the fifth floor. Before I could second-guess myself, I spotted Molly stepping out of the room at the end of the hall and ran toward her.

"Is that Rochelle's room?" I asked, out of breath. "I was just coming to check on her."

Molly nodded. "She's sound asleep. I just brought her some extra blankets." She nudged the door open so I could see Rochelle huddled under the blankets carefully tucked around her. "I brought her some clothes right after you guys got here, but she must have fallen asleep the minute her head hit the pillow."

"Griff took his time getting her out of interrogation," I said. "We were in St. Louis the day before we picked her up, but he said the longer we waited, the more she would see us as her rescuers and trust us faster. I thought it was cruel. She was probably uncomfortable and scared."

"She's comfortable now," Molly said. I couldn't tell whether she disapproved of Griff's treatment toward Rochelle, but I doubted it. "We'll take care of her."

"She'll just be in the way here." I turned away from Rochelle's sleeping figure. "She's not like us."

"And here I thought you'd be happy to see her." Molly pulled the door shut with a soft click. "Did you really care about the Aumonts, or did you just pretend to care so you'd have a roof over your head?

"They took care of me and didn't ask for anything in return. Yeah. I cared about them." I was tired of her questioning my motives in Maibe, but I also didn't want her to think I would be a threat to her friendship with Rochelle. "That's over now though. Loyalty to the Defiance means no other family."

Molly studied me, and I wondered what she saw. "I know it's hard for you to believe, but Rochelle and I were best friends once. The older we got, the more distractions she had. Todd and Max with their stupid projects, and Kat and Kinley, who didn't like me. Here it's just the two of us. Please don't ruin that for me."

"I don't have time to hang out with Rochelle. But I still don't understand why you want her. You already have Griff, he'll buy you anything you want, and you have as much power in the Defiance as I do."

"It shouldn't surprise me you don't understand. What do you know about family?" She laughed. "Rochelle is the closest thing I've ever had to what a sister should be. She's patient with me, we can talk about things, she knows what I've been through, and she understands." A genuine smile spread over Molly's face. "I can't wait to show her around, introduce her to everyone, and take her shopping to decorate her room."

"And get the passcodes?" I prompted.

"If it comes up, it comes up. I'm not going to pressure her right away." Molly gripped my arm and led me down the hall toward the stairs. "I want Rochelle to feel comfortable here. If she doesn't feel like a prisoner, in time, she'll come to like this place just like us. She'll choose to join the Defiance."

"And if she doesn't?" The farther I moved away from Rochelle's room, the harder it was to breathe.

"She will." Molly propelled me forward. "Because she'll see that she has control over her life with us. She can decide for herself to use the research the only way that will end this war. People don't have to get hurt if they make the right choice and join us."

"The only way that will end the war? Don't you mean releasing the virus to wipe out everyone standing in our way?" I pulled my arm away from her. "How else are you going to scare people into giving up the fight?"

"Rochelle and I will figure that out. You trust her to do the right thing. Don't you?"

"You're really going to do whatever she says? Even if you disagree?"

"Maybe you should stop worrying about my plans and help Griff find the pendants. I'm beginning to think you two don't know what you're doing." She opened the door to the stairwell. "If I were in charge of the Defiance, I'd be holding the research in my hand by now."

"What would you do? March up to the TCI and ask for their pendants?"

"Something like that. Good night, Charlie." She slammed the door in my face.

I stumbled back against the wall of the landing. As much as I hated to admit it, Molly was right. Underneath Griff's tough demeanor and hunger for power, he really wanted to help people, and that slowed him down. Molly, on the other hand, didn't care about anything but getting what she wanted. If she were in charge, the Defiance would control the country by the end of the year.

# CHAPTER 11

# ROCHELLE

*April 8, 2091*

The sun was slanting across my bed, and there was a chill in the morning air. It had taken me a minute to remember where I was. I swallowed over my scratchy throat and realized I must have caught whatever Max had in the days leading up to our mission. Not wanting to cry, I pushed Max out of my mind, found a towel, soap, and clothes waiting for me on the card table in the middle of my room, and crossed the hall to the communal bathroom for a shower. I let the warm steam chase away my chills. Taking my time to dress in the sweatpants and T-shirt Molly had laid out for me, I wondered if Keppler would come to visit. He had been unhappy to see me, but I didn't know if that was because he had a fight with Griff about bringing me here, or if he was disgusted with me for getting caught by the Defiance.

Footsteps padded into the bathroom, and the shower in the stall next to mine turned on. Not wanting to run in to anyone, I gathered up my stuff and walked into the bigger room. I paused at the mirror over a row of sinks, noting my pale face and puffy eyelids. If I had been crying in my sleep, I didn't remember.

When I entered the hallway, I noticed the door to my room was slightly ajar, even though I had closed it. If someone decided to rob me, they would be disappointed to find I didn't own anything. Taking a deep breath, I pushed the door the rest of the way into my room.

"Rochelle." Molly sprang out of the folding chair and smiled. "You found the things I left for you. I'm glad you're getting settled in."

Despite my warm clothes, I shivered. "What do you want?" It seemed so long ago that we were best friends.

"Please don't be mad." Molly brushed her long blonde hair over her shoulder and approached me. Her physical appearance hadn't changed a bit, from her perfect makeup to her stylish skirt and blouse. It was her casual greeting after everything she had done to my family that sparked my annoyance.

"Don't be mad? You kidnapped my sister." I backed away from her outstretched hand. "You locked her in a freezer in a junkyard and didn't tell me where to find her. She could have died."

"If you would have just listened to me, none of that would have happened." She looked down at her shiny black shoes. "I crossed a line though, and I'm sorry."

Trying to determine whether she was sincere, I noted her bowed head and slumped shoulders. "I don't know anything about the passcodes you asked about in December. If I did, I would have gladly traded them for my sister."

"Let's not worry about that right now." Molly nodded toward the table. "I brought you breakfast. You must be hungry."

I stared at the tray of pancakes, scrambled eggs, bacon, and orange juice on the table. Molly had once given me a tea that made me hallucinate that someone was searching my house. "Maybe later. I'm not feeling well."

"Don't say that so loud." Molly darted around me and closed the door. "Around here, the sniffles get you locked in the basement for quarantine."

I rubbed my heavy eyelids and shook my head. "I don't understand."

"Griff is terrified of the fever." She took my arm and guided me to the table. "You're probably just hungry."

"But I already had the fever. I can't get it again." I sat down in the chair she'd pulled out for me.

"We both know that, but Griff is selective about which scientific facts he believes. It's annoying, and his policies make the Defiance less efficient." She broke a piece off my pancake and stuffed it into her mouth, then swallowed it down with a sip of juice. "See, it's safe. Have some breakfast."

I stared again at the food in front of me. It looked better than the breakfast they served at the AEI, but I didn't have an appetite.

"Rochelle?" Molly touched her wrist to my forehead. "Maybe you are a little feverish. Don't worry, I'll cover for you." She retrieved a blanket from my bed and draped it around my shoulders. "I'll tell Griff you need to catch up on your sleep and adjust to your new room. I'm sorry he left you in interrogation for three days. If I had known, I would have come to get you myself."

"Griff said he would find out what they did with Max." I cleared my throat. "Do you know if he did yet?"

"Max?" She slid a chair over and sat down next to me. "Rochelle, I don't know anything about how you got here. It was a surprise from Griff, and I still don't know how he pulled it off."

"Max and I were on a trip." I chose my words carefully to avoid saying anything about the TCI. "Some Defiance guys surrounded us. They had a picture of me from the Maibe paper. They dragged him away and said they would kill him."

She studied me with her eyebrows raised and mouth open to ask a question, but she patted my arm instead. "If Griff said he'll find out for you, he will."

Blinking back tears, I nodded. "Is Keppler here?"

"I'm sure he'll be by to see you one of these days. He's always busy writing, or working on cars, or going to the gym with Griff." She shrugged. "I thought maybe the two of you had a falling out because he took your pendant."

"He never had my pendant." I stood to get away from her. "Stop trying to confuse me."

"Rochelle, I'm not . . ." Her eyes met mine and she looked away. "I'm sorry."

"No, you're not. You don't understand." Tears streamed down my face, but I talked through them. "You're the reason why Kat won't speak to me, and why Audrie won't let me go home to visit Kinley or Todd. You took my family away from me, and if Max is gone, I'm all alone."

"That's not true." Molly guided me to my bed. "I'm here for you."

I sat down and huddled in my blanket. "This isn't supposed to be happening. I just want to go back and change everything I've ever done. I want my dad."

"It's okay, Rochelle." She rubbed my back while I cried. "I miss my dad too. I understand."

"Your dad died from the fever. My dad was murdered. *Your* dad poisoned him. Whether he meant to or not, he killed his best friend over pendants and passcodes, and now I don't have my dad and I need him."

"I didn't know about any of this back then." Her voice was shaking. "I don't believe my dad would have hurt Auggie on purpose. He cried after the funeral."

I looked up, and her eyes were brimming with tears. "We're in this mess because our dads couldn't agree on how to use the research," I said. "I don't want to repeat that."

Molly sniffled. "Neither do I. Please help me, Rochelle. I don't want to hurt people, but it's so much easier to solve all our problems if I do."

In that moment, my old friend sat in front of me. She was no longer power-hungry and violent, but scared and confused.

"You don't have to stay here. You don't have to be a member of the Defiance," I said, even though I knew it was probably useless. I couldn't even talk her out of joining the Defiance in the first place.

"I have nowhere else to go." She wiped away tears with her sleeve. "There's no going back. But that doesn't mean we can't do the right thing now."

"Please, just think about it." I took her hands in mine. This was my chance to help her. To get her away from the Defiance and the pendants. "If you decide to leave, I'll go with you and we'll figure the rest out together."

Molly shook her head. "We can do good things here. All Griff and Charlie ever want to do is fuel the war and take over more land. I want to get the research. Then all we have to do is threaten to create the super virus, and everyone will back down and the war will be over. We can restore peace and save lives."

I shook my head. "That's dangerous. What would you do if someone tests your threat? If you infect even one person with that virus, we're dealing with something worse than the fever in a matter of weeks."

"No, Rochelle." She squeezed my hands. "They're all so scared after the fever, so they wouldn't risk it. Plus, we'll develop the vaccine just in case."

"There is no just-in-case. If we unleash something like that . . ." It would be an act of pure evil. My friend wasn't completely gone. She still had a conscience and knew the difference between right and wrong. She told herself her intentions were good, but the promise of power would persuade her to cross the line. If she stayed with the Defiance, I couldn't help her.

"We can talk about that another time. You should be resting." She brought me tissues to dry my face.

I lay down and shivered despite the thick warm blankets. "Will you stay with me?" I didn't want to be alone, but I also didn't want her to have the chance to make any more bad decisions.

"Of course. I have so much to tell you." She pulled a chair over to my bed and sat down. "I'm so glad you're here, Rochelle. We'll figure this out together."

Closing my eyes, I nodded. Nothing happens by chance. Maybe this was my opportunity to help Molly. Maybe the only way to help my friend and save the world was by joining the Defiance.

# CHAPTER 12

# CHARLIE

*April 9–10, 2091*

G riff slid the map toward Molly. "Once we make our way up the East Coast, the country will be ours. Then we'll get the rest of the pendants." He had called an emergency meeting with Molly and me to inform us that the pendants would be our secondary goal.

Molly slid the map back. "The pendants should be our priority over everything else. We're wasting time and resources on this war when the research could put us in control overnight."

"We're winning the war." Griff returned. "It could take years to figure out this pendant mess."

"That's because you don't know what you're doing," Molly retorted.

Griff turned to me and shrugged.

A sense of relief swept through me. Griff's obsession with the pendants was finally over. Rubbing my eyes, I sat back in my chair and opened my notebook on the table. I didn't expect anything worth taking notes on, and I wouldn't be able to concentrate even if there was. I had barely slept the night before as I tried to decide what would be the best thing for Rochelle. When I returned to her room this morning and Molly told me Rochelle was still resting, it had become clear that Molly didn't want me anywhere near Rochelle, which only made the situation more challenging.

"I thought you would bring Rochelle to the meeting." Griff raised his eyebrows at Molly.

"She's still catching up on her sleep after that horrible ordeal you put her through. You could have shown her better hospitality." Molly brushed her hair behind her shoulders. "She'll be here for Friday's meeting."

"Perfect." Griff gave her a big smile. "Aren't you glad Charlie and I found her for you?"

"Of course. Maybe she'll be able to talk some sense into you two." Molly turned to me. "Don't you think she'll bring some much-needed perspective to our meetings?"

I yawned and shrugged. "I guess we'll find out."

"What's wrong with you?" Molly snapped. "Did you stay up too late writing your little newsletter?"

"Let him be." Griff folded his map. "Charlie's writing is our secret weapon. As long as we have him, we'll win for sure."

"Whatever." Molly stood. "I've had enough of you two. I'm going to visit Rochelle and talk to someone reasonable." She turned on her heel and strode out of the room.

"What's bothering you, kid? You look like you haven't slept in days."

"I'm fine." I closed my notebook. "I've just been catching up on a lot of work after all those days on the road."

"Don't worry about this Molly-and-Rochelle situation." He punched my arm. "We'll turn them against each other. It'll be a good lesson for Molly. You know, teach her that getting what she wants isn't always what she imagined it would be."

"I guess. But what about Rochelle?"

"What about her?" Griff laughed. "I guess it's up to Molly. If she wants to keep her around, whatever makes her happy. If she decides she's a traitor, we'll get rid of her."

"After everything we went through to bring her here?" I

stood and picked up my notebook. "You would just eliminate her because Molly gets tired of her?"

"You know how it is, Charlie. Rochelle grew up with a family that actually cared about her. It'll be hard for her to fit in around here." He stood and shrugged. "There's not much we can do for someone who can't give all their loyalty to the Defiance. But maybe she'll surprise us." The scowl on his face signaled there was more to the conversation than he was letting on.

"Is that what you think about me?" I asked. "That staying with the Aumonts for a few months makes me less loyal?"

"You tell me." He shoved his chair under the table. "The pendant you gave me, the one that says 'Spero.' Was that Auggie Aumont's pendant?"

"Yes," I replied quickly, afraid to let Griff hear any hesitation. "Who else's would it be?"

"Adam Welch's, according to the notes taken by Molly's dad. She happened to look into it last night and brought it to my attention this morning. Welch should have had Spero and Optimus. Auggie should have had Pessimus." His scowl relaxed to a frown. "What's your explanation for that?"

"Molly's dad must have written something down wrong." I didn't need an excuse, only logic. "The pendant I brought you was in Auggie's truck. I did exactly what you asked and brought it here. Don't tell me you think I met Adam Welch and he gave me his pendant."

Griff smiled. "No, that would be crazy. But Molly's pendant said 'Tomorrow,' Zimmer's said 'Better,' and my dad's said 'Instruo,' as the notes indicated. Molly just thought there was something to it, so I had to check."

"But we're done with the pendants, like you said a few minutes ago." The hope I had felt earlier melted away.

"I said they were secondary to the war. I'll never be done with them." He ran his hand back and forth over his hair. "Think about it, kid. Those pendants are my inheritance. They're all my dad left me. Wouldn't you do the same in my shoes?"

I wanted to argue with him, but it had never worked before, and I knew he was still suspicious of me, thanks to Molly. "I guess so."

Griff squeezed my shoulder. "I knew you'd understand. We're brothers, right?"

My stomach churned. It was a combination of concern that he had to ask that question and knowing this would be our last conversation as brothers. I couldn't leave Rochelle at the mercy of Molly and the Defiance, and I couldn't fulfill Lareina's plan with Molly snooping into which pendant I should have found. Everything was about to change and there was no going back.

"Right," I said. "I think I just need to take a day off and get some rest. Then I'm with you for the next step."

"Sleep all day if you need to. And don't worry about the Spero pendant. We'll figure out why Auggie had the wrong one." He pushed me toward the door. "Maybe it'll lead us to the break-through we've been waiting for."

I nodded, not wanting to give away how close he was to the truth. Without another word, I walked halfway down the hall to my room and closed myself inside. Tossing my notebook onto the bed, I sat down with my face in my hands. My foot nudged the backpack on the floor. The day I returned to Kansas City, I had stuffed it full of all my notebooks containing the stories and journals I'd written as a child and those I'd secretly compiled during my first stay with the Defiance. I didn't intend to leave them behind again and kept them packed in case I needed to make a quick getaway.

If I stuck around any longer, Griff would discover my real motives for returning. Molly would make sure of that. More importantly, if I didn't get Rochelle out of here, she wouldn't live much longer. She was a good person, and she wouldn't be able to handle Griff and Molly like I could. Whether Lareina wanted to believe it or not, getting Rochelle away from the Defiance was the only right thing to do. I wouldn't sacrifice her even to save the rest of the world.

---

Standing on the rail of the fire escape, I gripped the ledge under the nearest fifth-floor window and slid one foot onto the thin ledge of brick that my legs stretched to reach. I cast a glance over my shoulder at the alley below where the car I'd parked waited, hidden in the darkness. Taking a deep breath, I slid my other foot onto the ledge and eased my way under Molly's window. I had heeded Molly's warning to stay away from Rochelle's room all day in fear that she would push Griff to probe deeper into my deception.

Rochelle's window was a foot away, but I couldn't reach it while I still held on to the nearest ledge. This was my only chance to talk to Rochelle, and, more importantly, to get her out. Taking a deep breath, I pushed from one ledge and flailed for the other, catching it with one hand and pulling myself the rest of the way across the building. Reaching up over the ledge with one hand, I knocked on Rochelle's window and waited. It was three in the morning, the streets were quiet, and I hoped everyone except Rochelle was sleeping. My fingers went numb against the cold concrete, and I wished I had worn gloves. I knocked one more time and contemplated sliding back to the fire escape before my grip would fail me.

A loud grating sound snapped my attention to the glass pane above as it slid open. "Aumont. Down here."

"Keppler?" She stuck her head out the window and looked down. "What are you doing?"

"I need to talk to you." Pushing myself up with my toes, I wrapped my hands over the sill and into the warmth of her room. "Can I come in?"

She took a step back. "Sure, but how . . ."

Before she could finish, I hoisted myself up and through the window. Spending so much time at the gym with Griff had its benefits.

Rochelle stood in front of me, arms wrapped around herself, shivering. "I was asleep, and in my dream I was home in Maibe and Todd was knocking on my window."

"Sorry to disappoint you." I slapped my tingly hands against my legs.

"I didn't mean it that way." She lunged forward and wrapped her arms around me. "I don't care which side you're on. You're still my friend and I've missed you."

"I'm on your side." I hugged her back, then gently squirmed my way out of her iron grip. "Are you okay? Did they hurt you?"

"I think I have the flu or something, but Molly has been taking care of me." She took a big step away from me. "We've been talking a lot, and I think I'm supposed to be here. She needs a friend."

"No, Aumont, she's using you. And so will Griff. We have to get out of here before they hurt you."

Rochelle walked over to her bed and sat down. "Why should I believe everything you say and nothing Molly says?"

"Think about everything she's done in the past year to hurt you and your family. She tried to force you into the Defiance. That's what she's still doing now." I looked down at my shoes. "And she kidnapped Kat."

"I remember you played a part in that last one." Rochelle's green eyes held me in place. "I've known Molly my whole life. We've been through a lot together."

"You and I have been through a lot together too, and you know

I would never hurt Kat." I took a step toward Rochelle and held out my hand to her. "I can explain it all, but we have to get out of here first."

"Have you been reporting to Audrie like you agreed to do?" She clenched one hand in the other. "Or are you having too much fun writing Defiance propaganda?"

"I haven't called Audrie because there's a mole in the TCI feeding Griff information, and I'm scared I'll get caught. He's already suspicious of me because his informant said I'd signed that agreement." It took everything I had to keep my voice low and even. "Griff told me to write the newsletters, but I also like having my writing recognized. I know it was wrong, but I'm done with that, and I'm getting us both out of here."

"I'm not leaving." Rochelle cleared her throat. "I'm not afraid to report to Audrie, and I can stop Molly from using the pendants to hurt people. We're going to make decisions about the research together. This is my only chance to clean up this mess."

"It's not your mess, and Molly isn't going to listen to you any more than she listens to Griff. She does whatever she wants, and all she cares about is power. You don't know what these people are capable of."

"I can learn." Her eyes locked with mine. "You did."

"I can't stay here either." Turning away from her, I decided how much to reveal. "Griff is always questioning my loyalty and expects me to do terrible things. Before we came to St. Louis, I was supposed to kill an innocent man because he didn't have the information Griff wanted."

A moment of silence passed before she spoke. "Did you do it?"

My face burned with shame because she had to ask that question. "No. I pretended. And if he finds out, I'm dead. So I have to go, and I'm not leaving you here."

"Can't we just stay for a week or two?" She sniffled. "Long

enough for me to find a way to help Audrie end this so I can go home?"

"I don't have that much time and neither do you. This is our only chance to run. Please, Aumont. I have a car down in the alley."

"If I run, I'll never get to go home." Rochelle coughed into her sleeve. "If I don't do something, I'll never see Kinley or Kat again."

"Aumont, I know neither the TCI nor the Defiance will ever have all the pendants, whether we help or not." There had to be something I could say to convince her to leave. "But all we have to do is get in the car, and we can be home in a few hours."

Hope sparkled in her eyes for a second, then drained from her face and deflated from her body. "I can't go back to Maibe. It would be dangerous for Kinley. If I agree to leave, will you go back to New York with me?"

"I'll take you there, but I can't stay. Once I leave here, I can't ever stay in one place for more than a day or two. If Griff found me in Maibe, he can find me anywhere."

"That can't be your life." She pressed one hand to her forehead. "The TCI can protect you. If you come back to the AEI with me, you'll be safe from them."

"Because they did a great job of protecting you." I couldn't disguise the frustration in my voice.

"That was my fault. I should have talked Max out of it." She squeezed her eyes shut. "Now I might never see him again."

"What do you mean?" I asked.

"Max was on the assignment with me," she whispered. "They dragged him away and said they would kill him."

"No way." It was hard to get the words out, and suddenly all I wanted was to work on the time machine with the friend who called me his brother—not someone who controlled me like Griff, but someone who cared about me. It had taken almost a year for me to figure out the difference. "Max is smart. He got away. We'll go to New York and he'll be there."

Rochelle turned away from me and walked to the window. "How did you get up here?"

"Mostly the fire escape. Reaching from one windowsill to the next is a little tricky, but I'll help you." I found a hoodie in the closet and kicked a pair of tennis shoes to Rochelle. "Put these on. It's cold outside."

She did as I told her, and we both jumped when a door slammed above us and footsteps creaked overhead. We had to get out of there before too many people started their day.

"Just someone going to the bathroom. We still have time." I slid one leg out the window and ducked my head under the glass pane. "Just watch me and you'll know what to do." Lowering myself until my feet found the ledge below, I slid along the building, pushed myself to the next windowsill, and finally landed on the solid surface of the fire escape.

Rochelle slid halfway out her window, looked down at the alley, and then at me about ten feet away from her. "I can't do this. I'll fall."

"It's just like climbing out of your window at home. You did that all the time." My voice was so loud in the still night I feared someone would hear us. "I'll help you." Climbing back onto the rail, I gripped the fire escape with one hand and leaned out as far as I could toward Rochelle.

She nodded and found her footing on the thin ledge as I had minutes before. "I didn't climb out of my window all the time. Only for emergencies."

"Whatever you say, Aumont." I watched her feet inch toward me in painful slow motion. She made it to Molly's window, rested her forehead against the wall for a second, then reached for my hand.

Her feet slipped as my hand gripped her wrist, leaving her dangling with one hand on the window ledge. She didn't scream but looked at me with calm, trusting eyes.

I linked my fingers tighter around her wrist. "Let go of the ledge and get ready to brace your feet against the rail. I'll pull you in."

Rochelle took a deep breath and let go. She swung toward me, and the bottom of her shoes caught the rungs of the rail and slid downward. Once her hand found the top of the rail, I jumped down from my perch and pulled her over onto the landing.

"Are you okay?" I gripped her elbows to steady her.

Rochelle smiled and nodded. "Let's not do that again until I'm feeling better."

I laughed. "Let's not do that again at all."

A light came on in Molly's room, and we pressed ourselves against the brick wall.

"She might be going over to my room to check on me," Rochelle whispered.

I took her hand, and we ran down the fire escape and to the car. Hands shaking, I pulled the passenger door open for her, then jogged around to my side. Glancing up, I glimpsed a silhouette in Rochelle's open window before sliding into the car and speeding out of the alley.

# CHAPTER 13

# ROCHELLE

*April 10, 2091*

"Aumont." A hand nudged my shoulder. "Aumont?"

I opened my eyes and looked at Keppler, who sat in the driver's seat of the parked car. After leaving Kansas City, we had decided to go out of our way and drive west for an hour so we could disappear into a more rural area. I had been telling Keppler about news from Maibe and explaining life at the AEI. I didn't remember falling asleep.

"We're a mile from the Nebraska border. Once we cross it, we're out of Defiance territory. This is as close as I'm willing to go on the road. We're safer walking the rest of the way through these fields." He turned to me. "Are you feeling up to that?"

I nodded even though my head was heavy and I wanted to slip back into sleep. "What if Griff and Molly think we went back to Maibe and they go there looking for us?" It had become my greatest fear that the people I cared about would get hurt because of a mistake I made.

He stared out the windshield at miles of thick grass still brown and tangled from the winter. "They know we wouldn't make it that easy for them. And they know Kinley wouldn't welcome me back after I left with the Defiance. We'll only be in Nebraska long enough to find a train station." He reached for his bag in the back seat. "You can sleep all the way to New York."

I knew he was taking a huge risk every step of this journey. If anyone along the way decided to check his arm, there would be no hiding the Defiance brand. He was putting everything on the line to get me to safety, and any doubts I had earlier about trusting him had evaporated. He was the same Keppler who had lived with my family for almost a year.

"I'll be fine. Let's go." We both got out of the car and trudged into the field. It was late enough for the sunrise, but thick clouds blocked much of the light from getting through. I pulled my hood over my head, shoved my hands into my pockets, and kept walking.

"Aumont?" Keppler's voice startled me after ten minutes of walking in silence. "I understand Kinley has plenty of reasons to be upset with me, but does she think I . . ." He stopped walking and turned to me. "Did she believe I was helping the Defiance? That I'd lied to her the whole time just to get a pendant or some passcodes?"

I couldn't give him a good answer because I didn't know. Instead, I shook my head. "I think she was just upset and scared for you. I don't know. There was so much happening at once."

Keppler nodded and looked down at his shoes. "I always knew I'd mess things up. I hoped it wouldn't be like this though."

"I wish you would have just let her help you." I sighed. "Why didn't you tell us you planned to go back to the Defiance? Especially since it was just to work undercover?"

"Because I knew you wouldn't like it." He shoved his hands into his pockets. "I had to go, Aumont. If I had let Kinley hide me, Griff would have come to Maibe looking for me, and I couldn't let him hurt any of you."

"That makes sense. But Molly keeps saying you brought a pendant with you—"

"Don't listen to her," Keppler snapped. "She's trying to manipulate everyone."

Before I could ask another question, voices shouted to our right. "Hey, you two. Stay right there."

Keppler gripped my arm. "We have to run. Come on."

He caught my hand and pulled me along with him. I tried to pretend I was on my morning run with Max, but it was hard to catch my breath. The crunch of footsteps behind us only got closer as my arm reached out to hold Keppler's hand as he picked up speed.

"Stop." The voice was at my ear. A hand wrapped around my arm and yanked me back, severing Keppler's grip from mine.

I struggled against strong hands that held my arms behind me and watched two men, twice Keppler's size, tackle him fifteen yards in front of me. I couldn't breathe. I was about to lose two of my friends in the same week.

"Check his arm," the man holding me in place shouted to the others.

Each of the men held one of Keppler's arms, but he kicked and twisted in every direction to escape. One of them shoved his face into the ground as the other yanked off the sleeve of his jacket.

"He has the brand!" the man shouted, pointing to Keppler's arm.

"It's not what it looks like!" I shouted in the loudest voice I could muster. There had to be a way out of this. "We both work undercover for the TCI. Neither of us are with the Defiance. I can show you." My captor let go of my left arm, and I pulled it free of my hoodie. Lifting the sleeve of my T-shirt, I exposed my entire arm between the shoulder and elbow. "Please don't hurt him."

The man behind me turned me away from Keppler so the two of us were speaking face-to-face. "Did that guy kidnap you? You don't have to cover for him. We can help you if you're in danger."

I shook my head. "We're working together. We have to report back to the TCI. If you just let me make a phone call, I can prove it." It was a gamble, but I hoped Audrie would vouch for Keppler. She couldn't abandon him when he was helping me.

"If that's the case, we'll have to turn you over to the local police and let them follow up." He raised his chin and shouted over my head, "Go easy on him. He might not be one of them."

The three men loaded us into the back seat of a car, and one of them drove us to a small-town police station. I asked Keppler if he was okay, but he just shook his head and worked on bending his glasses back into shape. Once inside, they separated us. I was escorted to an office-like room where I gave a policeman our names along with Audrie's name and phone number. He promised to contact her, but he had to follow protocol until he had answers, so he took me to a holding cell where Keppler was sitting on a bench inside.

I sat down next to my friend and waited for the officer to secure the door and walk away. "They're going to call Audrie. We'll be out of here soon."

"You'll be out of here." He pulled his crooked glasses off his dirt-smudged face. "She's not going to help me. I didn't keep up my end of the agreement."

"You're helping me right now." I reached for his hand, but he pulled it away. "She'll tell them you aren't Defiance."

"But I am Defiance. It only took me days to fall right back into it." He slowly lifted his face until his blue eyes met mine. "That's all I'll ever be."

"You know that's not true."

He shook his head, looked away, and returned to fidgeting with his glasses. I scooted closer to him until our shoulders touched, and we sat in silence.

Some time passed before footsteps approached. The police officer I had spoken to earlier appeared outside our cell.

"I've verified everything you told me." He pulled his keys from his belt and unlocked the door. "The TCI asked me to keep an eye on you two until they get here to pick you up. Come out here where you'll be more comfortable, and I'll order some pizza."

I sprang to my feet, relieved that Audrie had spoken for both of us. Keppler stood but remained slumped and despondent as we followed the officer to a lounge area with a couch, two cushioned chairs, and a small TV.

He leaned down next to the couch and picked up the bag Keppler had brought with him. "This belongs to you. Hang out here, and I'll get you guys some board games or something."

Keppler took the bag and sat on the couch, clutching it even after the officer left. "What do you think Audrie had to tell them to get us from a jail cell to pizza and board games?"

"The truth." I sank onto the under-stuffed cushion next to his. "We're not with the Defiance. We're with the TCI."

"I don't want to be with either of them." Keppler rubbed his hands over his face. "The Defiance does some pretty messed up stuff, but at least I know what they stand for. What does the TCI want out of all this? I think I would have been better off with the border militia. Who knows what the TCI will do when they get ahold of me?"

"Let's not worry about that for now." I found his hand and squeezed it. "What's in your bag?"

"Everything I regretted leaving behind the first time." He opened the bag to reveal a dozen notebooks.

"All of your writing." I smiled.

"Among other things." He pulled out the biggest notebook, opened the front cover, and slid a photo out of the folder pocket.

I studied the two people in the photograph. A little boy, maybe eight years old, with dark hair, held the straps of his book bag where they came over the front of his shoulders. Next to him, a girl, even younger, with curly blonde hair and a pink satchel over one shoulder, grinned at the camera.

"Is that you?" I could see the resemblance in the pointed nose, and chin, and dark hair with the boy in the photo and Keppler sitting next to me.

He nodded. "And my sister, Isabelle. This was one of those rare good days when my mom was . . . herself. She did our laundry the day before and made us breakfast in the morning. She didn't yell at me about putting the dishes away in the wrong places, or letting Isabelle eat crackers on the couch. She just wanted a picture of the first day of school. On days like that, I pretended I had parents who actually took care of me. It was a chance to catch my breath before the next round of yelling and hitting while trying to raise my sister."

"I wish I would have known you then. Someone should have helped you." No matter what Kinley believed about Keppler, I had to convince her to let him move back in with us when all of this was over. His parents and sister had died in a car accident last year, so we were the only family he had.

"Why would they? People in my town shunned my sister and me. They didn't want to deal with my dad, and they had their own families to take care of. That isn't selfish, it's smart." He slid the picture back into the notebook. "The first person who ever helped me was Griff. I guess that's why I was stupid enough to trust him."

"Now that I've met him, I think I would have trusted him too. He's not a bad guy, just misguided about his ideas on how to fix the world."

Keppler nodded. "I'm afraid there isn't a peaceful way to fix the world. Maybe we would be better off just to live with it broken."

"Maybe we just have to be patient." I shrugged. "Change happens slowly. We can figure all of this out."

"We never figure anything out." He placed the notebook in his bag and let it slide to the floor. "We just keep making everything worse."

"We're going to get home. Both of us." I rested my head back against the wall. "We'll tell Audrie everything we know, and she'll find a way to use it to put an end to all of this pendant stuff. We'll let the adults deal with all of it like we should have from the beginning."

He rested his head next to mine.

"Audrie told me she regrets how she handled things in Maibe. She'll give you a break."

He didn't reply, and I couldn't stop remembering all the times Audrie had scolded Kinley for letting Keppler move into our house. She didn't like him from the day she met him.

I closed my eyes and swallowed over my scratchy throat. I understood Keppler's fear of the TCI. He hadn't kept up his deal with them, but he had helped me escape, and they had to give him some credit for that. Max said Sid thought writing the newsletter didn't look good for Keppler, but wasn't everything different now? I pulled my icy hands into my sleeves, wishing Max could be here to make us laugh, but fearing I would never see him again.

# CHAPTER 14

# CHARLIE

*April 11, 2091*

I paced from one end of the room to the other knowing Audrie would be arriving any minute. My head screamed at me to get out of here, pretend I was going down the hall to the bathroom, and just keep walking out the back door. But I couldn't leave Rochelle alone, especially if she was about to find out if Max survived their assignment.

Rochelle was resting on the couch, and I was glad she was finally getting some sleep. We had spent most of the night watching TV and playing board games since we were both too anxious to be alone with our thoughts. When Rochelle spoke, she talked about Max. She said they weren't as close at the AEI as they'd been in Maibe. Max had become friends with almost everyone he had classes with, and they were interested in the science projects and inventions no one in Maibe cared about. It didn't bother her that he had other friends; she only felt guilty for not trying harder to talk him out of the assignment that took them to the Defiance rally.

"What time is it?" Rochelle sat up and rubbed her eyes.

I stopped pacing and glanced down at my watch. "It's early in the morning. How are you feeling?"

"A little better." She smoothed her hair back into a ponytail.

A soft knock on the door snapped our heads in that direction.

The door opened and Audrie walked into the room. Without a word, she rushed over and wrapped her arms around her niece.

"Are you okay?" Audrie said, ending the several minutes of silence. "Are you hurt?"

"I'm okay." Rochelle broke the hug and wiped her eyes with her sleeve. "Aunt Audrie, did you find Max? Is he okay?"

I held my breath and waited for the answer I feared.

"He's safe, kiddo." Audrie pressed her hand to Rochelle's forehead. "A little beat-up but mostly worried about you."

Tears streamed down Rochelle's cheeks, and she covered her face with her hands.

Audrie pulled her back into her arms and looked at me with tired eyes. "Charlie, are you okay?"

My mind ricocheted from relief that Max was safe, to shock at Audrie's sincere concern. I nodded. "How much trouble am I in for not calling with a report?"

"I've been putting in a good word for you." She sighed. "Please tell me you have a compelling reason for not calling."

I nodded again, hoping the threat of an informant would count as a good enough reason.

"We'll talk about it later. For now, I've convinced my boss you're valuable because of how much you know about the Defiance." She pulled a wad of tissues from her pocket and handed them to Rochelle. "I'll help you as much as I can. But for now, let's get out of here. We have a long drive back to New York."

She was taking me back to New York. I reasoned that had to be a good sign. Maybe I hadn't blown my chance at freedom just yet. Audrie helped Rochelle to her feet, and I followed them to the front of the building where a big man in a gray suit chatted with the two police officers who had been taking care of us.

He turned as we approached and nodded at Rochelle. "I see you've made it back to us in one piece, Rochelle. I knew you were the right one for the assignment. I think you deserve a day off before we meet to discuss your observations."

"Thank you, Head Agent MacCormack." Rochelle looked him in the eye but remained close to her aunt's side.

I studied Agent MacCormack. He was tall with broad shoulders and a head of thick dark hair. My heart stopped for a minute when I got a clear look at his face and realized that was exactly what Griff would look like in thirty years. Griff had once told me that after his mom passed away, his uncle Mac was always there for him when his dad wasn't. Was it possible his uncle was a head agent in the TCI?

"Charlie? Are you ready?" Audrie's hand on my arm snapped me back to reality.

Flinching, I stepped away. "Yeah. Yeah. Let's go."

My feet followed the others outside while my brain screamed at me to run. I didn't know what it meant if Griff's uncle was in charge and had sent Rochelle and Max to a Defiance rally. Would he be Griff's inside guy? Would he risk his title and reputation to help his nephew? If he was helping him, why didn't the Defiance have all the pendants yet?

"Go ahead, Agent Aumont. You and Rochelle need some time to catch up. Take the day off and spend some time with your niece." MacCormack turned to me. "Charlie can ride with me. We have plenty to talk about."

"You don't have to do that." Audrie forced a smile, and Rochelle looked at me with concern. "He can ride with us if you have other stops to make."

"My schedule's clear. We'll be fine." MacCormack's heavy hand clamped my shoulder. "Right, kid?"

"Right," I croaked. If my suspicions were correct, it confirmed that wherever I went, Griff always found me in one form or another.

Audrie took a step toward us. "Sir, if you don't mind me suggesting, Charlie is going to need a place to stay so he'll be close by to answer our questions. Max doesn't have a roommate right now and they already know each other."

"Thank you, Agent Aumont. I'll keep that in mind." He dismissed her with a nod. I believed Audrie was doing everything in her power to help me, but it also appeared there was little she could do to change her boss's mind.

Rochelle gave me an anxious wave and walked to the first car with Audrie. MacCormack gestured to the other car, and because I figured running would only prove my allegiance to the Defiance, I got in the passenger seat. For ten minutes, we drove in silence. I watched bare fields pass alongside the desolate highway.

"You signed an agreement with the TCI in December, and we haven't heard from you in four months." He turned to me, watching the road with his peripheral vision. "What went wrong?"

I would have rather explained this to Audrie, but that wasn't an option. "Griff Spencer, the leader of the Defiance, told me he has an informant in the TCI. He knew about the agreement I signed, and I was afraid he would find out if I followed through with it."

"Is that right?" He shook his head. "Rest assured, I'll find the mole, and Griff won't be hearing anything else about you. You'll be safe with us."

I let out the breath I'd been holding, but the knot in my stomach didn't relax. "Am I in trouble?"

"Depends how helpful you are." MacCormack turned back to the road. "How well do you know Griff Spencer?"

"Pretty well." It took everything I had to keep my voice steady.

"Well enough to see the family resemblance." He laughed. "I can tell by the look on your face. If it makes you feel better, my superiors know, and I expect you to keep it to yourself. I care about the kid, but I don't support what he's doing. He's always been a little troubled. I tried to help him, but when he ran away from home at sixteen . . . well, I suppose you know the rest of the story."

If MacCormack was anything like Griff, showing fear would be my downfall. "Most of it. Do you and Griff still talk?"

"Don't get smart with me, kid." He pinned me in place with his eyes as we hurtled down the highway. "He's my nephew, and I talk to him when he'll take my calls. I've been trying to convince him to turn in the pendants he's collected and walk away from the Defiance in exchange for immunity."

"Immunity?" If there was a way out for the leader of the Defiance, there had to be a way out for me.

"You know, so he'll get in far less trouble than he would if he gets caught as things stand today." MacCormack looked up at the rearview mirror, but I could feel his peripheral vision on me. "Is immunity something you're interested in?"

The knot in my stomach released as my body relaxed back into the seat. If I cooperated with MacCormack and did everything right, I could go home. If Kinley found out I was a hero who helped take down the Defiance, she would understand I hadn't betrayed her. I could get my family back and pursue my dream career as a real journalist.

"I thought so." He slowed down as we passed through a town, and he gestured to people walking on the sidewalk in the sunshine. "You're smart enough to choose your freedom over some dream of power. I wonder, then, what inspired you to write that newsletter for the Defiance?"

My stomach clenched. "It was a direct order from Griff. I was afraid he would kill me if I didn't comply." It was mostly the truth.

"I see." He raised one eyebrow at me. "So, now that he can't hurt you, you're willing to work with us and tell us everything you know?"

"Yes." If this was my opportunity to stop the Defiance and stay out of trouble, I had to take it. "And then when we're finished and you don't need me anymore, I can go home?"

"It depends on how everything plays out." He held the steering wheel steady with one hand. "I'll do everything I can to keep you out of prison if you keep your word to tell me everything you know."

I didn't believe him, but there was nowhere to run. All I could do in the moment was cooperate and hope for the best.

"We have a long trip ahead of us. Why don't you start at the beginning. Why did you join the Defiance?"

# CHAPTER 15

# ROCHELLE

*April 11, 2091*

"I'm sure he'll be scared." Audrie's voice mingled with the whistle of the tea kettle in the next room. "He's been stuck with MacCormack all day. Poor kid. Who knows what scare tactics he's been using on him."

I pulled the covers up to my chest and sank back into the pillows in Audrie's guest room. By the time we had parked in front of her apartment, I was visibly shivering. My aunt had sent me to take a warm bath and gave me a set of pajamas to wear. She promised to call Sid to find out if MacCormack had returned with Keppler. I reached for my charm bracelet on the nightstand. She had followed through on her promise to keep it safe, along with my necklace from Todd.

"Thank you, Sid. I'll get over there to check in on him as soon as I can tomorrow. Okay, talk to you later." Audrie entered the room with a cordless phone pressed between her ear and shoulder, a mug in one hand, and a thermometer in the other.

"What did Sid say? Does he know where Keppler is?" I told Audrie about Keppler's fears since he hadn't kept his agreement, as well as my own worries about what that meant for him. "I'll tell Head Agent MacCormack that Keppler helped me. He doesn't deserve to be punished."

"It's okay, Rochelle. Take a deep breath." She set the mug down on the nightstand and held out the thermometer. "Charlie will be okay."

I opened my mouth for the thermometer and held it under my tongue.

"MacCormack took my suggestion to put Charlie with Max. He called Sid earlier and asked him to stay late so he could show Charlie around." The thermometer beeped and she pulled it from my mouth. "One hundred point six. That's not bad, but we'll go to the doctor first thing in the morning just in case."

"Is he in trouble?" I played with the charms on my bracelet. "For being in the Defiance?"

"It's a good sign that Head Agent MacCormack is letting him stay. That means he's avoided the worst of it. He must be cooperating." She sat down on the bed and handed me the mug. "Tea with honey and lemon, just like your grandma made. It always worked when I had a sore throat."

"Thank you." I took a sip, but the brief comfort transitioned to homesickness. It was the first time I had ever been sick away from home. "Can I call Kinley?"

"Rochelle, you know those calls are for Sundays only, and it's late." She looked down at the phone still clutched in her hand. "I called her the minute I found out you were safe and assured her you would call this weekend."

"But she'll worry until I talk to her." I took a deep breath to keep my composure. "Please. I don't feel well, and I miss her."

Audrie's face softened and she sighed. "I don't want her to worry any more than she already has. Just this one time. Give me a minute to talk to her, and then you can have all the time you need."

I nodded and watched Audrie dial my familiar home number. Sipping my tea, I listened to the muffled ring coming through the phone held to my aunt's ear. Just when I thought Kinley wasn't home, the ringing stopped.

"Hi, Kinley. This is Audrie." My aunt sat up straight. "No, everything is fine. Rochelle is here with me at my apartment and wants to talk to you." Audrie smiled. "Of course. I'll put her on the phone."

She traded the phone for the mug and left the room to give me some privacy.

"Kinley?" I pressed the phone tight to my ear, desperate to hear my cousin's voice.

"Rochelle, I was so worried. Are you okay?" Her voice shook.

"I'm okay. I promise." Even though I wanted to tell her everything, I knew even mentioning my slight fever would cause her to worry all over again, and I couldn't do that to her.

"Audrie told me you went on an assignment and you were missing." She paused and cleared her throat. "What happened?"

My aunt told me in the car that she had been open and honest with Kinley in their previous phone calls. Kinley knew the facts about my abduction, but she didn't know about Keppler's role in my escape. Audrie and I had agreed to keep that part from her until we knew what MacCormack planned to do with him. I didn't know whether it would make her feel better to know he was with the TCI now, or if she would worry that I was in more danger with him around.

"I went undercover because I wanted to help the TCI and I didn't want Max to go alone. I thought we'd be safe together, but the Defiance was looking for me and they took me in for interrogation. I got away and called Audrie."

"I was so... I thought..." Kinley sniffled into the phone. "Sorry. Just... give me a minute to pull myself together."

"Kinley, I'm okay. I promise. Don't cry." Our conversation continued like that for fifteen minutes. My cousin cried, and I assured her over and over that I was safe and unharmed.

"I don't want you to ever leave the school again unless you're with Audrie every second," Kinley said when she had calmed down enough to speak. "And tell Max I forbid him from doing anything like that again."

"I promise I won't leave again. And I'll tell Max what you said. He'll listen to you." The conversation was making me worry about her instead of providing the comfort I needed. "Kinley, is everything okay in Maibe? Are you feeling okay?"

Audrie looked into the room, eyebrows raised, but I only shrugged.

"Me? Of course I'm okay." Kinley forced a laugh. "Now that I know you're safe, nothing else matters."

I switched the phone to my other ear. "Are you sure? Because you sound tired and stressed."

Kinley sighed. "Just the usual. I wish Kat would talk to me when I call her. I have an important test in a couple of weeks that determines whether I pass to the next level of my program, and I'm a little nervous about it."

"I know what you mean. I have finals in a few weeks." Until I said it out loud, I hadn't considered what a week of missed classes would do to my grades.

"We'll both study and everything will be okay." Finally, Kinley's usual confidence returned. "I have your midterm report card on the refrigerator. I'm so proud of you. I knew you'd be able to keep up at that rigorous school."

"My semester report card will be even better." I would have to study nonstop, but if it made Kinley feel better, it was worth it. "I miss you."

"I miss you too." Tears returned to her voice. "Hug Max for me. As crazy as it sounds, I even miss him hanging around the house all the time."

"I will. I love you." Part of me wanted to keep her on the phone all night, but I was tired, and her groggy voice indicated she should have been sleeping hours ago.

"I love you too. Can you put Audrie back on the phone?"

"Sure." I held out the phone to Audrie, who was still standing in the doorway. "She wants to talk to you."

My aunt came over and took the phone. "Hi, Kinley . . . yeah, just a minute." She mouthed, "Be right back," and left the room.

Miserable and lonely, I brushed away tears. Not even Kinley could fix my problems anymore. She had enough problems of her own, and I knew she wasn't telling me everything.

"Hey, what's wrong?" Audrie stood in the doorway.

I took a deep breath and sat up. "Aunt Audrie, can I go visit Kinley? Just for a few hours?"

"That's the same thing she just asked me." My aunt walked to the bed and sat down.

"What did you tell her?" I reached for a tissue.

Audrie shook her head. "I can't arrange anything for right now."

"But I have to see her. She doesn't sound like herself, and Kat won't talk to her. She only has me, and I can't leave her all alone." I fumbled through an explanation. "She was crying just now on the phone, and that's not like her." My cousin was always in control of everything and rarely let her emotions get in the way or impede her ability to get her point across. She should have been yelling at me for doing something dangerous, not crying because I was safe.

"I know she's a little stressed right now, kiddo. She told me about her test. But now that you're back, she'll be okay." Audrie reached for my hand, but I pulled it away. "I'll bet she'll be more herself when you talk to her again on Sunday."

"You don't understand," I said. "I'm supposed to take care of Kinley and Kat. My dad always said I was supposed to be the glue that held our family together, and then he left me here to figure it all out. I still need him, but he's not here."

"I know. I miss him too." Audrie pulled me into her arms and held me while I sobbed. "He would be so proud of you."

When I couldn't cry anymore, I wiped my face with my sleeve. "I don't know what I'm supposed to do."

"You're supposed to be a seventeen-year-old kid." My aunt brushed my hair back from my face. "Let the TCI take care of the pendants and passcodes, and let me take care of you. Your only responsibilities are to get good grades and stay out of trouble."

It would be easier to just forget about the pendants and dream about my future instead. Then again, was there a future if the TCI failed? "But Audrie—"

"No buts," she interrupted. "You're here because it's a safe place for you. I don't care what MacCormack or anyone else says. You are not responsible for those pendants, and you're done being involved in all of this."

"Head Agent MacCormack is already mad." I huddled closer to my aunt. "He expected me to do better on the assignment. You heard him earlier."

"You should have never been on that assignment in the first place. Let him be mad." Audrie pulled the blankets up to my chin. "He forgets sometimes that he doesn't rule the universe. If this is the way the TCI treats kids they promised to help, I'm sorry I ever joined them in the first place."

"But it's your dream job." I'd never heard my aunt express discontent with her position at the TCI, but the way it came out so naturally indicated she had at least thought it before.

"Some things are even more important than my job." She leaned forward and kissed my forehead. "For now, you need to stop worrying and get some sleep. Tomorrow will be better."

I used to believe it would be, before Molly told me about the pendants, before I made bad decisions that put everyone I loved in danger, and before I had to leave home to fix everything I'd broken. Now, every tomorrow brought a new problem and offered no solutions for the old ones.

# CHAPTER 16

# CHARLIE

*April 11, 2091*

**"A**lmost there, kid." MacCormack clapped my shoulder, and I sat up straight in my seat. "Agent Dotson is meeting us to take you to your room."

The car carried us down tree-lined streets lit by old-fashioned streetlights. Throughout our day on the road, I had cooperated and told him everything, from the first time I met Griff, to Griff's obsession with the pendants, and how I had escaped and returned to the Defiance. We stopped once for lunch and only one more time for a bathroom break, so I couldn't escape any of MacCormack's questions. Not that I tried to avoid any of them. He didn't know anything about the Spero pendant I'd given to Griff, and that was the only information I intended to keep to myself. If my freedom and chance of a future depended on my honesty, then I would reveal every detail I knew about the Defiance except for that, if it meant keeping the Aumonts safe.

For the last hour of the drive, I dozed off until I woke up from a nightmare about Griff finding me. I had overheard MacCormack's phone call with Sid. He ordered Sid to stay at work and be ready to show me around and take me to Max's room "for now." After the relief of telling MacCormack my entire story, the uncertainty of "for now" raised my anxiety once again.

"The information you provided will be really helpful." He

extended his hand to me. "We'll meet again in a few days to discuss questions I have, or anything you may have forgotten."

I shook his hand, too tired to think about anything but my head sinking into a pillow. MacCormack pulled the car along the curb where Sid Dotson waved on the sidewalk. I had only met Audrie's work partner once when he came with her to Maibe.

"This is your stop." MacCormack put the car in park. "See you in a couple of days, kid."

I pushed my door open and swung my bag over my shoulder.

"Agent Dotson," MacCormack spoke through my open door. "Show him around and get him to his room. We'll do more to get him acquainted with this place in the coming weeks."

"You've got it, sir." Sid took a step back so I could get out of the car. "Welcome to the Advanced Education Institute."

Instead of the big school I had envisioned, the AEI was only several buildings along a tree-lined path. I clutched the strap of my bag with one hand as MacCormack drove away.

"Max is going to be so happy to see you." Sid cleared his throat. "He's been a little under the weather this week. Worried about Rochelle, I think."

Overwhelmed and tired, I nodded. "What am I supposed to do here?"

"I'm not quite sure what Head Agent MacCormack has planned, but I would think, eventually, you'll join the other students. That'll give you a few weeks to settle in before the summer semester starts."

Memories of Kinley spending hours tutoring me in algebra and basic science flashed through my mind. Even with one-on-one help, I barely understood the lessons. I wouldn't be able to keep up with the classes here or anywhere. I hadn't been to a real school since I was eleven.

"I know it sounds like a lot right now, but it'll all fall into place." Sid put a hand on my shoulder and nudged me toward the cement pathway. "Let's get you to your room. Everything will be less overwhelming after you get some sleep."

As we crossed campus, he gave me a quick tour by pointing out all the dormitories and academic buildings. I was too anxious about my own future to pay attention. I felt alone without Rochelle, and I couldn't wait to see Max. He would find a way for us to laugh about the entire situation, and he'd give me a proper tour in the morning. He could provide the perspective I needed like he always did.

Sid's voice broke into my thoughts. "I work with a small group of gifted students a few evenings a week. Max is one of them. His latest project was 3D printing some fake pendants. It actually turned out pretty good. Anyway, maybe you could come along with Max. He said you helped him with a lot of projects in Maibe."

"Yeah. Sometimes." I barely knew what I was saying. I'd told Max it was a bad idea to make fake pendants, but he did it anyway. Now both the Defiance and the TCI had fake pendants. That was something I had forgotten to tell MacCormack.

"Here's your building." Sid led me through the front door into an open space with a giant TV, pool table, a few Ping-Pong tables, and chairs arranged into groups. "This is where everyone hangs out in their free time. There are some quiet rooms on the other side for studying or group work." I followed him to a stairwell. "There's a laundry room and a communal kitchen downstairs." He started up the stairs. "Max is on the second floor. There are two more floors after that, all dorms."

We entered a hallway lined with doors and passed two of them before Sid knocked on the third. A murmur of voices and laughter came through the ceiling above us, a door slammed down the hall, and still no one answered the door in front of us.

"Maybe he's hanging out with friends—" Sid started as the

doorknob clicked and Max peeked out through a crack in the door. "Hey, Max, I have a new roommate for you."

The door opened the rest of the way and Max stood in front of us, rubbing his eyes. His hair was long enough to stick up in places, his shoulders slumped, and his eyes were sunken in his ashen face.

"Keppler?" Max squinted and shook his head. "How did you get here?"

Sid smiled and nudged me forward. "Rochelle ended up in Kansas City. Charlie helped her escape the Defiance, so he's with us now."

Max perked up. "But she's okay? She's not hurt?"

"She's perfectly fine and staying at Audrie's tonight." Sid took Max's elbow and guided him back into his room. "Are you feeling any better than yesterday? You still don't look well."

"I'm feeling better. Just a little tired." Max smiled, but it wasn't his usual goofy grin. The Max I knew was a jokester who never took anything seriously, had more energy than a puppy, and never stopped looking for an adventure. The Max in front of me was lethargic and broken down.

"Okay. Get some sleep, and if you're not feeling like yourself in the morning, I'm taking you back to the doctor." Sid patted his shoulder.

"Yeah, thanks." Max winced. "I'll be fine in the morning."

While the two of them talked about a project Max was working on, I walked around the messy room. There were bunk beds against one wall, a futon against the other, and two desks by the window in between. The rest of the room reminded me of Max's garage workshop. There was a microwave surrounded by old computer parts, a stack of radios next to the futon, and several dead plants on an overturned box. A carpet of clothes, tools, and wires covered most of the floor except where pathways led to the beds and a bathroom.

"Charlie? Anything you need before I go?" Sid nudged my arm and I jumped. "Just stick around here tomorrow until Audrie or I can get over here to go over the rules with you. I'll let you two get some sleep, and I'll check in tomorrow."

I nodded and Max followed Sid to the door, closing and locking it behind him.

"I'm working on a more high-tech security system." Max slid the back of a chair under the doorknob. "We have to use this for now."

"Is it that dangerous around here?" I thought reuniting with Max would calm me down, but he was only making me more nervous.

"Only for me. I'm dealing with a bully situation." He tenderly touched a hand to his ribs. "You saw Rochelle? She's really okay?"

"She was locked up in interrogation for three days." Unexpected anger bubbled in my chest. "Griff and Molly could have done anything to her. Why would you go on a mission like that knowing she'd go with you? Knowing you were putting her in a dangerous situation with the Defiance?"

Max trudged to one of the desks and rifled through a stack of papers and books. "Maybe the country wouldn't be such a dangerous place if you weren't writing things like this." He held up an issue of the Defiance newsletter I had written a few weeks earlier.

I snatched the folded paper and shoved it into my pocket. "What about it? You knew I had to pretend to be one hundred percent loyal to the Defiance."

"That didn't sound like pretending to me." Max cringed, accentuating the fading bruises along the right side of his face and under his eye. "It sounds like you're having a great time launching your writing career."

"It better not sound like pretending. Think about what you're saying. You're the one who's making fake pendants so the bad guys can get to the virus faster."

"They're just decoys." Max pressed a hand to the side of his face. "The real ones have a computer chip in them to make them work. I can't replicate something I'm not allowed to tear apart."

It was the same thing Griff had said about his fake pendants, but the thought of more pendants, real or fake, opened the door to scary possibilities. "It's still a bad idea. Just like making trackers. Just like saying yes to a TCI assignment you weren't ready for, and dragging Rochelle into it."

"All right. I get it." He shuffled to the bed and sat down. "Everyone already told me I'm a failure and a loser. If that's all you have to say, I'm going back to bed."

The fact that Max backed down so easily shattered my own fight. "I'm tired. Let's just talk about this tomorrow."

"Tomorrow," Max groaned. "I have to go for my run at six so I can get to the lab to pitch my final physics experiment. Just don't touch anything and I'll come get you for lunch."

"What about breakfast?" I hadn't eaten anything since lunch today.

"I don't have time for breakfast. There's a jar of peanut butter around here somewhere." He lay down on his bed and pulled the blankets over his head.

Feeling more alone than I had when I was eleven and wandering the streets, I scooped up a blanket from the futon, turned off the light, and climbed up to the top bunk. Too tired to care that I didn't have a pillow, I folded my arms under my head and tried not to think about what tomorrow would bring.

PART 2

# TROUBLE AROUND
# EVERY CORNER

# CHAPTER 17
# ROCHELLE

*April 12, 2091*

"Did they say anything about the passcodes Molly asked for in December?" Agent MacCormack sat back in his desk chair while I sat next to Audrie in his meticulously organized office.

"No," I said. "Neither of them mentioned any of that."

"And you still have no idea what those passcodes could be?" He raised his eyebrows and leaned forward.

"That's correct." I looked down at my hands folded in my lap.

"And you have no other observations from your recent experience with the Defiance?"

"No, sir. I've told you everything already." It took all my self-control to keep my voice even. I had spent part of the morning at the doctor's office only to learn I had a virus that I'd be able to recover from on my own. On our way out of the clinic, Audrie received a call from MacCormack ordering both of us to report to his office. Then I spent an hour answering his irritating questions.

"In that case, it seems we're done with this conversation." He flashed a fake smile. "I hope you feel better soon. I expect you to report to classes first thing tomorrow."

"Yes, sir." I stood and Audrie followed.

"Not you, Agent Aumont. We have a few things to discuss." MacCormack gestured to her chair.

"Of course." Audrie pulled me into a side hug. "Get some rest and call me if you need anything."

I nodded and left the office, rushing through the lobby and outside into a cloudy late morning. At least the heavy rain had stopped. For a minute, I leaned back against the door, watching my classmates rush from building to building as they changed classes or went to lunch. I needed to see Max and Keppler. Checking in with them would help me forget my tense meeting with Head Agent MacCormack and stop worrying about what he was saying to Audrie. Was I in trouble, or was she?

"Rochelle!" Evie's delighted voice bounced down the sidewalk. "I thought you'd never get back."

I spun around in time to meet her hug.

"Are you okay?" She held my shoulders. "What happened?"

"I'm okay." I smiled in response to my roommate's relief. "It's a long story, but the Defiance took me back to Kansas City. My friend Charlie Keppler was there, and we escaped together. He's staying with Max. I'm on my way to check on them."

"I'll go with you. Max has lunch right now, so we might be able to catch him between classes." She linked her arm with mine, and we walked quickly toward Max's dorm building. "I've been worried about him the past few days."

"Why?" If Evie was worried about Max, something had to be really wrong.

"He hasn't been feeling well. He's been throwing up for three days, but he still comes to class. I don't think he's taking care of himself, so I got him one of those fancy sports drinks with electrolytes." Evie glanced over at me. "Also, Henry is leading the others in harassing him about the mission, calling him a failure and worse. He's always alone when he eats, when he walks to class, and when we have workshop with Sid."

"What about all of his friends?" I slowed down as we approached Max's building.

"'Friends,' is a tricky word, don't you think?" Evie pulled the door open, and we entered the lobby of Max's building, deserted since everyone was in class. "You can't really label someone a friend until something bad happens and they stick with you."

"Right." Where did that logic leave me with Molly? Had I abandoned her when she needed me to stick with her?

"I like Max better without all of his rude friends anyway." She smiled. "I'm beginning to understand why you're friends with him."

The front door swung open, and I turned in time to see Max run into the building, covered in mud.

"Have you seen him?" He put his hands on top of his head to catch his breath. "Henry? Has he come in?"

"No." I studied my friend, trying to make sense of the situation. "Max, what happened?"

The front door opened again and Henry, also covered in mud, growled, "You thought I wouldn't look for you here? Some genius."

Max took off running and Henry followed, pushing past Evie.

"Come on." I ran toward the stairwell after them, not bothering to wait for Evie.

"Let go of me," Max insisted as I made a sharp turn onto the landing between the basement and the second floor.

Henry twisted one of Max's arms behind his back. Max's other arm held the railing in front of him, pushing back with all his strength to prevent Henry from shoving him over it.

"Henry, let him go," I shouted.

"Not a chance." Henry didn't look at me, and Max's eyes pleaded for help. "You've probably been corrupted by the Defiance anyway."

Evie gasped as she came upon the scene, and we looked at each other, trying to determine whether we could restrain Henry without pushing Max over the railing.

"Hey, what's the problem?" I heard Keppler's voice before I saw him. He came up the stairs carrying a laundry basket stacked with folded towels and clothes.

"It's not your concern," Henry growled. "Keep walking."

"Listen, I just got here, and this guy is my roommate." Keppler set the basket on the landing and raised his eyebrows at me, but I could only shrug. "If you kill him, I have to get used to a new one, and I don't want to deal with that."

Henry laughed. "Max doesn't have a roommate. No one can stand him. You'll thank me for this."

Keppler looked at Max and tipped his head toward the wall. "We're not just roommates. We're also brothers."

Max shifted his weight to the side and kicked Henry in the shin. Henry gave Max a shove, but they twisted in the struggle, so Max stumbled back against the wall and slid to the floor.

Henry lunged for Max, but Keppler stepped between them and slammed his fist into Henry's abdomen.

I darted around Henry, who was doubled over coughing, and helped Max to his feet. Any crush Henry claimed to have on me had vanished during my brief absence. The anger in his eyes indicated that, to him, I now had the same rank as Max, but I didn't care.

Max squeezed my hand and stepped forward. "Remember when I told you I have a brother in the Defiance and you didn't believe me? Meet Keppler."

"You're not in the Defiance." Henry straightened up and faced Keppler. "And you're definitely not his brother."

Keppler lifted the sleeve of his T-shirt to reveal the brand on his arm. "I'm going to let you go this time, but if you get near either of my friends again, I'll show you how the Defiance deals with problems. We're a lot more creative than dropping a guy down a flight of stairs."

Henry glared at Max but didn't take a step with Keppler between them. "Fine. I'll leave. But I'm reporting all of this."

None of us said anything as he disappeared down the hallway. Max leaned back against the wall, hand still clutching mine. Keppler shook his head and picked up the laundry basket.

"Max. What did you do?" Evie broke the silence.

"Nothing," he groaned. "He's been throwing things at me, tripping me in the hall, and shoving me into things all week. When I was on my way to lunch, he jumped out from behind the building and pushed me into the mud, so I got him back. I tried to stay out of trouble, Rochelle. I swear. But I just couldn't take it anymore."

There was something wrong with Max, from his tired voice to his slumped posture to his miserable expression. He wasn't the confident friend who was excited about our assignment to attend a Defiance rally.

Max rubbed a hand over his face and took a step away from me. "I have class in a few minutes. I need to shower quick." He pulled himself up the stairs, leaning heavily on the railing.

I turned to Keppler. "What's going on with him?"

Keppler shrugged. "I'm not sure. We've been arguing since I got here."

"About what?"

"I write for the Defiance, and he makes fake pendants for the TCI. I don't think he should go to class when he got up in the middle of the night to throw up, but he says he has to go because of his important projects. And he told me not to move anything in his room, but I can't live in that disaster. He's going to flip his lid when he walks in there."

"Don't worry. I'll talk to him." I'd never known Max to be so temperamental, and it surprised me he wasn't excited to see Keppler.

"You're really in the Defiance?" Evie studied Keppler, more curious than alarmed.

"Yeah, I mean, I was undercover," Keppler fumbled. "That stuff I said wasn't true. Not for me, anyway."

She nodded and extended her hand. "I'm Evie Rubio, Rochelle's roommate. Welcome to the Advanced Education Institute."

"Thanks." Keppler shook her hand. "Charlie Keppler."

"It's nice to meet you." Evie glanced at her watch. "I have to get to class, but I have something for Max." She fished a bottle of sports drink out of her bag and put it in Keppler's laundry basket. "Tell Max to feel better soon, and make sure he stays hydrated." She waved and hurried down the hall.

"At least you have a nice roommate." Keppler shifted his basket. "Mine is questionable."

"Max isn't feeling well. We should go check on him before he leaves for class."

"Do we have to?" Keppler sank to the nearest step.

"It can't be that bad." I sat down next to him.

"He said he didn't have time to show me where to get breakfast because he had a project or something. There's supposed to be a jar of peanut butter in the room, but I've been cleaning all day and haven't found it yet. And I'm hungry."

I sighed and looped my arm through his. "Give me a few minutes to check on Max and then we'll get something to eat."

"Aumont, I don't want to stay here." Keppler slumped forward. "That MacCormack guy said he wants to help me, but I don't think he liked my answers."

"Did you tell him the truth?"

"Yeah. I told him everything I know." He rubbed one hand over his face. "But it wasn't enough. He wants to meet in a few days to talk about the things I forgot, and if I don't get this exactly right, I'm going to prison. But if I don't go to prison, I'll start classes in the next semester, and there's no way I'll pass any of them. Then what happens?"

"It'll be okay. Just take a deep breath." There wasn't much more I could say. "I agree Head Agent MacCormack is intimidating, but you're doing everything he's asking, so we just have to take all of this one day at a time. For now, let's go talk to Max." I needed them to get along. We had enough problems to face.

He nodded but his face remained pinched with worry. I understood Keppler's suspicion of MacCormack because I felt the same when I'd first met him, but I was also worried about Max. I stood and started up the stairs, feeling powerless to help any of us.

# CHAPTER 18

# CHARLIE

*April 12, 2091*

I followed Rochelle up the stairs, dreading Max's reaction to my morning of cleaning. Knowing Griff would hunt me down should have been my primary worry. Concern about MacCormack and his plans for me should have come in a close second. But all that mattered was that Max no longer accepted me as his friend. This wasn't like the last time we had fought. Back in Maibe, he had called me *hermano* for months before I found out it meant "brother." I'd snapped at him because it reminded me of Griff. We didn't speak for a few days, and then I apologized. But this time I didn't understand what I had done wrong.

Rochelle knocked on the door to Max's room, then opened it. Max was sitting on the futon wearing sweatpants but no shirt or socks, and his face was in his hands.

"Max, are you okay?" Rochelle approached him.

He shook his head without looking up. "I know I said I like it here, but I changed my mind. I want to go home."

Rochelle sat down and wrapped her arms around him. "I know it's been a rough week, but at least the three of us are back together now. This must be a sign that everything will be okay."

Max sat up and blinked his watery eyes. "It was a huge mistake to take that assignment. I wasn't ready for it, and I was so scared I would never see you again."

"I was scared for you too." Rochelle's eyes landed on the dark bruises that ran up and down Max's ribs and shadowed his face. "How did you get away?"

"They beat me up and left me on the side of the road. They said I was lucky and to tell whoever sent me not to come back, so I walked to the nearest house and the farmer let me use his phone to call Sid." Max shivered and looked at me. "I couldn't find my hoodie. Have you seen it?"

"Yeah. It's right here." I lowered the laundry basket to the floor and pulled out the hoodie, still warm from the dryer, from a stack of folded clothes.

"Thanks." Max smiled as he pulled it over his head. "I should really get to class. I'm already late."

"Max, wait." Rochelle caught his hand and gently pulled him down beside her. "You need to stay here and get some rest. I'll call Audrie, and she'll excuse you from your afternoon classes. She can take you to the doctor tomorrow."

"I've already been to the doctor." He groaned as he sat back against the cushion. "They said nothing was broken."

"But you've been throwing up for three days." She leaned back. "That's not good, Max. You can't keep going like that."

"It's just stress from worrying about you." He started to sit up but winced and fell back.

I wanted to point out that he was still throwing up last night after finding out that Rochelle was safe, but I didn't want to create an additional conflict.

"Either way, you're exhausted. You need to sleep." Rochelle stood, patted her pockets, then turned back to Max. "Can I borrow your phone?"

"It's in the front pocket of my bag." He pointed to the backpack by the door.

"I'll call Audrie, and I'll be right back." Rochelle squeezed my arm, fished the phone out of Max's bag, and then vanished into the hall.

Not sure what to do next, I plucked the sports drink Evie had given us out of the basket. "Do you want something to drink? Evie thought this would make you feel better."

Max's eyebrows furrowed, but he nodded, so I handed it to him.

"Thank you." He took a sip. "The way I treated you last night wasn't fair. I'm just struggling, and that's not your fault."

"I'm sorry about what I said too." I sat down next to him. "It wasn't your fault that assignment went wrong either."

He sighed and nodded. "Things were going pretty well here until MacCormack asked us to go undercover. It surprised me because he doesn't like me. He doesn't think I'm qualified to be here and that I only got in because Audrie and Sid pulled some strings. But I have better grades than most of the kids here, and Rochelle and I make a great team in our skills class, so I figured we'd finally gotten his attention."

"Is there any chance he sent you because he doesn't like you?" The thought twisted my stomach.

"That would be too suspicious." Max's serious expression signaled he hadn't dismissed the theory. "My biggest problem right now is Henry Davis. Thanks for helping me out, by the way."

"Davis?" I shook my head. It was a common enough last name.

"As in Brandon Davis's son," he confirmed. "He's no more qualificd to be here than me. He only got in because his dad traded a pendant for Henry's safety."

Brandon Davis's pendant was with the TCI, and if Max knew it, that meant all the adults had to know it too, including Griff's inside guy. "How long has he been here?"

"Almost a year now." Max sat up, watching the emotions play over my face. "Why?"

Before I could decide where to begin, Rochelle walked through the door. "Audrie said she'll take care of everything, and she'll bring us some lunch in a little while. At least she's out of her meeting with Head Agent MacCormack. I don't like that guy."

"Why not?" While I was suspicious of everyone, I'd never heard Rochelle admit she didn't like someone. Not even Molly.

"I don't know." She sank down next to me. "He's so grumpy. I know he's mad that I didn't learn more about the Defiance, and I think he's blaming Audrie for us not figuring out the passcodes yet. That's the only reason he let me come here in the first place, and I've failed."

MacCormack didn't like Max or Rochelle. Both of my friends could have died on the assignment, but the head agent acted like that was a normal risk for students—teenagers who weren't trained agents—to take.

"Now you look like the one who's about to throw up." Max forced a smile, but it vanished when I didn't respond. "What's wrong?"

"I have to tell you guys something," I said.

Rochelle and Max leaned forward. "What is it?"

I took a deep breath. "Agent MacCormack is Griff's uncle. He says he's trying to get Griff to turn over his pendants and walk away from the Defiance. But Griff has an inside guy in the TCI who has been giving him tips about where to find Brandon Davis so he can get his pendant."

Max's eyes brightened, and he perked up almost like his old self. "Does the TCI know about MacCormack and Griff?"

I shrugged. "MacCormack said they do, and I'm supposed to keep my mouth shut about it. It's probably some kind of test to see if he can trust me."

"We won't tell." Max took another sip from the bottle.

"But the TCI has Brandon Davis's pendant." Rochelle pulled a tissue out of her pocket, reminding me she hadn't been feeling well the last few days. "Why would Griff's inside guy tell him it was still out there?"

"Maybe he's not actually helping him." I shrugged. "Maybe he just wants to keep him busy. Spread his attention thin so he can't succeed with the pendants or the war."

"Or maybe he's trying to control the whole situation somehow." Max frowned. "That's how they found us so easily at the rally. This informant told Griff that Rochelle Aumont would be there, and they were waiting."

I nodded. "Griff was expecting her. He definitely knew something."

"So, the TCI is using us?" Rochelle rested her head against the back of the futon. "But what do they get out of it?"

"It got me here." A gate opened in my brain and scenarios flooded my thoughts. "Maybe the informant thought you and Molly would figure out the passcodes, and then I would bring you back. Maybe it was some kind of trade between Griff and his informant."

"I don't think the entire TCI is using us, but I'm suspicious of MacCormack. What if he's in on all of it with Griff? What if Griff wanted you to end up here so you could be his informant?" Max stood, his face went blank, and then he tottered one way then the other.

I caught his elbow, and Rochelle jumped up and wrapped her arm around him.

"We can talk about all of this later. You should be in bed." Rochelle led the way, and I steadied Max as he crossed the room.

"I'm all right, guys. I just stood up too fast." Max sat back against the pillows Rochelle fluffed for him. "Between my physics project and Henry, it's just been a long day."

Rochelle sat on the edge of the bed and touched the back of her hand to his forehead. "You're not going to any classes tomorrow, and we're both taking the weekend off from our morning run and anything strenuous. If we're both feeling better on Monday, we'll go back to our normal schedules. Deal?"

"Deal." Max sighed. "Maybe we should let the TCI solve their own problems. We've all told them everything we know. That's all we can do. Right?"

Rochelle looked up at me. "What do you think, Keppler?"

I knew I was a dead man, whether at the hands of the TCI or the Defiance. It was only a matter of time. But Rochelle and Max didn't have to share that fate. "I think we should cooperate the best we can and let MacCormack deal with the rest." As long as no one found out about Lareina's Optimus pendant, we had won anyway.

"What if he tries to send us on another assignment?" Rochelle fidgeted with the charm bracelet on her wrist. "If there's an informant around here, how do we know who we can trust?"

"We'll refuse to go." Max settled into his pillows and closed his eyes. "Maybe then he'll send us all home."

I nodded. "And we shouldn't trust anyone here anyway. For now, we only trust each other, and the three of us will survive this together."

Rochelle tucked Max under his blanket and comforter, and for half an hour we sat in silence, listening to the rain patter against the window. When Max had fallen asleep, Rochelle lay down on the futon.

I pulled the blanket from my bed and covered her with it. "Are you feeling any better?"

"Yeah. I just didn't sleep well last night." She closed her eyes. "And I'm worried about Audrie. After we talked with MacCormack, he made her stay, and she sounded tense when I called her earlier. I don't want to get her in trouble."

"You didn't do anything wrong, Aumont." I sank to the floor next to the futon. "I'm sure Audrie knows how to handle herself around here."

"Yeah. Maybe." She sat up. "I just feel so guilty, like I ruined things for Kinley and Kat, and I don't want to do the same thing to my aunt."

Before I could say anything, a soft knock came from the door and Audrie peeked inside. "Hey guys, can I come in?"

Rochelle jumped up, crossed the room, and hugged her aunt as if she hadn't seen her in a year.

Audrie shifted her armload of bags to one side so she could return the hug. "What's this for?"

"I'm so sorry I got you in trouble."

"Rochelle, no one's in trouble." She kept one arm wrapped around her niece and held up a paper bag with her other hand. "I brought you guys some soup and sandwiches. Hopefully, that'll make everyone feel better."

"Thanks." I took the bag and carried it to the desk I'd cleared earlier.

"Do you want to stay for a while?" Rochelle pulled her aunt toward the futon.

"I have a little time. Maybe the rain will slow down." Audrie slid the shopping bags off her arm one at a time. "Charlie, the rest of this is for you. There's a pillow, a couple of blankets, a toothbrush, and a few changes of clothes. If you need anything else, just let me know and I'll get it for you."

"Thank you." I took the bags from her with a sense of hope and relief. If she bought me a pillow and toothbrush, that meant she expected me to stay long-term, and even though I didn't want to stay at the AEI, it was better than the alternative.

"Are you settling in okay? I know this place can be a little overwhelming at first." She sat down on the futon with Rochelle.

"Yeah, I think so." I stumbled over my words, surprised by her sincere concern for me.

Audrie gave me an understanding look then nodded toward Max, who was sound asleep in bed. "If I didn't have to go out of town this weekend, I would take all of you to stay with me for a couple of days."

Rochelle nodded. "Maybe next week."

"It may be a month or two before I have another weekend off." Audrie sighed. "But I'll be teaching more during the week, so I'll be around campus if you need anything."

"Why is your schedule changing?" Rochelle turned to her aunt.

"It changes based on the TCI's current goals." Audrie brushed Rochelle's hair behind her ear. "It happens from time to time. Nothing to worry about."

"Are you sure it's not a punishment from MacCormack?" Rochelle insisted.

"I'm absolutely sure." Audrie clutched one hand in the other. "I made an appointment for Max to see the doctor tomorrow morning. I'll take him, and then I'll check back in with all of you before I leave for my assignment tomorrow afternoon."

"Audrie?" I took a few steps toward her. "What should I be doing right now so MacCormack won't send me to prison?"

She gave me a sympathetic smile. "When he requests to meet with you, be early to the meeting and give him the best answers you can. Otherwise, stick with Max and Rochelle. They'll show you the ropes. Right?" She hugged Rochelle with one arm. "I promise everything will be just fine."

Rochelle smiled and nodded, but we had both recognized something familiar in Audrie's promise. It was the exact same tactic Kinley used when she wanted to protect us from all the real world's problems and dangers. By no fault of her own, Kinley hadn't been able to keep that promise, and I doubted Audrie would be able to either.

# CHAPTER 19

# CHARLIE

*April 16, 2091*

"The information I wrote in the newsletter is all based on fact." I sat in MacCormack's office, doing my best to answer his questions without revealing the information I wasn't willing to share: I had turned in a pendant to Griff, and the final pendant was in Maibe with Lareina. "I was only writing the truth. That's why the Defiance has been successful at recruiting."

"So, you were aware your writing was being used as a recruiting tool?" He jotted something on the notepad on his desk. "Did you realize how integral it's been to the Defiance's success in the war?"

"Sort of." I looked down at my shoes. "I tried to stay out of all that. I was only there to gather information."

MacCormack laughed. "Are you sure about that? It's hard to believe Griff's right-hand guy wouldn't be up to date on all the progress."

"We disagreed on the Defiance's priorities." I gripped the armrests of my chair to control my temper. The head agent had already asked the same questions in the car. He doubted my story. "I agreed with his ideas to help kids without families. I didn't want any part of the rest."

"And that's why you went back." He looked up at me, eyebrows knitted together. "You were invested in at least part of his plan."

"No." I stood. "I went back to gather information for the TCI."

It was the story I'd decided to stick with because any mention of protecting the Aumonts would complicate my explanation and give MacCormack more ammo to twist my motives.

"Really? Is that why you made it a priority to call Agent Aumont and report your findings?"

"I already told you, I didn't call because I was afraid Griff's informant would find out. Did you figure out who the mole is yet?"

"Sit down," MacCormack barked, and I dropped into my chair. "It sounds like you and Griff were pretty good friends. Would he have believed his informant over you?"

I considered Griff's recent behavior: doubting my loyalty to the Defiance and questioning the pendant I had given him. "He's been paranoid lately. Something about traitors and leaders from history. He was questioning me, and I hadn't even done anything suspicious."

"Questioning you about what?" MacCormack walked around his desk.

"His informant told him I'd signed an agreement with the TCI. I told Griff I'd never acted on it, which was true, but I knew I was running out of time. He wouldn't let it go."

"So, it was good timing for Rochelle to show up when she did." He sat down in the chair next to mine. "Where would you have run if she didn't bring you back here?"

"I don't have anywhere else to go. No home. No family." It was the truth. Nothing Rochelle or Max said could undo what I had done. "I gave all that up to become your informant."

"I see." MacCormack smiled. "Well, I'm glad it all worked out then. It's like you were meant to come here."

"Yeah, nothing happens by chance," I muttered. Had MacCormack played a part in Rochelle's kidnapping, knowing I would return her to New York? There were so many factors he had

no control over in that scenario. He hadn't known I didn't want
Rochelle anywhere near the Defiance. And there was no way he
could know that I would survive outside of the Defiance territory
with a brand on my arm.

"What was that?" He stood and smoothed his suit.

"You're right. It all fell into place. I'm lucky, I guess."

MacCormack nodded. "I think that's enough for today. We'll
meet again on Thursday."

I stood, ignoring the nagging voice in my head that demanded
I tell the head agent about Griff's fake pendants. That was another
detail I had left out. I didn't like that the TCI had allowed Max to
explore that possibility, and I didn't want to encourage any more
of it. A bunch of fake pendants could only complicate things.

"If you think of anything else, you know where to find me." He
clamped his hand over my shoulder. "Stay out of trouble, kid."

MacCormack walked me to the door and opened it. "Henry,
come on in."

I came face-to-face with Max's bully standing in the hallway.
Henry glared at me as we switched places, and then the door
closed behind me. It had been four days since my encounter with
Henry, and so far he hadn't bothered either of my friends, but I
worried he'd confront them when I wasn't around.

Head foggy from MacCormack's questions, I shoved my hands
into my pockets and left the building. The warm sun on my face
pulled me back to reality. It would be a great day to stay outside,
but I didn't feel like walking around alone, so I headed back toward
my dorm building.

I had spent Friday taking care of Max while Rochelle was in
class, and I hung out with them for the rest of the weekend while
they caught up on homework and studied for tests. They took a
break on Sunday morning for church, but we listened to it on the

radio because Audrie wasn't around to take them. My dad always said religion was a scam, but nothing I heard sounded fraudulent to me.

Although I was glad both of my friends were feeling better, my day was lonely when they were in class. I'd met them for lunch but spent the rest of my day doing laundry, writing, and meeting with MacCormack. Despite all that, Rochelle and Max wouldn't be done with their classes for another hour.

As I passed the mailbox on my way into the building, I remembered there was something I still had to do. The last time I'd spoken to Lareina, I let her believe I was staying with the Defiance and would bring Rochelle into our plan to steal and destroy the research. She wouldn't be receiving her usual Monday-night phone call, and I needed her to understand why I backed out of our plan. After all, she had trusted me with the Spero pendant, so I owed her an explanation.

Using the key Audrie had provided, I unlocked the door to my shared room and kicked off my shoes. I tore out a blank piece of paper from one of Max's notebooks, put on my crooked glasses, sat down at my desk, and picked up a pen.

*Lareina,*

*I know I promised to bring Rochelle into our plan and move forward with it, but everything changed more quickly than I could keep you informed. Griff and Molly were planning to use Rochelle for their own purposes and then dispose of her when she was no longer useful. She wasn't safe there, and I had to get her out immediately.*

*Griff and Molly also discovered documentation of which scientist had which pendant. Griff spoke to me about it just before I left.*

*Rochelle is safe, and I'm working with the TCI now. I think it's as close as we can get to being on the right side without trying to figure this out on our own. For now, it's best that what's hidden remains hidden.*

*That would be best for everyone. I'm sorry this didn't work out the way you wanted it to, but maybe it's for the best. Nothing happens by chance. I really tried to make our plan work. I'm not giving up, just changing strategies based on the information I have at this time. I'll be in touch.*

*Charlie*

I didn't want anyone, especially Rochelle, to find out about the Optimus pendant. To accomplish that, I needed to convince Lareina to go along with a new plan. I had to make her understand that our decision impacted the lives of many people. It wasn't like her journey to Maibe when she could just run away and leave the mess behind her. If we made the wrong choice, everyone in Maibe, the people we both cared about, would pay the price.

This was the best explanation I could give her at this time. I spent twenty minutes searching for Max's envelopes and stamps. After locating them under a box of granola bars on the dresser, I addressed the letter to Lareina at the Maibe Home for Children. By the time I dropped it in the mailbox outside and lay down on the futon for a nap, voices passed in the hallway, and then the doorknob jiggled.

I sat up as Max and Rochelle walked into the room. "Hey guys, how was class?"

"Overwhelming." Rochelle dropped her bag and sat down beside me. "I'm so far behind."

"She's been worrying all day." Max tossed his bag onto his bed.

"She thought you'd still be in your meeting with MacCormack, or that he would tie you up and throw you in a river."

"Max! I didn't say that last part." Rochelle patted my arm. "How did things go with MacCormack?"

I shrugged. "He asked me a lot of the same questions again. He's either testing my memory, or he thinks I'm lying to him. I'm pretty sure he doesn't want me here."

"Same for me." Max laughed. "It's okay. The guy is a power-hungry psycho. We don't need his approval."

"But I do need his help if I'm going to stay out of prison."

"It's all going to work out. He's letting you stay at the AEI, so he clearly knows you're on our side." Rochelle pulled me into a hug. "Being kidnapped by the Defiance wasn't great, but it was worth it to get you back."

"I'm glad it worked out this time, but let's not do it again." I squirmed to get away from her, but she pinned my arms to my sides. "Do you want some help with your homework?" Most of her assignments were way above my understanding, but I could help proofread her writing and find information in her textbooks.

"Are you sure you can see with those glasses?" Max tilted his head to imitate the way the glasses fit on my face.

Rochelle let go of me and sat up. "I can ask Audrie to get you new ones."

"It's fine." I stood. "I can manage for a while." The less Audrie and the TCI were involved in my life, the better.

"Let's study outside." Max picked up his bag. "There's a picnic table on this side of the building."

"Great idea. The fresh air will be good for all of us." Rochelle was still worried about Max. Although the doctor had said it was just a stomach bug and Max was mostly back to acting like himself, he still wasn't eating much.

I picked up Rochelle's bag with one hand and pulled her to her feet with the other. After everything we'd been through together, it felt wrong not to tell her that Lareina had the Optimus pendant. It had been hard enough not telling her last December about the agreement I'd signed with the TCI, or my plan to return to the Defiance. I had kept those secrets to protect her and keep her home with her family. Although I'd failed, this time I would succeed at keeping Rochelle and the world safe from any plans the Defiance had for the research. All I had to do was keep one little secret and convince Lareina to do the same.

# CHAPTER 20
# ROCHELLE

*April 17, 2091*

A udrie hadn't told me the whole truth. It couldn't be a coincidence that her schedule had suddenly changed after our meeting with MacCormack. She was being punished because I hadn't delivered any new information to the TCI.

My legs propelled me down the trail past the trees, tinged green with incoming leaves. Max and I decided to run after classes since it would be warmer than our usual time in the early morning.

As much as I wanted my aunt to tell me the truth, I wanted it even more from Kinley. On Sunday when I spoke to her on the phone, she was more despondent. She asked me questions, so I did most of the talking, and when I asked about her week, all she said was that she'd been studying and picking up extra shifts at the hospital. As far as I knew, she hadn't spoken to Alexander, it bothered her that Kat wouldn't respond to her letters or phone calls, and she was really worried about her big test coming up. I missed her so much I cried after hanging up the phone.

"Rochelle . . . slow . . . down." Max's breathless voice pleaded.

I stopped and turned around. He walked toward me with his hands on his head. It was only the second day we had resumed running, and he still wasn't back to his usual energy level or good humor. The doctor decided it was just a stomach bug or something he ate and said he could return to normal activities after twenty-four hours of not throwing up.

"Sorry. I just got lost in my thoughts and forgot where I was for a minute." It felt good to run and convince myself I could leave my worries behind if I were fast enough.

"It's all right. Do you mind if we sit down for a while?" He pointed to a waist-high retaining wall a few feet into the brush.

"Sure." I realized we were at the abandoned hospital, which meant we were only half a mile from campus.

The expansive building sprawled through the trees. Its shadow engulfed us as we approached, blocking out the last warmth of the setting sun. A cacophony of birds squawking and rustling in the nearby trees shattered the peace of the evening.

"They must roost here." Max looked up, but there was nothing visible through the thick tangle of trees. "Things are so different out here in the evening compared to morning." He sat down on the wall and winced.

"Do you need some water?" I offered him the bottle I was carrying even though he insisted we wouldn't need it. He was more concerned with carrying his TCI-issued phone in the band on his arm in case of an emergency.

He nodded and took the water. "Thanks."

I braced one foot against the wall and slowly leaned in until my knee met my chest. The hospital's dark windows stared down at me, and I shivered. Despite the buildup of discarded tires and piles of old junk that had been dumped here for the past fifty years, I could imagine what it looked like when it was open. A now-cracked walkway must have been lined with flowers and surrounded by a well-kept lawn. The hospital was toward the edge of the woods to provide its former patients with the peace of nature, although the highway was less than a mile from its main driveway.

"I've been wanting to investigate since we got here to find out if it's really haunted." Max's voice pulled me out of my imagination. "We never have any free time though."

I sat down next to Max. "I know what you mean. I won't be ready for finals in two weeks. I missed so many classes while I was away."

"You caught up on all your assignments over the weekend." Max nudged me with his elbow. "I'll help you study for your precalculus test, and you'll be fine with everything else."

"I'm still nervous about it." My heels bounced off the wall with each swing of my leg. "I can't disappoint Audrie, and I definitely can't disappoint Kinley. After everything I've put her through, my grades are all I have left to make her proud."

Max shook his head. "Kinley would still love you even if you failed every one of your classes. And there's no way she blames you for any of this."

"I know, but she's just—"

"Just like you," Max finished.

I laughed. "Very funny. But seriously, I'm worried about her. She's working too much and is stressed out, and I'm not there to do anything about it. I don't want her to worry any more than she already did when Audrie told her I was missing."

Max's eyes went wide. "She actually told Kinley about that?"

"She had to, Max. Kinley would have known something was up when I didn't call that Sunday." I lowered my voice even though no one was around to hear us. "Audrie let me break the rules and call home the night we got back to her apartment. It took me fifteen minutes to calm Kinley down and convince her I was okay. I was really careful when I told her about my time with the Defiance. She doesn't even know Keppler is here because I don't know if that would make her feel better or make her worry more."

Max scratched his head. "What did you tell her then?"

"That I was in Defiance interrogation for a few days, and then I escaped and called Audrie to come get me." I ignored Max's raised eyebrows. "I didn't lie to her. I just left out a lot of information. It'll be easier to tell her in person eventually." The last thing I wanted to do was keep things from my cousin, but it was for her own good. She wasn't even angry at Audrie for letting me go on the assignment like I'd expected her to be.

Max's phone let out a high-pitched ding, and he pulled it free of the band on his arm. "It's from MacCormack." He flipped the phone open and read the screen. "It says, 'Report to my office immediately. Bring Charlie and Rochelle with you.'"

My chest clenched. "That doesn't sound good. Why would he want to see all three of us?"

"Only one way to find out." Max flipped the phone shut and stood. "We'll go get Keppler and face whatever it is together."

---

"It's been brought to my attention that you two were involved in a fight after cornering one of your classmates in the stairwell of your building." MacCormack glanced at Max and Keppler.

The three of us stood in front of the head agent's desk. He hadn't asked us to sit down, so we didn't.

"According to my witness, Charlie made threats that invoked his connection to the Defiance and," MacCormack's glare landed on Max, "you had the nerve to call in sick and take that afternoon and the next day off."

Max stepped forward. "Head Agent MacCormack, that's not—" MacCormack held up his hand and Max fell silent. "I'm not finished. Rochelle, the scores in your classes have slipped a full letter grade since the midterm."

I knew it was because the assignments I'd turned in yesterday hadn't been graded yet, but I just nodded.

"You should know by now this isn't your small-town school. I expect better from you, and if you can't pull it together and meet the standards of the AEI, you won't be returning for another semester. Max, the stakes are higher for you. If I have to call you to this office one more time, you're off to the reform school you were originally bound for. Charlie, if you cause trouble at my school, you'll be sent to a prison designed specifically for Defiance kids. Take my word for it, that won't be a pleasant place to spend the rest of your life."

Max opened his mouth again, but I caught his hand and squeezed it tight.

MacCormack's eyes gleamed with malice. "Am I clear?"

"Yes, sir," I answered for all of us.

"Good. Now for the consequences of your recent actions." MacCormack folded his hands on top of his desk. "There will be an announcement tomorrow morning that the AEI will be hosting a meeting for state leaders to discuss the circumstances of our country, or what's left of it. They'll arrive next Thursday and stay for the banquet on Saturday evening. It's my intention to involve all students in next Saturday's events, but you three are to remain in your rooms. Plan ahead so you have food to get you through the day." He looked at each of us in turn. "If any of you are caught outside of your building, the consequences will be as previously mentioned."

Keppler's head bowed in defeat. Max's hand gripped mine so tight it hurt, and I knew it took everything he had not to argue with the injustice of MacCormack's declaration.

"Understood?"

"Yes, sir." Keppler and I responded in unison. Max nodded, probably afraid of what would come out if he opened his mouth.

"Then you're all dismissed. I recommend you study for your finals. Your future depends on it." He smirked and shuffled the papers on his desk.

Unable to breathe, I rushed out of the room, pulling Max with me because he hadn't loosened his grip on my hand. I made it through the front door and outside before sinking to the ground, forehead against my knees, gasping for air.

"Rochelle?" Max's voice sounded far away.

"It's okay." Keppler's shaking hand landed on my shoulder. "Focus on one breath at a time. I'll count with you."

The minutes we sat together counting my breaths in and out felt like hours. Finally, I lifted my head and blinked away tears I hadn't noticed before. "We're being punished for things that weren't our fault."

"I know. It's not fair." Max squatted with his arms wrapped around his knees. "We'll tell Audrie or Sid. They'll fix it for us."

"No." I wiped my face with the back of my sleeve. "What are they going to do? MacCormack is their boss, and Audrie is already in trouble because I failed to figure out the passcodes and get any information from Molly. The changes to her work schedule are a punishment, and I don't want to make things worse for her."

Keppler sank back against the wall next to me. "Aumont's right. They don't have any more control over this than we do. MacCormack wants us to get in trouble so he can get rid of us, so all we can do is stay out of trouble."

"What's stopping him from making something up?" Max lowered himself to the ground with his legs folded underneath him.

"He can't send you guys to prison. There has to be something . . ." I choked on the rest of my words. The TCI was supposed to save my friends, not destroy their lives.

"No one is going to prison." Keppler didn't sound as sure as I wanted him to. "MacCormack has evidence for those other things. Not accurate evidence, but probably enough to prove we're not meeting the standards of this place. From now on, we'll stick together and avoid everyone so they can't accuse us of anything. You guys will ace your finals, and MacCormack will move on to a real problem."

Max and I nodded, and then we sat in silence for several minutes. I didn't understand why the head agent was suddenly targeting us. The cloud-covered sun had already sunk behind the building, giving way to the encroaching shadows.

"Do you think Alexander is coming next week?" Max sat up and slid forward.

Keppler rubbed his face. "Why would he?"

"MacCormack said state leaders are coming for the meeting." Max shrugged. "Isn't Alexander running for governor?"

"I don't know." Keppler stood. "If he is, I'm sure he's not the only candidate. What are the chances he'd come here?"

"It doesn't matter." The twinge of hope that I could hug Alexander vanished. "Remember, we have to stay in our rooms."

Max bounced to his feet and offered me his hand. "We have to stay in our rooms on Saturday, but they're coming on Thursday."

I took his hand and stood. "Let's just go and get something to eat so we have time to study."

"That's a solid plan." Keppler took a backward step down the sidewalk. "We'll feel better after we eat something. We've dealt with worse. We can handle this situation."

His voice told me everything would be okay, but his expressionless face warned that we were at the beginning of a losing battle.

# CHAPTER 21

# CHARLIE

*May 1, 2091*

The words on the page in front of me blurred. I took off my glasses, which had been crooked since my encounter with the border militia. Rochelle sat next to me, head bobbing as she read her psychology notes for the thirtieth time. Across the table, Max studied his physics book with his head on the table.

Two weeks had passed since MacCormack's warning, and we'd been successful in not drawing any more negative attention. Rochelle, Max, and I had fallen into a simple routine. The three of us ate breakfast together, then I returned to the dorm to write or read a book while Rochelle and Max went to class. I met them for lunch and returned to my earlier activities before joining them on their three-mile run, just to get out of the room. After dinner, we went to the library where I helped them study when I could. Rochelle's literature and psychology notes were interesting, but I didn't understand a word of Max's physics or advanced calculus.

I replaced my glasses and tilted my head so I could see through both lenses at the same time. I glimpsed 11:15 on the clock across the room. "Guys, it's late. Maybe we should call it a night."

"But my first two tests are tomorrow," Rochelle groaned.

"You probably know those notes better than your teacher does." I turned my attention to Max. "And didn't you know most of that stuff before you even got here?"

"Thanks for the pep talk." Max closed his book. "But knowing it for fun and knowing it to stay out of reform school are two different things." He had been moodier today and hadn't eaten much but wouldn't admit he wasn't feeling well.

"Sleep helps your brain process information. It's in Aumont's notes." I glanced around the room once packed with studying students but now only speckled with a handful of people. "Everyone else is sleeping right now."

"Keppler's right. I'll sleep with my notes under my pillow just in case it actually works." Rochelle gathered her materials into a pile.

"Good idea," Max relented. "Do you think I'll dream about physics equations?"

"Probably." I wasn't going to argue.

Rochelle stood and slid her books into her bag. "I wish my precalculus test was tomorrow. I want to get it over with, but I'm going to have to think about it all week."

"I'll help you study again tomorrow." Max crammed his book into a bag overflowing with wadded-up paper. "Can I borrow your history notes? Mine are terrible, and most of them are missing."

"No problem." Rochelle swung her bag onto her shoulder, and the three of us made our way to the door.

Every time we went outside, I feared we would run into Henry Davis. Part of me thought MacCormack would send him to stir up trouble, while the other part of me decided the head agent was just doing his job and didn't have anything against us. He had called me to four additional meetings, during which he questioned me about the Defiance. I answered them, and it was easier than I expected to avoid saying anything about the Optimus pendant or Griff's fake pendants. MacCormack was actually more interested in Griff. He wanted to know what he was afraid of, what made him angry, who and what were most important to him, and how he would react to my decision to help the TCI. I decided he was building a psychological profile on his nephew. Although MacCormack was civil and polite in our sessions together, I would leave anxious about whether my answers, which were absolutely true, would be acceptable enough to earn immunity from the severe consequences.

As always, we walked Rochelle to her building, and once she was safely inside, we continued to ours. On our way through the lobby, Max opened his mailbox. It was usually empty, but tonight he pulled out a single envelope.

"It's for you." He held it out to me. "Who from Maibe knows you're here?"

I wanted it to be from Kat or Kinley, but I knew it was a reply to the letter I had written. "Lareina."

Max's eyebrows slid halfway up his forehead. "Why is Lareina writing to you? How does she even know you're here?"

"Remember how I needed that pendant from her to regain Griff's trust?" I started walking toward the stairs and waited for Max to catch up. "She gave it to me on the condition I stay in touch with her. The last time I talked to her, she told me not to blow my cover. She wanted me to stay and make Rochelle part of the plan."

"She didn't want you to get Rochelle out?" Max opened the door and walked into our room.

"She's kind of obsessed with this pendant stuff." I locked the door behind us. "It's like what happened to Griff except she wants to destroy the research instead of use it. I guess that's better."

"I'm glad you didn't listen to Lareina and helped Rochelle escape instead." Max kicked off his shoes. "Rochelle's asked me a few times why Molly thought you had a pendant."

I sat down with the unopened letter in my hand. The betrayed looks on Kinley's and Rochelle's faces when I had stood next to Molly flashed through my head. "What did you tell her?"

Max sighed. "That Molly would say whatever it took to get her attention. That she was trying to manipulate her like always."

"Good. She has enough to deal with." I studied the neatly printed address on the envelope in my hand. "Griff figured out that I brought him the wrong pendant."

"No way." Max sat down next to me. "How?"

"Molly's dad kept record of it in his notes. Molly looked into it after she talked to Rochelle." I sighed. "That was another reason I had to get out of there. Griff was asking questions and getting suspicious."

"It doesn't matter now. You're here." Max squeezed my shoulder. "And even knowing who should have which pendant won't matter because Lareina won't be on their list, so everything's fine." He nodded to the envelope that I gripped in my hands. "Are you going to open it?"

I nodded, dreading what I would find inside, but opened it and unfolded the letter anyway. Lareina had to understand that with my cover blown by Molly's evidence, sooner or later I would be questioned under torture, and there was a risk I would say something that would lead the Defiance back to Lareina and her pendant.

*Charlie,*

*I trusted you with the most important thing in my life, and I shouldn't be surprised you let me down just like everyone else. Sure, I can keep my pendant hidden, but that's only a temporary solution. I know better than anyone that not having a key doesn't stop people from opening a door. If the Defiance wants the research, they'll get to it with or without my pendant.*

*You should have just told Rochelle about the plan. She*

*would have helped you cover for that little problem, and we would be in a much better position to get to the research before the Defiance. Now the world is a more dangerous place, thanks to you. From now on, I want to work with Rochelle on this. You have one week to tell her everything before I write her a letter explaining it all myself.*

*Lareina*

"That doesn't sound good." Max looked up from the letter. "Do you think she's right about unlocking the research without the pendants?"

"No. We're not talking about a regular door here." This was why the fake pendants made me nervous. Just because they didn't work yet, it didn't mean someone wouldn't figure out how to make them work in the future. "This is high-tech, fortified stuff."

Max nodded but didn't meet my eyes. "What are you going to do?"

"Nothing." I crumpled the paper and tossed it into the trash can. "Lareina's all talk. She thinks she knows everything about the world. According to her, the Defiance is a bunch of evil thugs and she's good because she can survive without a family. She doesn't need anyone, and the only way I can redeem myself is to steal the research, and now that's never going to happen."

"Isn't she the one who needed a bunch of people's help to survive?" Max sighed. "I'm lucky my *tío* and *tía* took me in when my parents died. I can barely take care of myself in this place. If I had ended up on the street, I would have been in the Defiance the minute I got hungry, and that wouldn't have taken long."

I smiled. "Maybe we would have been brothers even then."

Max laughed. "When I figure out time travel, we could experiment with different scenarios and find out."

"Or we could prevent all this from happening and stay in Maibe."

"Even better." Max walked to his bed. "How are we going to stop Lareina from telling Rochelle? I know the mailman. He's interested in time travel. Maybe I could distract him while you intercept Rochelle's mail."

"I don't think Lareina is actually going to write to her. She doesn't want the TCI involved, and as long as Rochelle is here, Lareina will be afraid she'll spill the secret." I kicked off my shoes and pulled off my hoodie. "Do you think I did the wrong thing by not sticking around to make Lareina's plan work?"

"You couldn't make it work." Max sat down on his bed and pulled off his socks. "There was no way you could get the rest of the pendants from the TCI, and Griff was about to figure out you were working undercover. You had to get out of there. Lareina should understand that."

"I guess Lareina is harmless compared to MacCormack. Part of me feels like he's setting us up for failure, but I have no evidence, so I might just be paranoid." I turned off the lights and climbed up to the top bunk. "He doesn't like us, but we need his help. It's a good trap, but I don't know what he's getting out of it."

"Keppler, what's the chance we're both going to prison?" Max's voice was small and shaky below me.

I sank into my pillow. I was as uncertain as he was. "Higher for me than you. MacCormack knows you're smart and can help the TCI. Once he has all the information he wants from me, I'm useless."

"Next semester, we can team up in Sid's workshop class. We'll collaborate on a project and create the newest, most innovative spy gadgets. He'll want both of us working for the TCI when he sees what we can accomplish, and we'll graduate from spy school together."

I didn't respond. Instead, I pulled my blanket over my head and closed my eyes. The last thing I wanted was for Max to end up on the head agent's bad side because of his association with me, but maybe it was already too late for that. Then again, even my worst nightmares didn't come close to imagining the trouble Max was about to face because of me.

# CHAPTER 22

# CHARLIE

*May 3, 2091*

"Can you stop that?" Max didn't look up from his calculus book. "I'm trying to study."

"Sorry." I tossed the ball I'd been bouncing off the wall to the other side of the futon and lay down. "Don't you think we should take a break for lunch?"

It was almost two o'clock and we hadn't eaten since breakfast. I had mostly been stuck in the room for the past day and a half while Max and Rochelle went about their separate finals schedules. Right now, Rochelle was in the middle of her physical fitness test, which meant doing a set amount of sit-ups, push-ups, and timed runs that culminated into a timed obstacle course. Max had come back from that test earlier, which I figured accounted for his gloomy mood. "Rochelle will be done with her test in like twenty minutes." Max's desk faced the window so I couldn't see his expression. "It won't kill us to wait for her." Before I could respond, two loud knocks came through the door.

Max didn't move. "Tell whoever that is to go away."

"Am I your butler now?" I got up and trudged to the door. Preparing myself to face Henry or MacCormack, I pulled the door open. My jaw dropped and the words evaporated from my brain when I saw Todd and Evie standing in front of me.

The last time I'd seen Todd was four months ago. He'd still been recovering from his injuries from the Defiance work camp

Molly had sent him to. But now he looked like himself. His light-brown hair was combed to one side as always, and he was in good shape from helping his dad unload lumber and shingle roofs. Todd smiled and raised his hand in hello.

"Hey, Delgado." I turned to Max, whose head was bent over his book. "Todd is here."

"Very funny, *hermano*. If you want to distract me from studying, you're going to have to come up with a more believable story than that."

"Studying?" Todd laughed as he entered the room. "I've never seen Max Delgado study for anything in his life."

Max stood so quickly he almost toppled over his chair. "Todd. What are you doing here?"

"He came to my room looking for Rochelle." Evie took a step into the room. "I figured you two could help him out."

"Evie, hey." Max stood up straight and ran a hand over his hair. "Help. Yeah. Rochelle. I know where Rochelle is."

"I'll take that as a yes." Evie looked at me and shrugged. "Todd, I leave you in semi-capable hands. Max, I'll see you at the final tomorrow." She waved and disappeared into the hall.

"I think she likes you." Todd tilted his head toward Max.

"She has a funny way of showing it." Max shook his head. "She usually acts like she's annoyed with me."

"That's rough." Todd put a hand on Max's shoulder and turned him back to the desk. "What are you studying?"

"Advanced calculus." Max pointed to the book and notes scattered across his desk. "It's my hardest class this semester."

"That looks way more complicated than the college calculus class I took." Todd squinted at the open book. "This is like something from another planet."

"I can't argue with that." Max laughed. "I'm happy to see you, but what are you doing here?"

"I came for the State Leaders Conference with Alexander. He was going to hold some kind of competition to determine which council member would come along to assist him, but everyone else backed out." Todd smiled. "I think they know how much I miss Rochelle."

"Are you here to help Alexander or to visit Rochelle?" Max shoved one foot into his shoe.

"Can't I do both?" Todd looked at his watch. "Alexander told me to meet him at the dining hall for a late lunch around three. He's in some kind of welcome meeting with the other leaders, so he doesn't need me right now."

"We're going to lunch soon too." Max slid his arms into his jacket. "But we'll find Rochelle first. She's in the middle of her skills test now. Did she know you were coming?"

Todd shook his head. "I wasn't even sure I was coming until my dad finally okayed it yesterday."

"She'll be so surprised. I can't wait to see the look on her face." The usual energetic Max I hadn't seen for a couple of days returned as he bounced around the room looking for his key.

"Charlie, it's good to see you." Todd extended his hand and shook mine. He seemed more at peace than the last time we'd spoken. I was glad he'd recovered.

"It's good to see you too." I knew Rochelle wrote to him every day, so he was probably aware of everything that had happened and why I was here. For a second, I considered asking him what Kinley had been saying about me, but then I decided I didn't want to know the answer.

Max put a hand on each of our shoulders and steered us toward the door. "We'd better hurry or we'll miss Rochelle crossing the finish line."

On our way to the skills course, Todd told us about the college calculus and architectural drawing classes he was taking through a distance learning program. He enjoyed both of them more than the English and history assignments Emma still expected him to keep up with. When he wasn't studying, he was working with his dad. According to Todd, Maibe was boring without us.

"There it is." As the skills course came into view, Max explained the obstacles they had to climb, cross, and crawl under before running a three-mile course in an allotted amount of time. "I did mine this morning and I'm still exhausted."

"And you haven't eaten lunch yet?" Todd surveyed the complicated obstacle course as we approached Sid, who held a stopwatch in his hand. "Usually, you've had lunch at your house, Rochelle's house, and my house by now. Are you feeling okay?"

"Yeah, just trying to shake the side effects of a stomach bug I had a few weeks ago." It was better than the shrug he would have given me had I asked the same question. "Hey, Sid, how's her time?"

Sid turned to us, nodded at Todd, and held up the stopwatch. "She got through the obstacles in record time. She should be finishing up her run any second now."

"Todd, stand behind Keppler." Max took his arm and pushed him behind me. "If she sees you too soon, it might distract her and mess up her time."

He didn't protest and remained behind Sid, Max, and me as we waited another thirty seconds. Ahead, Rochelle sprinted out of the trees, not slowing down until she'd passed the finish line by eight feet.

"That's two minutes under time." Sid held up the stopwatch with one hand and high-fived Rochelle with the other. "Nice work!"

"Two minutes!" Max took Rochelle's hand and held her arm above her head. "You left my time in the dust."

Rochelle coughed and pressed her hands to the top of her head. "I've . . . never run . . . so fast . . . in my life." She tried to brush mud off her filthy jacket but gave up. "You guys can go eat if you want. I need to shower first."

"Not a problem. But before you go . . ." Max spun her around to face Todd.

"You see him too, right?" She rubbed her eyes but remained frozen in place.

"Surprise." Todd grinned and closed the space between them.

Rochelle sprang forward and the two of them were glued together, so lost in their own world that the rest of us no longer existed to them.

Sid rested one hand on Max's shoulder and the other on mine. "I know you guys have friends here for the conference. Just make sure you're still following MacCormack's rules."

"We will," Max assured. He had informed me that the head agent warned both Sid and Audrie about our supposed unacceptable conduct. They both believed our side of the story but advised us to do as we were told. "We won't leave our rooms for even a second on Saturday."

"Good. I want both of you in my class next semester." Sid slid the stopwatch into his pocket and walked back toward campus.

A raindrop splashed against my forehead, and I pulled my hood up.

"Todd. Rochelle." Max raised his voice even though they were only a few feet away from us. "It's starting to rain. Maybe we should get inside."

They both looked up and reluctantly separated from their embrace. Rochelle ignored the tears streaming down her face, and Todd pretended to scratch his nose to discreetly brush his tears away.

"You guys go meet Alexander for me." Todd didn't take his eyes off the girl he hadn't seen for four months. "I'll walk Rochelle back to her room, and we'll be there when she's ready."

Knowing time with Todd was exactly what Rochelle needed, Max and I agreed.

"This is it. He's going to ask her out." Max fell into step beside me as we started toward the dining hall. "I'll bet you twenty dollars."

"I'm not betting on that. It's going to be hard for them when Todd has to leave."

"Don't worry about that for now. Hopefully, seeing him will help Rochelle get through a few more months." He pulled the door open, and we darted into the warm, dry building. "She's so homesick. If her grades weren't so important to her, I'd advise her to fail on purpose so MacCormack would send her home."

"Do you miss home?" I knew the AEI had lost its glow of adventure for Max, but he didn't talk about his family or Maibe like Rochelle did.

He nodded as we passed through the hang-out area surrounding the dining hall. "I miss my *tía's* cooking and helping my *tío* fix things. I even miss my little cousins messing with my stuff." Max stopped outside the door to the dining hall. "I'd give anything to be walking the streets of Maibe with nothing to do but think about my next invention, but I've accepted that we're either here or somewhere worse."

"Yeah." I pushed the hood off my head and ran a hand over my hair. "Me too." Seeing Todd had left my brain scrambling for ways I could go home, but unlike Max, I didn't even know whether I had a home in Maibe anymore. But that didn't matter because he was right. We were both stuck at the AEI if we wanted any kind of freedom at all.

"Come on." Max nudged my arm. "It won't help to think about it."

I followed him into the dining hall where we checked in, loaded our trays with warm food and mugs of coffee, and sat at a table with a good view of the only entrance.

"I thought you were hungry." Max scooped a spoonful of mashed potatoes into his mouth.

I looked down at the pizza I'd been craving all afternoon. "We should have asked Todd if he told Alexander I'd be here. Maybe he doesn't want to see me."

"Why wouldn't he want to see you?" Max spoke around the food in his mouth.

"Because I talked him into signing that agreement with the TCI. Kinley never wanted me to go undercover in the first place, and she only found out through Audrey after I left. Now Kinley hasn't spoken to Alexander since Christmas."

"You really think you're the reason for that?" Max shook his head. "They've had disagreements before. Alexander won't blame you."

"I still left him to clean up the mess and explain everything to Kinley," I said.

Max stopped eating and lowered his spoon to his tray. "Alexander knows it was mostly out of your control. He'll forgive you."

I looked down at my tray, trying to decide whether I would be able to forgive someone in a reverse situation. Probably not.

"There he is." Max stood and waved.

I looked up and watched Alexander approach the table, trying to read his expression and body language. He looked the same, from his broad shoulders to his neatly cut brown hair and his kind blue eyes. He was a little thinner than I remembered, but he was standing up straight and smiling.

"Hey, guys. Long time no see." He clasped Max's outstretched hand and they quickly hugged. "Are you showing these people how smart you are?"

"I think so." Max grinned. "I'll know for sure after my calculus final tomorrow."

"That's like multiplication for you. Piece of cake." He turned his attention to me. "Charlie, you have no idea how relieved I was when Todd told me on the train that you'd be here. I've been worried about where you ended up."

"You have?" My chest ached, but I maintained eye contact. "I'm sorry about how it all happened. I didn't know Molly was coming. I had to play along—"

"I know." He rested his hand on the top of my head, a familiar, comforting gesture. "It's not your fault. I'm just glad you're safe."

"But you and Kinley . . ." I couldn't finish.

"You heard about that?" Alexander sat down in the chair next to me. "Kinley and I had been on shaky ground for a while, and it had nothing to do with you. I should have talked it all over with her. That was my responsibility, and I messed it up."

"She really hasn't spoken to you?" I couldn't look him in the eye. "At all?"

"We talked a little yesterday." He rested his hand on the back of his neck, which meant he didn't have good news. "I've been taking her seedlings from the greenhouse all week for her garden." When Alexander wasn't busy as Maibe's mayor, he ran a plant nursery and landscaping business. When I lived in Maibe, I helped him in the huge greenhouse on his farm and sometimes worked with him on landscaping projects in town. "Yesterday she happened to be home, so I told her I would be coming here, and I thought I would see Rochelle if she had anything to send. The conversation was civil for a few minutes, and then it dissolved into her accusing me of making decisions about you and Rochelle without talking to her, and me being so busy with my political ambitions that I wasn't there to help her like I'd promised. I lost my temper and told her she was so obsessed with work and studying that she wouldn't have time to talk with me unless I was one of her patients." He shook his head. "I'm not proud of that. The first thing I'm going to do when I get home is find her and apologize."

"She has to give you some credit." Max slid into the chair on the other side of me. "Who else would bring her apology plants?"

"If I had been thinking clearly, I would have brought her a bouquet of roses. I'll do that the minute I get home." Alexander smiled. "Enough about my problems. How are you guys?"

Max and I exchanged a look, and then Max explained everything we'd been through with MacCormack and the threats he'd made.

Alexander glanced around the empty dining hall. "Can you guys keep something between us?" We nodded, and he continued in a lowered voice. "A friend of mine from the leaders of Nebraska coalition is a really good lawyer. I told him about Max getting caught making trackers and Charlie's affiliation with the Defiance, and he's interested in taking on your cases. From the conversations we've had so far, he thinks he could get you both off with community service, which means we don't need the TCI."

"You mean, we could go home and do the community service there?" Max struggled to keep his voice quiet.

"That's the plan." Alexander smiled. "We're not there yet, but if we can get things rolling, you two will be home by Thanksgiving."

"What about MacCormack?" With Alexander around, I already felt safer. He was barely an adult at twenty years old, but he was putting a plan in place to help us, unlike the adults in the TCI.

"For now, stay out of trouble," Alexander said. "But don't worry about his threats. I'm not going to let any of that happen. When you guys leave here, you're going home."

I nodded. It was hope for the future I didn't know existed, but a nagging voice in the back of my head wondered if Alexander was truly a match for MacCormack. And even if he did get us out of the AEI, I still had to worry about Griff for the rest of my life. Things couldn't remain as they were forever. Whether Alexander's plan worked or MacCormack won, everything was about to change.

# CHAPTER 23
# ROCHELLE

*May 3, 2091*

**M**y reflection in the bathroom mirror watched me through tired eyes as I pulled a comb through my hair. The low murmur of Todd's voice carried on a conversation with Evie on the other side of the door. As long as I could hear him, it wasn't a dream. He was really here. Every night since I'd arrived at the AEI, I prayed for a miracle so I could safely visit the people I loved. It was a big request, but I knew God was better at solving problems than the TCI. Quickly, I pulled on a clean T-shirt and sweatpants, fastened the necklace from Todd around my neck, and clipped the bracelet from my dad on my wrist. Taking one last look in the mirror, I exited the bathroom into my room.

"That's incredible. You must be some kind of math genius." Todd sat at my desk, tipping the chair back so it balanced on two legs.

Evie laughed as she tossed books from her bed into her bag. "I don't know about that, but I was at the top of my class until Max got here. This is the first time I've had any real competition." She zipped her bag and slung it over her shoulder. "I should get going. I have a final in fifteen minutes. Nice to meet you, Todd." She shook his hand. "See you later, Rochelle."

"Good luck." I walked over to my bed and sank onto the edge of it.

"Long day?" Todd lowered the front legs of his chair to the floor.

"Long week, and I still have my precalculus test tomorrow. Everything's been rough lately, but now you're here and none of that matters."

Todd smiled so big his dimples showed and his hazel eyes sparkled. "I can help you study after we eat. Alexander doesn't need me much until tomorrow."

"That would be great." I brushed my wet hair off my shoulder. "Max is trying to help me, but it's hard for him to explain something that's so easy for him."

"Perfect. That means we can spend some time together." Todd walked over and sat down next to me. "And I'll be able to give Kinley an accurate report on your health."

"You told her you were coming?"

"Of course. I've been looking out for her like you asked. The best way to do that was to ask her for help with my calculus homework." Todd had written me detailed letters about how he'd spent three days fixing the leaking roof that was never leaking, or hours repairing the sticking screen door he could have fixed in a few minutes just so he could hang out with Kinley. "We talk all the time now. So, when she asked me to spy on you, I naturally said yes."

I laughed. "I talk to her every Sunday. She knows I'm okay."

Todd shrugged. "She's worried you're leaving things out."

"Interesting." I turned so I could see Todd's face. "I'm worried she's leaving things out. What do I need to know?"

"It's just like I wrote in my letters." He stopped, knowing he couldn't hide anything from me when we were sitting in the same room. "She's barely home. If she's not in class, she's at the library studying or taking extra shifts at the hospital. Her headaches have been worse the past few weeks. Emma and I have been taking her food because we don't think she's been cooking anything for herself. We both check on her every day though, so try not to worry."

"Poor Kinley." I played with the hummingbirds on my bracelet. "I miss her and Kat so much."

"I almost forgot. I have news about Kat. I actually talked to her on Tuesday. She asked Emma to put me on the phone."

"What did she say?" Usually, Kat only talked to Todd to ask if Emma was home, so I hoped this meant she was progressing toward calling Kinley.

"She asked me about you." Todd's eyebrows slid together. "I told her to answer your letters, but she said she couldn't. She just wanted to know you were okay."

"That must be a good sign, right?" Maybe Kat wouldn't stay angry with me much longer. "Did she say why she won't answer my letters?"

"No." Todd took my hand, and the hummingbirds on my bracelet jingled against each other. "Don't worry. Emma is doing everything she can to convince Kat to reach out to you or Kinley. But she's also trying to patch things up between Kinley and Alexander, so she has a lot to deal with. I don't know how she can be so patient with everyone. If I were in her shoes, I would have lost it by now."

I hadn't considered how much we had put on Emma's shoulders by asking her to be our go-between for Kat on top of Kinley and Alexander. "I owe her big time."

"She'll be happy when you get home." Todd sighed. "She said you're a good mediator, and the two of you together can bring everyone to their senses."

"I hope so." I rubbed my hands over my face to clear my head. "If I ever get home. Todd, how am I going to say goodbye to you?"

"Shelley, I just got here." He managed a smile big enough to show his dimples. "Plus, we're together right now and we never thought this would happen."

"You're right. I'm wasting our time thinking like that." It was so good to have Todd next to me, but it was so awful knowing it couldn't last. "You have to be hungry. We should get to the dining hall." I stood but Todd didn't move.

"Actually, Rochelle, before we go, there's something I've been planning to ask you for a long time, but I wanted it to be in person." His face drooped into a serious expression.

"Okay." I sat down next to him and waited.

"Rochelle . . . I . . ." Todd looked down at his fiddling thumbs and then back up at me. "Would you . . ." He rested his forehead in his hand. "I've practiced this a thousand times. I'm sorry."

"It's okay." I patted his knee. "You can ask me anything."

Todd nodded. "Because we're best friends, right? We always have been?"

"We always will be." I braced myself for bad news I didn't want to hear, but I couldn't think of anything we hadn't already discussed or written about.

"Unless we upgraded." Todd stood. "To something better."

I rubbed my forehead. "Sorry, Todd. I think I'm too tired to follow this conversation."

"No, it's my fault. Let me try again." Todd took my hands in his and pulled me to my feet. "Rochelle Aumont, I can't even remember a time before I loved you because I don't really remember anything before kindergarten." He closed his eyes. "Will you be my girlfriend?"

"Yes, Todd." I laughed out of relief that nothing was wrong and disbelief he had actually asked the question Max and Kat had been anticipating for years. "Of course I'll be your girlfriend."

"Really?" His hazel eyes studied my face.

I squeezed his hands. "You thought I'd say no?"

Todd sighed. "I've had recurring nightmares about what would happen if you did."

"You know we can talk about anything." I pulled him into a tight hug. "How long have you been worrying about this?"

"Almost two years. I was going to ask you at the homecoming dance, but then it got canceled because of the fever, and I was afraid that was a bad sign." He rested his cheek against the top of my head. "And then you got sick, and ever since all of this pendant stuff started it never felt like the right time."

There was no arguing our lives had been complicated. "I'm glad you asked now. Perfect timing."

We separated from our long embrace and spent a minute just looking at each other.

"What do we do now?" Todd finally broke the silence.

"Hold hands whenever we want." I smiled and reached for his hand. "And probably get to the dining hall before Max theorizes that we ran away to get married."

Todd took my hand. "Max and his theories."

---

"I'm pretty excited about the food here," Todd said as we walked across campus hand in hand. "The food shortages are just getting worse at home." His letters had outlined what he couldn't reliably find at the grocery store due to shipping disruptions caused by the war with the Defiance. At first it was citrus fruits and some vegetables, mostly things people barely noticed. But recently, the shortages expanded to essentials like flour, sugar, milk, and eggs. Fortunately, there was no shortage of cows and chickens around Maibe, but still not enough to meet the prewar demand for the entire region.

"I miss dessert the most." He held the door open for me. "Emma started substituting for the ingredients we don't have with things like applesauce and honey, but the cakes and cookies she makes aren't the same as before."

"They manage to get everything here." I felt guilty looking at all my options in the dining hall after reading about Todd's sacrifices. "It's not really fair."

"You gave up a lot already. You deserve good food."

When we arrived at the dining hall, I checked in and showed Todd how to check in as a guest.

"There they are!" Max exclaimed when we were finished.

I waved and glanced around at a room of empty tables except where Max and Keppler sat in the middle of the room. As we approached them, Todd didn't let go of my hand like he used to in Maibe.

"Something's different." A big grin spread over Max's face. "You asked her, didn't you? I knew you'd figure it out, Todd." He nudged Keppler's elbow. "You owe me twenty dollars."

Keppler shook his head and looked away. "I told you we weren't betting on that."

I playfully smacked Max's arm with the back of my hand.

"Ow." Max laughed as he slid away from me. "Todd, did you see that?"

Todd smiled and shrugged. "If you annoy my girlfriend, there's nothing I can do to help you."

"I knew it." Max folded his arms and leaned back in his chair.

"Todd." Alexander's voice pulled our attention to him as he approached us with a tray piled with food. "I was starting to worry you got lost."

"The opposite." Todd laughed. "I found Rochelle."

"So I see." Alexander slid his tray onto the table. The bags beneath his eyes were more pronounced than ever, and I wished Kinley would stop being stubborn and accept one of the hundreds of apologies I was sure he had attempted.

I rushed forward and hugged him. "It feels like forever since I've seen you."

"It's been a long four months." He hugged me back, enveloping me in the safety I'd always felt in his presence. He had always been like a protective big brother to me. "It's so good to see you. I just wish it wasn't under such serious circumstances so I'd have more time to visit."

"The Defiance is winning the war, aren't they?" I sank into the chair next to Keppler.

Alexander nodded. "They're getting closer every day. Representatives from every state that isn't Defiance territory are here to discuss strategies to stop them, but from conferences we've had in the past, I'm worried about what that will mean." He sat down in front of his tray of food, and Todd sat down next to me. "You've all been great advisers to me at one time or another."

It seemed so long ago when I worked with him as a member of the town council in Maibe.

Alexander glanced around the room. "So, let's talk it over. But what's said here stays between us."

We all nodded. Todd gripped my hand under the table, this time as a comforting gesture.

"Many of the others want to find a way to appease the Defiance by giving them a piece of territory if they'll agree to stop."

Keppler sat up. "They won't stop. Don't believe anything they agree to."

Alexander nodded. "I'm with you. We know from history that appeasement won't get us anywhere. I'm here to propose we work harder to stop the Defiance's recruiting program and even pull some of those kids over to our side. We can't win unless we can offer the millions of kids without families something better than the Defiance. We should have been doing that a long time ago."

Keppler's head dropped until he stared at his empty tray.

Max and I knew he was thinking about the newsletters he'd been writing.

"What can we do to help?" I trusted Alexander. He had always been a forward thinker, willing to try new things instead of fearing change like so many others.

"I know kids on the street need the basics: food, shelter, and adults they can trust, which will require major changes to our current system. I want to use the Maibe Home for Children as a model for others across the country." Alexander took a sip of his water. "What else should I be considering to prevent kids from joining the Defiance in the first place?"

"A chance at a future. They all need school through twelfth grade and help getting into college or finding the right career," I said. I remembered what Molly had said before she joined the Defiance. She'd told me it was the only way she could compete with kids whose parents sent them to good schools and helped them apply to colleges. Without the Defiance, she didn't see any opportunities for her life.

"Great idea." Alexander gave me an appreciative smile. "I'll add that to the list."

"They need a family." Keppler lifted his head. "That's what the Defiance claims to be, but it's not, really. If you could prove there are people who'll take care of them and love them even if they make a few mistakes, most of them would be out of there in a heartbeat."

Alexander nodded. "I figured most of them are good kids, like you."

"Better." Keppler stood and picked up his empty glass. "I'll be right back."

Alexander watched him walk away. "Is he okay?"

Max and I looked at each other and nodded. What Keppler had done during his time in the Defiance would haunt him forever unless I could help him undo it all. There had to be a way to defeat the Defiance, and even though I loved Alexander's plan, I knew it all came back to the pendants, the passcodes, and who controlled the research.

# CHAPTER 24

# CHARLIE

*May 5, 2091*

I t hadn't rained all day, but the dark clouds outside my window promised a storm. I'd spent most of the afternoon watching cars drive past on the road outside. It only made me feel more trapped knowing that everyone else could go about their normal lives while I was confined to the dorm room that seemed to shrink by the minute. Then again, after all the recruiting I'd done for the Defiance, I deserved far worse. Why had I put so much effort into writing that newsletter? Max was right, I could have been less enthusiastic about it, and I didn't have to make my stories so compelling.

"I can't wait for this day to be over. Being stuck here is making me anxious." I pulled myself away from the window and flopped onto the futon.

Max rolled over on his bed to face me. "At least it's just one day, and we're together. Rochelle's all by herself."

Under normal circumstances, Max would have come up with enough projects to keep us working all day like we did in Maibe with his time machine. But today, he had spent the morning throwing up and the afternoon trying to sleep. I knew he was miserable, but I didn't know how to help him.

"Do you want to try to eat something? I can make toast." Using the illegal toaster would have been a small act of rebellion to get me through the afternoon.

"Thanks, but I'm not hungry right now," he groaned.

"Maybe you should go back to the doctor." I stood and walked over to him. "I'm starting to worry."

Max sat up, his face pinched in pain. "If I'm not feeling better tomorrow, I'll go. For today, I'm staying right here. I wouldn't put it past MacCormack to say I faked being sick to disobey his orders."

"What if it's serious?" I wished we could talk to Kinley. She would know what to do. I picked up Max's phone from the comforter. "Maybe we should call Rochelle again."

"Soon." He took the phone and slid it into his pocket. "I already have you worried. I don't want her to worry too."

"You're right. I just hate having all this time to think." I sank to the floor.

"You know it's not your fault the Defiance recruited so many new members." Max patted my shoulder. "They truly could offer what you promised, and no one else could. Alexander's right. It's a problem that should have been addressed a long time ago."

"But that doesn't mean I'm innocent in all this." I slumped against the side of the bed. "I made the problem worse. My whole life is a huge disaster."

Before Max could come up with a response, two sharp knocks pounded on the door.

"See." Max's eyes fixated on the door. "That's probably MacCormack checking to make sure we're both here."

"I hope it is him." Two more persistent knocks shattered the silence as I approached the door. "I'm coming." I intended to demand the head agent to get my friend the medical attention he needed. I unlocked the door and yanked it open. Before I could process the scene in the hall, two hands encircled my neck and squeezed.

Griff's face hovered in front of me as I fought to pull air into my lungs. "You didn't expect me to let you off the hook after what you did." His grip tightened. "If you were smart, you would be watching your back every minute of every day. Looks like you got pretty comfortable here."

*He can't be on TCI property*, I thought as blackness closed in at the edges of my vision. MacCormack promised I would be safe from the Defiance as long as I was at his school. If Griff could get to me here, I had nowhere left to run.

The room faded to darkness, and then I was on the floor, gasping for air. Griff stood over me with Alec and Tommy right behind him. All three of them laughed at me.

"Hey, leave him alone." Max stepped between me and the others.

"You don't want any part in this fight." Griff glared at Max. He towered over him by a head and outweighed him by more than a hundred pounds. "We'll deal with him somewhere else, no messes. Go back to sleep and forget about him."

Max rolled his shoulders back. "I can't. He's my brother. His problems are my problems."

Griff laughed. "I have to warn you, Charlie here is not a very loyal brother. This is your last chance to get out of my way."

Silently, I begged Max to back off as I tried and failed to sit up. Max didn't move.

Griff grabbed him by the shoulder and shoved him to the side. "Uncle Mac predicted that would be your decision. You two take this guy. I'll get Charlie."

"No." I forced myself up halfway. "Leave him out of it."

He responded with a kick to my torso and a boot to my face. Lying on the floor, I watched the ceiling spin one way and then the other. Griff yanked me to my feet and half carried me to the hallway, down the stairs, and out of the dorm. Tommy and Alec, each gripping one of Max's arms, shoved him forward in front of us.

The world appeared in blobs of gray interspersed with specks of colors I struggled to identify as buildings and trees. Concentrating on any one thought took a tremendous amount of energy, but I was alert enough to understand MacCormack had betrayed us. He wanted us dead, and he was going to let Griff do the job for him.

By the time my head cleared enough to gain my bearings, we were in the trees on the trail I had run with Max and Rochelle.

"How did you get MacCormack to let you come here?" I spit blood onto the ground.

Griff laughed. "He called and offered me a window of time to take you off his hands. He only wanted the pendants. Four fake pendants and I get to kill a traitor. Sounds like a fair deal to me."

"He'll know they're fake," I muttered. Suddenly, I wished I had warned the head agent. I doubted it would have saved my life, but it could have saved everyone else from the Defiance.

Griff shoved me through a cluster of branches growing over the trail. "He didn't figure it out during the meeting I just had with him. Examined the pendants and everything. Now, you're going to tell me all about how the TCI got the Pessimus pendant from Rochelle, and how you somehow found the Spero pendant lying around. If you can't manage that, your friend pays the price."

"Whatever MacCormack told you about the Pessimus pendant, he's lying." I struggled against his grip on my arm, but there was no opportunity to break free.

"Maybe he lied to you, but he's my uncle, my only family. He's known me since I was a little kid. I'm the one person he'd never hurt."

Max looked over his shoulder, but Alec yanked him forward.

"Even better, I have people in position to get the TCI pendants once Uncle Mac leaves the administration building. It's his mistake to trust me." Griff spit into the brush.

A burst of energy surged through me. I swung at Griff and hit him in the nose, but he returned with a punch that splayed me on the ground.

Tommy turned to view the commotion and tripped over a root. Max took the opportunity to kick Alec and break free, darting into the trees.

"If he gets away, you're done," Griff shouted.

Alec took off after Max, and my chest clenched in panic. I tried to get up and yell out a warning, but Griff's boot stomped on my back, slamming my face into the dirt.

Thunder cracked overhead, followed by three gunshots in quick succession.

Griff kicked me in the side. "Get up."

I tried, but my arms wouldn't hold my weight. Coughing, I collapsed back onto the ground.

"I said get up." He pulled me to my feet by the collar of my shirt. If I just had a minute to regain my strength, maybe I could disappear into the thick trees, find Max, and get away. There had to be a way to escape.

A rustling sound snapped our attention to the brush. Alec emerged from the budding foliage, dragging Max behind him.

Max looked at me, eyes wide and face contorted in pain. I scanned him for wounds that didn't appear on his head, chest, or torso. But blood soaked his pant leg between his ankle and knee.

"I said no guns." Griff yanked me with him as he approached Alec. "Do you want to blow the whole plan?"

"I stopped him, didn't I?" Alec let go of Max, who fell back on the trail, groaning. "If anyone heard, they'll think it was thunder."

"They'd better. Stop the bleeding," Griff barked. "I don't want them dead, yet."

Twisting myself, I attempted to kick Griff in the shin, but my leg didn't cooperate.

He kicked my legs out from under me, and I landed on my knees and elbows next to Max.

"Remember, Molly and the others are in position to get the TCI's pendants. We won't have another chance like this." He spit on me and laughed. "Even better, Molly has a plan to get those passcodes from Rochelle. I hope she's figured them out. I liked her for the short time I knew her, and I hate to think about what'll happen to her if Molly doesn't get what she wants."

"Leave her . . . out of it." I pushed myself up on my elbows.

"Worry about yourself." Griff leaned down so we were face-to-face. "We're going to go explore the old haunted hospital. Uncle Mac reminded me of how I used to sneak in there as a kid when I came to visit. When he found out, he told me I'd get killed playing in there. Maybe he thought it wasn't structurally sound, or maybe he thought the ghosts would get me."

Tommy tied a piece of his shirt around Max's leg, and Max yelled out something incoherent. Why couldn't he have just gotten out of Griff's way?

"Please." I couldn't let Max die. I couldn't let Rochelle face Molly alone.

Griff shook his head. "For someone who writes stories in his free time, you'd think you would have been able to imagine that betraying me would lead to an ending like this."

# CHAPTER 25
# ROCHELLE

*May 5, 2091*

I sat on my bed, looking at the grade report I'd found in my mailbox earlier this morning. Seven classes and seven A's. Five of them A+'s. I was exhausted and relieved, especially after finding out that Max had aced every one of his classes too. We had proven MacCormack wrong, and now all we had to do was stay in our rooms for a few more hours and then maybe we could stop worrying. A surge of hope spurred me to reach for my phone. I wanted to call Max to find out if he was feeling any better than when we had talked earlier.

Thunder rumbled outside, and I decided it wasn't such a bad day to stay inside. Maybe MacCormack had done me a favor by giving me an excuse to avoid whatever storm was approaching. I flipped open my phone, but before I could dial, a soft knock came from my door. Fearing Keppler and Max were bending the rules, I flipped my phone shut and rushed to the door. I pulled it open, ready to lecture them about the consequences of leaving their room. Instead, I took a step back, surprised by what I found in the hall.

Todd, wearing a shirt and tie, held a bouquet of daisies in one hand and hid the other hand behind his back. We had said goodbye last night because I wouldn't be at the banquet to see him before he left. "Todd, what are you doing here?" I took his arm and pulled him into the room. "I'm not supposed to leave my building, remember?"

"That's why I came to you." He smiled so big his dimples showed. "This MacCormack guy never said you couldn't have visitors, right?"

"No." I closed the door. "But I'm probably not supposed to."

"I brought you flowers." He held out the bouquet to me. "There's a flower shop next to my hotel."

I laughed and accepted the daisies. "Thank you. I'm so happy you're here, but aren't you supposed to be at the banquet?"

Todd shrugged with one arm still behind his back. "Alexander won't miss me for a little while. Did you get your grades yet?"

"Yeah." I hurried across the room and held up the report for him to see.

"I knew it." He pulled his arm into view, revealing a little green paper bag folded over on top. "Congratulations!"

"Todd, you don't have to buy me all these things." I opened the bag and pulled out a clear container with a chocolate cupcake decorated with green frosting.

"For the first time in my life I have some money, and you're pulling A's at the hardest school in the country. We'd be crazy not to celebrate."

I placed the gifts on my bed and threw my arms around my boyfriend. "I wish you could stay here." He would be on a train back to Maibe in the morning, and now we would have to say goodbye all over again.

"Even better, I wish you could come home with me tomorrow." He held me close. "Alexander is going to have to drag me onto that train to get me to leave you behind."

"I know how you feel." My TCI phone let out its chirping ring. "That's probably Max." I let go of Todd and walked to my bed. "He wasn't feeling well this morning, and I told him to check in later."

Finding my phone, I glanced at the unfamiliar number displayed on the screen. It wasn't one of the contacts in my phone, and no one else had ever called me.

Curious, I flipped the phone open and held it to my ear. "Hello?"

"Listen carefully," Molly's voice, distinct and unmistakable, commanded through the phone. "I have people outside your door and surrounding your building. Don't attempt to leave or they'll have to hurt you. You have thirty minutes to tell me the passcodes to the safe or the Defiance is going to pay a visit to that State Leaders banquet. Make the right choice and no one gets hurt. And don't hang up your phone or I'll take it as a refusal to cooperate."

Todd watched me, eyebrows raised, hazel eyes gentle with concern.

"Molly, listen to me. When I told you I don't know the passcodes, I meant it." I hurried to the window and looked outside but didn't see anyone. The last year and a half, however, had taught me not to underestimate Molly.

"I suggest you think fast. You have twenty-nine minutes to figure it out." The steady calm of her voice only made me more anxious. She knew she was in control. "No more games, and no more pretending to be friends. This is your last chance to give me the codes before I take other actions to get what I want."

"Okay. Okay." I turned to Todd, who had crossed the room with me.

"What's going on? Is that Molly?" He pointed to the phone.

I nodded. "She says the building's surrounded, and if I don't give her the passcodes in twenty-nine minutes, the Defiance will hurt everyone at the banquet."

Todd's face scrunched in thought, and he looked out the window. "There's no one surrounding us. I'll bet she's nowhere near here. Tell her to prove it."

"Is that Todd? What great timing that he's there to help you,"

Molly's voice screeched into my ear. "If he wants proof, here you go."

I lowered the phone and nudged Todd away from the window, not sure what to expect. Todd turned to me and opened his mouth, but before he could say anything, an obnoxious pounding on the door and the pop of rocks hitting the window made us both jump.

"Satisfied?" Molly laughed. "You have twenty-seven minutes. Quit wasting time."

"Okay. Just let me think." Heart pounding, I lowered the phone.

"Hang up," Todd whispered.

I shook my head, lowered the phone to my bed, and took Todd's hand. After pulling him into the bathroom, I closed the door behind us and leaned back against the sink.

"What am I going to do, Todd? I don't know the codes." I gripped the countertop to fight against the lightheadedness that was threatening to make my problem worse.

"Would you give them to her if you did?" He loosened his tie.

Sinking to the floor, I covered my face with my hands. "I don't know. Giving her the codes is wrong, but if she kills all the leaders at that banquet, that's clearly worse. That's the immediate threat." I dropped my hands. "The passcodes are no good without the rest of the pendants, so she can't hurt anyone that way, right?"

"Right, I think." Todd sank down in front of me. "Pretend we had the passcodes. What would Molly be able to accomplish if you gave them to her?"

"She would be able to unlock the safe to get the secure box that contains the research." I raised my eyes to meet Todd's. "But she would have to have all eight pendants to unlock the box. At least I think that's how it works. I haven't actually seen any of this, so maybe she can just take an axe to the box."

"Logically, if these scientists went through so much effort

to make the pendants work as keys, the box must be some kind of safe too." Todd shrugged. "Otherwise, what's the point of the pendants?"

"You're right." I rested my head back against the vanity. "So, all I have to do is give her the codes, and then she'll leave and no one gets hurt."

"But you don't know the codes."

"Don't remind me," I groaned.

"Sorry," Todd sighed. "Can't you just call Audrie and tell her what's happening?"

I shook my head. "Molly said if I hang up the phone, she'll send the Defiance into the banquet. We don't have landlines in our rooms, and we can't go into the hall." My stomach twisted, and I thought I was going to throw up. We were on our own. Todd and me against the Defiance.

"Okay, we can figure this out." Todd chewed on the inside of his cheek. "Do you believe she'll walk away if you give her the codes? She won't attack the banquet anyway?"

"She always keeps her word, but . . ." I stood, pushed the door open, and ran to my bed. I pulled the phone to my ear. "Molly, are you still there?"

"Do you know the codes?" Her voice rose in excitement.

"I'm working on that, but first, I need you to give me your word that when I give you the codes, you'll walk away and no one will get hurt."

"I promise, on the condition you give me the correct codes." Her voice was sharp and annoyed. "You should know I'm also on the line with someone who will enter them immediately to verify they work. You have twenty-two minutes and thirty-five seconds."

Placing the phone on my bed, I ran back to the bathroom, where Todd stood in stiff anticipation.

"What did she say?"

I pressed my hands to the top of my head. "She's on the phone with someone who will tell her if the codes work. We can't fool her. We need the real codes, and we only have twenty-two minutes."

"We can do this." Todd took a deep breath. "When Molly first asked you about the passcodes after Christmas, what did she say exactly?"

I closed my eyes and tried to remember her exact words. "She said her dad let my dad set the passcodes. Eric Bennet told my dad to enter the three most important things in his life. He thought he already knew the answer, but it didn't work when he tried to open it using 'Rochelle,' 'Kinley,' and 'Kat' as passcodes. So, all we know is that it's not our names."

"That makes sense." Todd rubbed his hands over his face. "He didn't want Eric Bennett to figure it out, and your names would have been obvious. So, what else was important to your dad that his best friend wouldn't guess?"

"He worked on his truck a lot." I scanned through memories of my childhood as I had done hundreds of times with Audrie. "Then again, he was in touch with Audrie, and I just found out about it last summer. It's like he had this whole secret life I didn't know about."

"What if it's not a secret? What if it's just before you remember? Maybe something to do with your mom?" His voice brightened.

"There are three words, so it could be her full name." I gripped his hand and relief swept through me. "Anna Josephine Aumont. Or he could have used her maiden name. It was . . . it was . . . I don't remember my mom's maiden name. She lost both of her parents before I was born. I never met them and . . ." My voice dissolved into tears.

"It's all right." Todd pulled me into his arms. "It must be something else. Your dad and Molly's dad went to college together, so none of that would have really been a secret. If he wanted someone he trusted to get to the research, he would have chosen something he was sure you knew. Something so automatic you wouldn't have to think about it."

"What if he didn't want anyone to get in?" I pulled away from Todd. "What if Audrie's right and I shouldn't be involved at all?" Annoyed, I flicked the tears off my face, causing the charms on my bracelet to tinkle against each other. It drew my eyes to the gold and silver hummingbirds on my bracelet. The answer had been on my wrist the entire time.

"We just have to stay calm," Todd was saying. "Maybe it's something—"

"Todd," I interrupted. "When my dad talked to me, how often did he call me 'Rochelle'?"

"Only when you were in trouble or when he was trying to be serious." Todd stared at me with wide eyes, a smile spreading over his face. "Most of the time he called you 'hummingbird.'"

I clutched my bracelet with my other hand. "And Kinley 'sunflower,' and Kat 'canary.' Molly said the codes weren't our names, but maybe . . ."

Todd nodded. "That has to be it."

"He gave us these bracelets right before he went to the hospital for the last time." I raised my wrist. "It had to be a clue, to remind me of what I already knew. He loved us, and he would do anything to make the world better for us." Lunging forward, I gripped both of Todd's hands. "We have to be right, because if we give her the wrong codes—"

"We're right. It makes sense." Todd looked down at our hands. "It's our best guess and we're running out of time."

I nodded. "But if we're wrong, we're probably going to die. Sorry I got you into this."

Todd leaned forward, and our lips touched for a second in a

quick kiss, our first real kiss. "Just in case we're wrong. But I'm pretty sure we're right."

A thousand emotions fought in my head, but Molly held a timer to doom in her hand. I stood and Todd followed. Holding hands, we walked into the next room, and I raised the phone to my ear.

"Molly?"

"Four minutes, Rochelle."

I squeezed Todd's hand and cleared my throat. "The passcodes are 'sunflower,' 'hummingbird,' and 'canary.'"

"You're sure?" Molly's earlier confidence gave way to skepticism.

Closing my eyes, I took a deep breath. "Yes."

"Stay on the line." A few seconds of rustling became silence.

"What did she say?" Todd whispered.

"She's checking to make sure they work." For several long minutes, I stood hand in hand with Todd, hoping for the best and preparing for the worst.

"I can't believe I'm saying this, but you were right," Molly said in a crackled voice. "You can now exit your room and building. The Defiance is leaving the premises, and no one else will even know we were there. As much as I wish we could have worked together, I've accepted you don't want any part of this. Have a good life, Rochelle."

After a loud click on Molly's end, I flipped my phone shut. "We did it. They're leaving. But now . . ."

Todd's smile faded. "We did the right thing. It was the only choice."

"When MacCormack finds out about this, I'll probably be on my way to one of those prisons he likes to talk about." I lifted my phone with a shaky hand, but before I could dial, it rang and Audrie's number appeared on the screen. I answered. "Aunt Audrie, I have to—"

"Rochelle," she interrupted. "Are Charlie and Max with you? Sid just checked their room, and they're missing."

# CHAPTER 26

# CHARLIE

*May 5, 2091*

"Where did you get the Spero pendant?" Griff's face hovered over me, out of focus.

"I already told you." My words slurred. It hurt to move my jaw. It hurt to move at all.

When my eyes came into focus, I stared at the cracked ceiling of the abandoned hospital. Turning my face to the open door on my left, I tried to remember how Griff had navigated the maze of hallways to reach the third-floor room. After the stairwell we'd turned several times, and the others had dragged Max further down the hall.

"You told me a story. I want the truth." He grabbed the front of my shirt and pulled me into a sitting position. "Do you expect me to believe you just found it in Auggie's truck when I asked for it? That everyone overlooked it until you got there?"

I wanted to give him an answer that would make the beating stop, but I couldn't tell him the truth. If he found out about the Optimus pendant, he would be in Maibe the next day and no one would be safe. Looking for a better story, I glanced around the room through the one eye that still opened but only halfway. Outside, the sky had darkened either due to the storm moving in or night approaching, but I wasn't sure.

Griff shook me. "Where did you get the Spero pendant?"

"When I ran away last year, I snuck onto a train." That much was the truth, but the rest would have to be fabricated. "I didn't realize it at first, but there was a girl hiding in the same cargo car. She told me a detective who worked for the TCI was chasing her because she had something they wanted." It was a good lie, but my head lolled back and I choked on my words.

"And?" Griff put a hand behind my head so it was easier for me to talk. He was enthralled by the story. It could work if I had the right ending.

"I asked her why, and she showed me the pendant. She was afraid of it. Thought it brought her bad luck, so I told her I could take it off her hands and restore her luck. She was superstitious and decided that must have been why we met." Taking a deep breath, I scrambled for a satisfying ending. "I jumped off the train outside Maibe because I lost my nerve and thought I'd get caught stowing away. She stayed on the train. I don't know her name or where the train took her."

Griff let go of me and I collapsed onto the cold tile.

"How did she get it?" He walked to the window and looked out.

I would have asked a question like that if I had really encountered the scenario in my story. I had to know the answer. "She was a thief. She took a jewelry box from a house she burglarized, and it was inside."

"Is that right?" Griff crossed the room and his boots stopped next to my head. "How am I supposed to believe you when I know you're so good at making up stories? What good are you to me if you can't tell me where to find the Optimus pendant?"

I tried to sit up, but I couldn't move my left arm, and my right arm couldn't support my weight. I didn't know how badly I was hurt, but warm blood soaked the right side of my shirt and pant leg.

"Optimus pendant?" I had to keep him talking to give myself time to form some kind of escape plan.

"*Spero optimus*. Hope for the best. We have Spero, but no one knows what happened to the Optimus pendant. Except maybe you." He nudged my arm with his boot. "Tell me where it is, and I'll let your friend go."

I wanted to save Max's life, but I couldn't send Griff to Maibe. I didn't believe he would let Max go anyway. "It could be anywhere. I only had the Spero one for insurance. I thought you would let me back into the Defiance, but then I was afraid you were still mad until you contacted me."

"Hey, boss." Tommy spoke from the doorway. "Molly's on the phone. It sounds like good news."

Griff looked down at me. "Take Charlie to his friend. When I get back, I'm getting a real answer."

Without a word, Tommy pulled me to my feet, zip-tied my hands behind my back, and forced me to limp to the room at the end of the hall. When we reached a dead end, he opened a door to our left and shoved me inside. The door slammed as I crashed to the floor.

"Keppler. Keppler, can you hear me?" Max's voice followed me into the darkness.

I opened my eyes and lifted my head enough to see I was in a room similar to the one I had just left. This one had a few chairs pulled out and a cool breeze coming through the partially broken window. Max sat on the floor, back against the wall and legs stretched out in front of him. My eyes landed on the bloody, improvised bandage tied around his leg.

"Are you okay?" I managed to roll onto my side. "Is it still bleeding?"

"I'm hanging in there." His shoulder shook slightly as he spoke. "I'm definitely more okay than you."

"How bad do I look?" All I knew was that I hurt more than I ever had in my life.

"Remember the first day we met and you helped me push my truck out of the mud, and I said you looked like a zombie?" He didn't wait for an answer. "You look way worse now."

Groaning, I shifted my weight but couldn't relieve the throbbing in my shoulder or numbness in my arm.

"Don't worry though." Max glanced at the door that stood between us and a murmur of voices in the hall. "I have a plan," he whispered. "I'm cutting through my zip tie with a piece of glass I found on the floor. I'm almost there. This vent . . ." He tipped his head in the direction of an air vent—maybe two feet across and a foot high—in the wall beside him. "There's more to the building behind us even though the hall ends here. My theory is that this room contained equipment that produced a lot of heat, so it needed a vent. I'm ninety-five percent sure this vent will lead us to an adjacent hallway. If I can pry it off on this side and kick it out on the other, we'll be small enough to crawl through. The others are bigger than us, so we'll have a head start while they figure out how to get to the other side of the building."

"I'll never make it through there." I couldn't even stand. "You go. You shouldn't be here anyway."

"When I ran into the trees earlier, I was going to get help." Max kept his voice low. "I would have come back to get you."

I tried to sit up and closed my eyes against the pain exploding throughout my body. "Yeah. I believe you would be dumb enough to come back."

"Who are you calling dumb?" Max feigned offense. "I'm the one with a plan. What do you have to contribute?"

It even hurt to smile. "Nothing, I guess."

"As I suspected." Max stopped at the sound of birds squawking outside. "They always settle in the trees out here at this time. Rochelle and I even talked about it one day when we were running. If I just had my phone, Rochelle would know where we are even if I didn't say a word."

"You had your phone in your pocket." Hope surged through my body.

Max glanced at the door. "It rang when we got here, so that Alec guy took it. It's been ringing every ten minutes since then, but they just ignore it."

"We're not getting out of this." My hope deflated. "We're both hurt, and we're trapped, and—"

"Go join the others," Griff barked outside the door. The knob jiggled. "I'll finish the job here and meet you guys at the car."

The moment Griff walked into the room, Max's phone started its obnoxious chirping in Griff's pocket. He pulled it out and glanced at the screen.

"Rochelle again," Griff said. "Let's have some fun." He slid the gun from his belt and aimed it at Max's chest. "Charlie, you're going to answer and get her to stop calling. Say anything you shouldn't and your friend is dead. Got it?"

I nodded. Griff gripped the front of my shirt, pulled me into a sitting position, opened the phone, and held it to my ear.

"Hello." I looked at Max, still and silent on the other end of Griff's gun.

"Keppler? Where's Max? Why aren't you in your room?" Rochelle peppered me with questions, her voice tinged with panic.

"Remember how Max wasn't feeling well this morning?" I glanced up at Griff and chose my words carefully. "He got worse, so I took him to the emergency room."

"Is he okay? The emergency room is twenty miles away. How did you get there?"

"Rochelle, listen." I paused long enough for the cacophony of birds to come through. "Everything is fine, and I promise we'll explain it all when we get back."

"Are you sure?" Her tone didn't indicate whether she had heard the clues or not.

"Yes, but the phone's battery is about to die, so I have to hang up for now." I didn't want to say goodbye.

"Okay," Rochelle agreed. "I'll talk to you soon."

I nodded at Griff, and he snapped the phone shut. "This is why I can't trust you. I would have believed every word if I wasn't the one holding the phone. Too bad Rochelle won't ever get that explanation." He tossed the phone out the broken window.

"Hey, that was my phone," Max snapped. "That's TCI property."

Griff laughed. "You don't need it anymore."

"Yeah. Yeah. I get it. You're going to kill us." Max kept an eye on the gun Griff had lowered to his side. "You've been saying that for hours now, but you haven't followed through."

"That's because your brother here hasn't told me what I want to know." Griff kicked me hard in the side. "Might as well just give up already. Rochelle gave Molly the passcodes, and we successfully recovered the TCI's pendants right out from under them."

"What are you talking about?" The force of my voice surprised me. "Rochelle doesn't know any passcodes."

"It turns out we were both wrong about that, kid. Molly turned up the pressure and Rochelle cracked. Maybe Molly's right, I should listen to her more often." He pointed his gun at me. "I guess I'm a bad judge of character."

"Wait," Max shouted. "You don't want to kill either of us."

"Oh yeah?" Griff turned to Max. "Why not?"

I held my breath, frozen with dread that he would try to save us by telling Griff the secret we both knew about the Optimus pendant.

"I'm six months away from discovering time travel," Max

blurted. "Imagine what you could do with that. Way better than some research that might not even work the way you think it will. I'll make you a partner. It'll be a four-way equal split between the three of us and Rochelle. We'll all make a fortune, and you can use the technology however you want."

"Time travel?" Griff turned his gun on Max. "Maybe I should get rid of you first."

"No, Griff." I fought through the stabbing pain that came with every breath. "I'll help you figure out where the Optimus pendant is. There must be a logical explanation."

"You're out of time." He turned back to me. "You both know too much."

"What if we know just enough?" Max shouted. "Kill us and some valuable pendant information goes with us."

"Delgado, shut up." The last thing I needed was for us to accidentally give up the pendant's location.

"What do you mean?" Griff glanced over his shoulder at Max.

Max shrugged. "Just that we could know things we don't know we know. Like Rochelle and the passcodes."

I needed another distraction and a real one met my nose. "Hey, do you guys smell smoke?"

"Both of you shut up." Griff snapped the gun back to me. "No more distractions." He glanced around the room, sniffed the air, and walked to the door. He opened it, and a haze of smoke wafted into the room. Griff swore and ran into the hall, slamming the door behind him.

"I thought he'd never leave." Max held his hands in front of him, free of his restraints. "Now we can get out of this place." He crawled to me and sawed through my restraints with the glass much quicker than he had his own.

"Do you not understand that the building is on fire?" I protested as he crawled to the vent. Had it been part of Griff's plan to burn the building with us trapped in it? His reaction didn't indicate he had expected the smoke.

"That's our lucky break. Do you think it got struck by lightning?" He yanked at the loose end of the vent. "Get over here and help me. There are only a few screws holding it, and they're really rusted."

"It wasn't lightning. One of those traitors is probably trying to take Griff out." In the chaos, I didn't have time to consider it any further. I crawled to Max, my left arm dangling. With my right hand, I gripped the top of the vent and we both put all of our weight into peeling it back. The screws popped and we clattered back onto the floor.

"Are you all right?" Max already had his legs through the opening, kicking the other side of the vent. "It's giving way. You're lucky your shoulder is dislocated. You'll be able to slide through like nothing."

The distinct clang of metal met my ears as I slid across the floor to Max. Knowing what was wrong with my shoulder only made it hurt more.

"I'll go first, and then I'll pull you through." He lay flat on his stomach and slid forward using his elbows until all of him vanished into the dark opening. "Okay, your turn," he shouted from the other side.

Coughing against thickening smoke, I pushed my legs through the opening and lay back with my arms at my sides. Hands gripped my feet and I slid forward. The door opened and Griff rushed into the room as my shoulder caught on the wall.

"Hey, get back here!" Griff shouted as he lumbered toward me.

"Turn your shoulder," Max ordered.

I slipped to the side by an inch, and Max yanked me away from Griff. My head plunged into darkness, then emerged in a dingy hallway.

"I can't get to the stairs," Griff yelled over an audible cracking. "Don't leave me here, Charlie. Please, kid, you have to help me."

Max and I looked through the opening at Griff's wide eyes and soot-smudged face. I'd never seen him afraid before.

"Can you squeeze through?" Max gestured for Griff to follow us.

Griff shoved his head into the vent opening, but both of his shoulders caught on the walls despite any twisting or turning. "I won't fit."

Max turned to me. "There are concrete blocks behind the drywall. We can't make the opening any bigger. Whatever you decide, I'm with you."

Griff was trapped, and I was powerless to change that. Max was in this situation because of me, and he couldn't walk without help. "I'm sorry. I have to get Max out."

"No, Charlie. Please don't leave," Griff pleaded.

"I'm sorry." I turned away from Griff's terrified face. "I'm so sorry." Despite everything he had done to hurt me, I didn't want to leave him behind. I didn't want him to die. "I'll get help. I'll come back."

Griff continued pleading as I pulled myself to my feet using a chair. Max got himself up on one leg, and with his arm around me for support, we stumbled down the hallway through choking smoke.

"This side of the building is a mirror construction of the side we entered." Max coughed. "That means we have to turn left, right, left and we'll be at the stairwell."

I ducked my head, searching for breathable air. "We won't make it. The smoke is getting thicker."

Max veered toward an open door, taking me with him. "This is the side of the building with balconies." He closed us in the room, and we limped to the sliding glass door. "Rochelle knows we're here. She'll send help. Until then, pray."

We collapsed onto the balcony, gulping the fresh air. From outside, I could see flames breaching the roof down on the other end of the building. We were three floors above the ground, too injured to climb down on our own, and running out of time.

# CHAPTER 27

# ROCHELLE

*May 5, 2091*

"I'll talk to you soon." I lowered my phone, trying to understand the rushed conversation I'd just had with Keppler. For the past fifteen minutes, Sid and Audrie had been frantically questioning Todd and me about what Molly had said and where Max and Keppler were.

"Was that Charlie? What did he say?" Audrie sat beside me on my bed.

Alexander, Sid, and Todd all stood in front of us, waiting for answers I couldn't provide.

"It was him, but none of it made sense. He said he took Max to the emergency room and everything is fine." I flipped my phone shut. "But Max's phone was dying, so he had to hang up."

"Max would call me if he was that sick." Sid checked his phone for the twentieth time. "He tells me everything." He slid his finger around the screen on his phone. "Why can't I track him?"

"They were both really worried about following that rule to stay in their room." Alexander pressed his hand to the back of his neck. "There's no way they left on their own."

"Max would have answered his phone. He always has it on him. And Keppler just called me 'Rochelle.'" It all had to mean something, and I had to figure out what.

"Max would trust Charlie with his phone, and Charlie calls you 'Rochelle' all the time when he talks to me." Audrie wrapped one arm around me. She had been surprisingly calm about me revealing the passcodes to the Defiance and was more concerned about my missing friends. "That's your name."

"He calls her 'Aumont' when he talks to her." Todd sank next to me and shrugged. "He only calls her Rochelle when she's not in the room. It's weird but true."

Audrie nodded and her forehead wrinkled. "What else did you hear, kiddo?" My aunt's voice kept me grounded. "Did it sound like he was in a hospital?"

Keppler had told me to listen. What had I heard in the background? Squawking birds. I'd heard that before.

"I know where they are." The realization pulled me to my feet as Audrie and Sid's phones let out an ear-piercing screech.

My aunt tensed up but relaxed as she read her screen. "It's just a fire out in the trees. We're supposed to shelter in place until the fire department takes care of it."

All the fear, panic, and confusion of the past hour congealed into a voice in my head that screamed: *Max and Keppler are in trouble. Get there now.*

I didn't think or take the time to explain anything to the others. Instead, I ran out of my room, out of the building, and across the lawn to the trail entrance. Despite the threat of smoke in the air, my feet pounded against the packed dirt I had run with Max almost every day we'd been at the AEI. The deeper I pushed into the trees, the more obvious the flickering orange glow in the direction of the abandoned hospital. By the time I raced into the clearing, fire had breached the windows on one side of the building, scorching the outside bricks in its greed for oxygen.

"Rochelle." The shouting behind me registered as familiar voices calling my name.

Scanning the building, I spotted two figures waving from a third-floor balcony. "Right there." I pointed at the balcony, not even bothering to turn around to see who had followed me. "We have to get them out of there."

"Rochelle." Audrie appeared in front of me, gripping my shoulders so I couldn't move. "The fire department is on the way. It's not safe."

I imagined the fire trucks speeding across town to reach us. They would have to assess the scene and set up equipment. "It'll be too late. We have to get them down now."

Sid and Alexander caught up with us in time to hear my argument with Audrie.

"She's right, Audrie. We have to get up there or those kids aren't going to make it." Sid waved to Max and Keppler. "Hang on, we're coming!" Between the constant rumbling of thunder and the roar of the fire, I could barely hear him right beside me.

Dodging Audrie, I jogged toward danger, spotting discarded tires and wooden pallets among the junk surrounding the building. Keppler and Max pressed themselves as close to the railing as possible to get fresh air. Each had one arm around the other's shoulders, so I couldn't tell who was supporting who. Under the first balcony, I stepped on something firm but springy.

"We're coming," I shouted, even though I doubted they could hear me. I knelt down and pulled on the metal panel, but it was too heavy to pry out of the dirt and vines that held it down.

"You guys get that side," Sid ordered as he ran past me. "Audrie and I will get the other side."

Todd and Alexander crouched one on each side of me and worked their fingers under the panel. Together, the five of us pried it away from the ground and leaned it against the building. Each square became a foothold that climbed from the ground to the base of the first-floor balcony.

"We can use these too." Alexander knocked on a wooden pallet even taller than him that was leaning against the building. "Can you guys help me get it up to the balcony?"

Audrie and I climbed the panel, used the spokes on the railing to pull ourselves up, and hoisted ourselves over and onto the balcony. We helped the guys get the first pallet onto our platform and waited for them to climb up with the second one. This one had narrower footholds, but I scrambled up anyway. We repeated the process until we realized the last pallet was two feet short of reaching the base of the next balcony.

"That's all right," Sid shouted over the exploding glass and approaching sirens. "Alexander and I can hold Rochelle's weight. Audrie and Todd, be ready to help Max and Charlie climb down."

Alexander and Sid got into place, and I climbed the pallet, shoving the fronts of my shoes between the wooden supports. Finally, standing on the top edge, I gripped the balcony rails and pulled myself up to the outer ledge of the balcony. Eye level with my friends, I realized getting them to the ground would be more challenging than I'd imagined. Max leaned heavily on Keppler, not putting any weight on his left leg. Keppler's face was bruised and swollen to the point I wouldn't have recognized him if he wasn't beside Max. He leaned into the railing, and I was afraid it was the only thing keeping him from collapsing.

"They shot him in the leg." Keppler coughed. It was impossible to get a breath of smoke-free air.

"It'll be all right," I assured. In the smoke and chaos, I didn't need any more of an explanation. My friends were alive, but we had to hurry. "Max, can you climb over the rail if we help you?"

With help from Keppler, Max got himself onto the rail, and I guided his good leg onto the pallet as he lowered himself. We descended a few feet, and then Audrie and Todd helped Max down the rest of the way.

"I'm going to need more help with Keppler." I didn't wait for an answer as I scrambled back up to the rail. A window down the line from us shattered, and I ducked instinctively. "Come on."

Keppler looked over the rail and shook his head. "Aumont, I can't. Griff is still in there. I promised I'd get him out."

"You'll die if you go back in there," I shouted over the deafening roar. "The firemen will have a better chance of getting him out."

"Rochelle, we have to get him down now," Audrie yelled a few feet below me.

Keppler took a step back. "I can't do it. My left arm isn't working. I'll fall."

"I'll help you." I reached for him. "Remember when you made me climb out of that window in Kansas City? We were up higher then, and you weren't afraid."

"I was a little afraid." He stepped up to the rail.

"We have to go." Audrie climbed up until she was next to me. "Come on, Charlie. We won't let you fall."

With my aunt's help, we got Keppler over the rail and lowered him down to the balcony one painful step at a time. Alexander and Sid shoved the pallet aside as giant raindrops collided with my face. We all coughed, but Max and Keppler's coughs were deeper and more desperate for fresh air.

"You guys are going to be okay." Alexander surveyed Max and Keppler, then turned to Sid and Todd. "You two climb down and I'll lower Max to you."

As glass shattered around us and the building groaned and cracked, we lowered my friends down to the next balcony, one by one. We repeated the process with Max on the first-floor balcony, and relief swept through me when he was safely on the ground with Todd and Sid.

Sirens wailed from the front of the building, but they had no way of knowing we were climbing down the back of the building.

Audrie and I helped Keppler to the rail just as fire burst through the glass door of the balcony next to us.

"That'll be us in another minute." Alexander hopped over the rail, planting his feet in the squares of the metal panel. "Get him over the rail and I'll carry him the rest of the way."

"You trust Alexander, right?" I asked close to Keppler's ear so he could hear me.

He nodded. Audrie and I helped him climb over and down until his good arm looped over Alexander's shoulders. By now, the rain had slickened the panel, forcing us to climb down more slowly than I wanted to.

Although the entire ordeal took less than fifteen minutes, it felt like years since my feet had touched the safety of solid ground. We made our way to the flashing lights at the front of the building. Max hobbled with help from Sid and Todd, and Alexander carried Keppler in front of him as if he were a child.

Audrie wrapped her arm around me and pulled me close to her. "Are you okay?" I nodded in response. "You are way too brave for your own good."

My aunt and Sid promised to find paramedics in the chaos, and I sank to the ground, a safe distance from the building, with my friends. The only shelter we had from the rain was a low-hanging tree that only blocked some of the moisture.

"See, Keppler? I told you she would figure it out and come save us." Max coughed and wrapped his shaking arms around me. "I didn't have much time to investigate, but I never saw any ghosts."

"Ghosts were the least of your worries." I hugged him. "It's a miracle we all got out of there in time." The dangers of what we had done to rescue my friends started to register as a knot in my stomach.

"I think it's too late for Griff." Keppler's voice shook as he stared at the building, now surrounded by firefighters working to put out the fire. "I shouldn't have left him. I promised to come back so he wouldn't be alone."

I slid closer to Keppler, wrapped my arms around him, and held him as he sobbed silently against my shoulder. He was bleeding and struggling to breathe, but his mind was somewhere else.

"You did everything you could." Max patted Keppler's back. "Maybe the firemen are getting him out right now." As much as I wanted Max to be right, the scene in front of me argued against it.

The three of us huddled together for warmth and comfort. Keppler didn't lift his head from my shoulder, and Max leaned against me, uncharacteristically silent. Of all the dangerous situations we'd been through together, this was the worst. Wrapping my arms more tightly around them, I rested my head against Max's.

Saving the world wasn't an adventure. It was an impossible battle three seventeen-year-old kids weren't equipped to survive.

# CHAPTER 28

# ROCHELLE

*May 5, 2091*

Several long minutes passed before the ambulance approached across the lawn. The red and blue lights were dulled by the persistent mist. Paramedics pried Keppler away from me, and it scared me that my friend, who didn't trust doctors and hated hospitals, didn't put up a fight.

After they took Max, Alexander's hands slid under my elbows and lifted me to my feet. "I'm riding in the ambulance with them. Audrie will bring you and Todd to the hospital as soon as she can." He hugged me. "I'll take care of them. It'll be okay."

Standing in the rain, I watched Alexander get into the ambulance. The doors closed, and the taillights crossed the lawn and disappeared down the tree-lined road leading to the highway. A hand squeezed mine, and without looking, I knew it was Todd.

"Don't tell me they came here on their own." It was Audrie's voice, not calm as usual, but just short of shouting. "They almost died. You promised Charlie he was safe with us, and yet the Defiance kidnapped him from his room and brought him here to kill him."

I whirled around to see MacCormack standing under a big umbrella, surveying the scene. Sid and Audrie stood in front of him, their backs to me.

"Or maybe Charlie had a part to play in their plan and something went wrong." MacCormack's eyes locked with mine. "Once in the Defiance, always in the Defiance. I feared that in Charlie's case, but I never would have believed he would be able to pull Max in. Now the question is, how much was Rochelle involved?"

"None of them were involved," Audrie protested.

"Then why was the tracking on Max's phone disabled? How did Rochelle know where to find them?" MacCormack tilted his umbrella back and glared at me. "I expect you and Rochelle in my office in ten minutes. Don't be late."

Audrie, Sid, Todd, and I trudged to MacCormack's office, soaked and shivering. My aunt tried to reassure me, but my only solace came from Todd's hand gripping mine. It took all my control not to cry when I had to leave him in the hall and enter the head agent's office with only Audrie by my side.

I sat next to Audrie across the desk from MacCormack. We listened to him concoct a story in which Keppler, Max, and I were working for the Defiance in an attempt to infiltrate the TCI.

"This is why we don't make the kind of exceptions we made for Rochelle and Max." MacCormack slammed his hand on the desk. "They weren't qualified to be here in the first place, and they came with malicious intent."

I stood. "That isn't true, sir. None of us are working for the Defiance."

"No?" MacCormack stood. "Then why did you play games with us? You said you didn't know the codes over and over, and then you conveniently gave them to the Defiance when they asked. What did you get in return?"

"Molly said they would attack the banquet, and I couldn't let her hurt anyone." I clutched my bracelet with one hand. "I didn't think I knew the codes, but then I had an idea."

"Liar!" MacCormack shouted, and I took a step back.

"That's enough." Audrie sprang to her feet and stepped up to the desk. "My niece is not a liar, and those boys have been so worried about following your rules, Max has been throwing up for weeks."

"Do you disagree with my assessment, Agent Aumont?"

"Your assessment that Rochelle, Max, and Charlie were helping the Defiance?" My aunt didn't back down. "Yes, I disagree with every part of that."

"Please, sir," I said. "Molly called me and made threats. I didn't even know she could call my TCI phone. I don't know how she got the number." I took a cautious step forward. "The Defiance hurt Max and Charlie." Keppler's first name felt weird on my tongue, but I couldn't risk any confusion. "They weren't working with them. They were trying to get away. Someone helped the Defiance, but it wasn't us."

"We'll investigate thoroughly, I assure you." MacCormack shook his head. "I sure hope your story holds up, or all three of you will be behind bars for the rest of your lives. Until then, you and Max are expelled, and all three of you are prohibited from setting foot on TCI property." He glared at me. "You have twenty minutes to pack your things and leave the premises."

"Head Agent MacCormack, there's no evidence to warrant that kind of punishment." Audrie took a breath and continued. "I've given my word that these kids would be safe here, and—"

"Agent Aumont," MacCormack interrupted. "Any agreements signed on behalf of Charlie, Rochelle, and Max are now void. You can accept that decision, or I can fire you for insubordination. Your choice."

Audrie looked at me, then turned back to her boss. "Then I quit." She pulled her credentials from her pocket and the gun from her belt and placed them on his desk. "I'll get my things from my office and be off the premises in twenty minutes. Let's go, Rochelle." She took my hand, and we walked into the hall where Todd and Sid waited for us.

"Agent Dotson," MacCormack shouted. "Get in here."

Audrie rolled her eyes. "He's going to ask you to supervise me while I pack."

Sid stopped halfway to the office, nodding in understanding before he continued inside.

"Audrie, what are you doing? You can't quit." I blinked hard. She wasn't crying, and I didn't want to either.

"I'm choosing my family over this job like I should have done a long time ago. It'll be okay." Her face softened. "You and Todd go pack for you and the boys, and I'll come find you. Sid will give us more than twenty minutes if we need it."

"But what are we going to do?" I didn't know what to expect, or how long I had before MacCormack fabricated the evidence he needed to send me to prison.

"We'll get to the hospital and take care of Charlie and Max, and once they're released, we'll go home."

All I had wanted for the past four months was to go home, but not like this. Not as a failure who got kicked out of school and a criminal under investigation. What would I tell Kinley?

"One thing at a time." Audrie seemed to read my thoughts. "Go pack and we'll figure everything else out later."

Todd took my hand, and we remained silent until we stepped outside. The sky had cleared and stars glowed overhead. A faint haze of smoke hovered over the campus.

"Your room or Max and Charlie's room?" Todd's voice interrupted the silence.

"Mine, I guess." I took a breath to steady my voice.

"It's okay. I'll help you." Todd wrapped his arm around me, and the warmth made me realize how cold I was. "Shelley, what happened in that office?"

"MacCormack said Max, Keppler, and I are all working for the Defiance and we're all going to prison. Audrie got mad and quit her job." I leaned into Todd for comfort and an anchor to life before it got complicated. "I came here to stop the Defiance and so I wouldn't put Kat and Kinley through anything worse than I already had. I keep trying to fix things, but I'm only making it worse and digging a deeper hole. Todd, why can't I get it right? What's wrong with me?"

"Nothing's wrong with you." Todd opened the door to my building. "There's something wrong with that MacCormack guy, and everyone should be able to figure that out."

"But he's in charge." I led the way to the stairs. "We're always caught somewhere between trouble and disaster. All these adults think they can tell us what to do about it, but they're only making things worse. I should have just gone with Molly from the beginning so I could have persuaded her to use the research the right way."

"You don't mean that." Todd fell into step beside me as we ascended the stairs. "It never would have worked."

"Why not? I know Molly better than anyone. I'm the only one who can stop her, and I've spent a year and a half running from that."

Todd shook his head. "I know you better than anyone. You blame yourself for things that aren't your fault. Molly isn't your responsibility, and if you went with her, I would have never seen you again."

"It's pretty selfish for us to let Molly terrorize the world so we can have a little time together before we both die from the super virus she'll unleash." I stopped in front of my door and observed the hurt look on Todd's face. "I'm sorry. I'm just scared."

"I know." He looked down at his shoes.

"Todd." He didn't look up, so I leaned in and kissed him on the cheek. "I love you, and I don't know what I would do if you weren't here right now."

"I love you too." He smiled. "We'll find a way through all this. I promise."

I nodded and opened the door to my room. After the psychological exhaustion of dealing with Molly, and then the physical exhaustion of helping to save Max and Keppler, followed by the meeting with MacCormack, all I wanted was to crawl into my bed and sleep for days. But it wasn't my bed anymore, and I had to get to the hospital to be there for Keppler and Max.

"Rochelle, what happened?" Evie jumped up from her bed. "Are you hurt?"

"No, I'm okay." For the first time, I realized what I must look like, clothes wet and dirty, hair tangled. "But I'm in some trouble. I got kicked out."

Evie shook her head. "No way. That can't be right."

"I have twenty minutes to pack." Tears burned the corners of my eyes, and I looked away.

"I can explain what happened." Todd's hands steadied my trembling shoulders. "Change into dry clothes and then we can pack."

"Okay. Good idea." I closed myself in the bathroom where I washed my face, combed my hair, and pulled on dry clothes. Feeling a little more in control of my emotions, I took a deep breath and opened the door.

"Is Max okay?" Evie asked.

"He was alert and talking," Todd responded. "I think he'll be okay."

I thought he would be okay too. It was Keppler who I was most concerned about. I had to get to the hospital and comfort him. Walking into the closet, I pulled down my duffel bag from the shelf.

"I can help if you want," Evie said. "What can I do?"

My roommate folded my clothes and piled them into my bag while Todd took his drawings and my photographs off the wall. I carefully stacked my cards and letters from home in my bookbag and left my TCI flip phone on my desk. My entire life at the AEI was packed in less than ten minutes.

"I'm going to miss you." Evie hugged me.

"I'll miss you too." I laughed so I wouldn't cry. "I've never had a roommate before, but you're my favorite."

She took a step back and smiled. "Is there any way I can contact you to make sure you and Max are okay?"

"Um." I still hadn't convinced myself I would return to Nebraska. Maybe I could just stay in New York with Audrie until my prison sentence started.

Todd stepped forward. "I can give you Rochelle's address and phone number. We'll be heading back to Maibe as soon as Max and Charlie can travel."

Evie handed Todd a pad of paper and a pen. He jotted down the information and handed it back to her.

"Take care of yourself, Rochelle." Evie clutched the notepad in her hand.

I nodded. Todd swung both of my bags over his shoulders, and we left my room for the last time.

"Do you really think it's a good idea for me to go back to Maibe?" I blurted in the hallway. "I don't want to mess up anyone else's life." Kinley, Alexander, and Audrie had all been preventing me from doing what I believed was right. They wanted me safe, and I didn't want to hurt them, but the only way to end the threat of the pendants and the Defiance was for me to take matters into my own hands.

"Our lives are messed up because you're not there." Todd shifted my bags so he could reach my hand. "I think all of this is a sign that you never should have left. Nothing happens by chance. Right?"

I was too tired and overwhelmed to decide whether getting

kicked out of a prestigious school was part of the grand plan of my life. "We better get to Max's room. Sorting out his stuff could be a little tricky."

I found it surreal how beautiful the sky was following the storm. The world around me was oblivious to my problems. Todd didn't say anything on our short walk to the boys' dorms, and that was okay with me. I needed quiet. Time to think. How had Molly and the Defiance so easily snuck onto campus while we were hosting a high-security event? How had they known where to find all of us without being noticed? Had MacCormack been involved, and if so, how much had we messed up his plan?

In Max's room, I found Keppler's bag, checked that all his notebooks were there, and added the new clothes Audrie had bought him.

"There's no way we can take all this stuff." Todd nudged an overflowing box with his shoe. "I know Max would say it isn't, but most of this is junk."

"We'll just pack the stuff he brought with him. The TCI can clean out the rest." I found Max's bag in the closet and handed it to Todd. "Can you get his clothes? I'll make sure there's nothing else important lying around."

While Todd was busy, I walked around the room, opening drawers and glancing under the bed. When I reached Max's desk, I picked up his physics notebook and something fell to the floor. I bent down and picked it up. It looked just like my dad's pendant, the one I had given to Audrie, from its shiny black surface to its triangle shape. The only difference was that the white lettering on this pendant said "Optimus." It must have been one of the fakes Max had made with Sid.

"Did you find anything else?" Todd asked from the other side of the room.

"Just his physics notes." I raised the hand still holding the notebook.

I shoved the pendant in my pocket. I didn't know if Max was supposed to have the fake pendant, and I feared he would get in trouble if I left it behind and MacCormack found it.

# CHAPTER 29

# CHARLIE

*May 6, 2091*

"Charlie, please." Griff gripped my shoulders so tight it hurt. "Don't leave. You took an oath. The Defiance forever."

"There were no pendants when I took that oath." I pulled away from him and pain seared through my ribs. "You weren't planning to unleash a deadly virus when I took that oath. You told me I'd have a family and that we'd help kids like us."

"None of that's changed," Griff snapped. "We just have a solid way of accomplishing it now. Don't look at me like you're so good and moral. You've stolen for us, you wrote our newsletter, and you didn't tell Uncle Mac about our fake pendants." He took a backward step and shook his head. "Then you left me behind to die."

"I didn't have a choice." I looked around for a place to run, but we were surrounded by trees in the thick woods. Nothing looked familiar and I didn't know how I got there. "I want out."

"There's no way out." He laughed. "You can't undo what you've done. You think you have a family to run back to? Wait until they hear what you've done. They won't take you back. Why would they?"

Wanting to escape the truth I feared, I took another step back and stumbled over a root. Griff's laughter followed me as I fell toward the ground.

"I want out," I screamed as I fell, trying and failing to grasp branches as I rushed past them on my way down. "I'll do better this time. I swear I'll do better."

My eyes shot open to a dimly lit white room. The sheet that covered me up to my chest pressed down on my body like a weight. Even the slightest movement of my head shot a piercing sting through every bone in my body, but I managed to maneuver enough to see the wires connecting me to beeping machines. How many of my bones had Griff broken? He'd clearly hurt me bad enough to warrant a stay in the hospital.

Taking shallow breaths, I continued my surveillance for a comforting detail to shut down my growing panic. To the left of my bed, Rochelle sat in a chair, head back against the wall and eyes closed.

"Aumont." My voice was a rusty squeak, but I needed her to wake up. I swallowed over my dry throat and tried again. "Aumont."

She opened her eyes, stared at me for a second, then sprang to her feet. "Hey. Are you really awake this time?"

"I hope so." My head was so foggy I didn't trust myself to distinguish between dream and reality. "I was in a forest with Griff. Then I was falling. Where am I now?"

"You're in the hospital. The other stuff was just a nightmare." Rochelle brushed her cool hand across my throbbing forehead. "Remember the fire and climbing down the balconies?"

A rush of memories swamped my brain. I'd been in an ambulance. Alexander said I would be okay, but the doctors wouldn't let him come with me. I had begged them to leave my left arm alone so they wouldn't see the brand.

My brain wavered between the dream and the truth. "Griff's right. I'm not good." My eyes slid down to my hospital gown, which left my arm exposed. "They'll know when they see it. I have to get out of here."

"Shh, it's okay." Rochelle gave my hand a light squeeze. "Alexander and Audrie explained everything. You'll be okay. You're safe."

Although it hurt, I shook my head. "I want to be a good person, but I can't get it right." I hadn't warned MacCormack about the Defiance's fake pendants, and now they had everything.

"You are a good person, Keppler." Rochelle's tired green eyes scrutinized me. "You take care of me all the time. You helped Max get out of that building."

"No, he helped me." Max had been in the ambulance with me, and then they took him. "Where is he?"

"Resting in the room next door." Rochelle's free hand gripped the rail on the bed. "They got the bullet out of his leg and took out his appendix. That's why he's been so sick lately. He went to the doctor twice, and they didn't figure out he had chronic appendicitis."

"Kinley would have figured it out." I wanted her here to tell me I'd be okay.

"Yeah, she would have." Rochelle rubbed a hand over her face. "She's way better at taking care of us than Audrie. I owe Kinley everything, and how do I repay her? I get kicked out of the best school in the country, and now I'm under investigation for helping the Defiance."

"What are you talking about?" I tried to sit up, but moving even an inch caused unbearable pain to explode through my body.

Rochelle took my hands in hers. "I gave Molly the passcodes, so now MacCormack is saying that you, Max, and I were working with the Defiance, and he's conducting an investigation to prove it. Max and I are expelled from the school and Audrie quit her job."

"But you didn't know the passcodes."

"The answer was always right here." Rochelle held up her wrist to reveal her charm bracelet. "Now I know my dad intended for me to fix everything if something happened to him. Getting the research to someone who can develop the vaccine is my responsibility."

"You got all that from a bracelet?" I squeezed Rochelle's hand to prove to myself I was really awake.

"That's all he left me. What else am I supposed to think?'"

Griff had said something like that once. The pendants were his inheritance.

Head spinning from everything Rochelle told me, my mind scrabbled to change the subject. "Max is okay? He's not sick anymore?"

"He's back to telling jokes and complaining they don't serve enough food in this place." She smiled. "He keeps saying everything will be okay now, but I'm scared."

"Did he tell you the Defiance has the TCI's pendants? They traded four fake pendants with MacCormack in exchange for me, and then they broke in and took the real ones the TCI already had." Now it was easy to believe that MacCormack was helping Griff. That was how he'd found me so easily and how Molly knew how to contact Rochelle.

Rochelle nodded. "Max told Sid all about that. MacCormack is denying it. He said there was no trade, and the pendants they had are still locked up in the safe. Audrie said we just have to wait for the investigation to bring out the truth."

"What I just said is the truth. Griff told me, and he wasn't bluffing." *You left me behind to die.* The accusation from my dream sent a shiver through me. "Did Griff . . ." I cleared my throat and tried again. "Are you sure he didn't get out?"

Rochelle shook her head. "No one saw him, but it'll take them a while to sort through what's left of the building."

Swallowing the lump in my throat, I closed my eyes. "I wanted out of the Defiance, but I didn't want him to die."

"I know," Rochelle whispered. "It wasn't your fault."

The realization that someone else could be to blame allowed my brain to connect the pieces. "I warned him she would stab him in the back. It was the first thing I told him when I got to Kansas City."

"You think Molly started the fire?" Her tone indicated she had thought about it before I said it. "But she loved him. She told me in Kansas City. Why would she hurt him?"

"She doesn't care about anyone. She just wants power. The fire started right after Griff sent his henchmen to meet up with the others. Maybe they had it planned the whole time, and . . ." My story was cut off by a deep cough that burned up and down my rib cage.

"Take it easy. They're still worried about your oxygen levels." Rochelle glanced at the numbers on the machines by my bed. "I don't know how the fire started, but I do know Molly cared about Griff in her own way."

Griff had called me his brother, and this was the second time he'd intended to kill me. I would have been dead if the fire hadn't started. Knowing I couldn't change Rochelle's mind, I focused on taking shallow breaths to avoid the pain. I understood she defended Molly for the same reason I had wanted to go back and save Griff. They had been our friends, and we cared about them even though they would sacrifice us to get what they wanted.

"When can I get out of here?"

"Hopefully tomorrow. As long as your lungs are okay and there aren't any signs of infection."

"What's all broken?" From the way I felt, I should have asked what wasn't broken.

Rochelle winced. "Four of your ribs, the bone under your left eye, and your nose. They want to do another x-ray on your jaw, and your left shoulder was dislocated but it's back in place now.

You have some stitches down the right side of your body to close up a deep gash."

"Is that all?" I tried to laugh, but it sent a jab of pain across my chest. "Aumont, if we can't stay at the AEI, where are we supposed to go?"

"Home, I guess." Rochelle blinked watery eyes. "But I can't face Kinley. I don't know what I'm going to do."

My chest clenched at the sight of Rochelle's hopeless tears. If she was afraid to face Kinley, where did that leave me? "Just tell her what happened. She'll understand."

"She shouldn't have to." Rochelle dried her face with her sleeve. "Kinley has made so many adjustments to her life because of me, and despite all that, she succeeds at everything she tries. I have nothing figured out, and I fail over and over again. All I ever do is embarrass and disappoint her."

"But she still wants you back, right?" I clenched and un-clenched my hand just to prove to myself I could move. "Does she know we're coming home?"

"Sort of." The uncertainty dulling her usually bright eyes stoked my own anxiety. "Todd and I called earlier today, but Emma answered. She said Kinley had a really bad headache, so I kept the conversation short when she put her on the phone. I told her we got into some trouble, so they're sending us home. I told her they pulled you from your undercover work and you're coming too."

"What did she say?" I braced myself for the rejection I feared.

"She said to travel safely and that we could talk about everything else when we got home." Rochelle rubbed her forehead in little circles like Kinley always did when she had a headache. "She didn't sound like herself, Keppler. I'm worried about her, but at the same time, I don't want to explain the new disaster I've created."

"You mean the disaster *we've* created." I reached for her hand, needing the comfort of human touch. "You can't take all the credit."

Rochelle took my hand and nodded. "Whatever happens, we'll stick together."

The sudden boom of something hitting the door made us both jump. The doorknob jiggled and the door opened revealing Max, in a wheelchair, rolling himself into the room. "Hey, guys. Did they bring you dinner yet?"

Rochelle watched him bump into the doorframe twice before going over to help him. "Max, what are you doing here? Where's Todd and Alexander?"

"I told them I was ready to sleep for a while so they could get something to eat. Then I escaped all by myself." Clear of the obstacles, he rolled over to my bed.

"You're supposed to be in your room resting." She leaned over the handles of his chair.

"I'm not tired. I feel great." He bent his head back to look up at her. "I am kind of hungry though. There aren't any snacks in this place. Now that we have all these spy skills, maybe you could sneak something in like a cheeseburger or a pizza, or both."

Rochelle laughed and hugged him from behind. "I'm so glad you're feeling better."

Max patted her hand. "My *tía* was so upset when I told her my appendix almost exploded, and the doctors didn't figure it out until I got shot. She wanted to yell at them over the phone." He shook his head. "Don't worry, *hermano*, we'll get you out of here tomorrow and then home for better medical care while you recover."

"Guys, I don't think Kinley is going to want me back," I said. Rochelle's promise to stick with me didn't make me feel any better. I didn't want her on my side if it meant damaging her relationship with her family. "But I don't have anywhere else to go."

"Kinley gets mad sometimes, but she's not a monster." Max's eyebrows slid together. "She's not going to throw you out when you look like that."

"I'm the monster." I choked on my words. "I deserve to be thrown out." No one else knew I'd lied to MacCormack about the Defiance having fake pendants. It wasn't hard to believe MacCormack would help Griff find Max and me, and reveal how Molly could contact Rochelle as part of a deal, but he wasn't working for the Defiance. MacCormack would never have made any trade with Griff unless he believed he was getting the real pendants in return. That meant I'd put the whole world in danger by allowing the Defiance to fool the TCI's head agent.

Max patted my arm. "If Kinley needs some time, you can stay with Alexander. It's less convenient because we won't be able to walk to each other's houses, but we'll figure it out."

"Doesn't any of this bother you?" I started coughing again, and Rochelle rested her hand on my forehead. "We almost died. We failed to stop the Defiance. And it's only a matter of time before we're behind bars for the rest of our lives."

"I'm a little sad we got kicked out of spy school." Max shrugged. "But I can't wait to go home and see my family. Everything will work out. Right, Rochelle?"

She nodded but didn't say anything. Max took her hand but didn't push her to agree more enthusiastically.

"Hey, guys." We all jumped at the sound of Audrie's voice. She stood in the doorway with a to-go cup in her hand. "Is Charlie awake?"

"He's been alert and talking for about ten minutes now." Rochelle smiled.

"That's good news. His doctors will like that." Audrie walked over and offered the cup to Rochelle. "This is for you."

"Coffee?" Rochelle asked hopefully.

"I compromised and bought you hot chocolate." Audrie smiled. "You need to get some sleep, kiddo. Max, Charlie, I'll buy you two anything you want to eat once we get out of here."

"Two hamburgers, extra large fries, an ice cream cone, and a large pepperoni pizza." Max grinned. "I'll share the pizza."

"I'll have to write that down." Audrie ruffled his hair. "Here's the plan. Tomorrow you'll both get discharged as long as the doctors don't find anything else concerning. We'll stay at my apartment tomorrow night to get some real sleep, and then Sid will fly us to Omaha on Tuesday. We'll take a train to Maibe from there."

"Wait. Fly, like on a plane?" Max slid to the front of the wheelchair. "Sid can fly planes and no one ever told me?"

"You mean that never came up?" Audrie wrapped an arm around Rochelle, who stood silently beside her. "He usually only flies single-passenger planes when we have to get somewhere quick for a mission. But he got us a bigger plane for Tuesday. We can all have our own window seat."

"Finally, things are looking up." Max glanced at Rochelle, eyebrows raised.

When Audrie wasn't looking, Rochelle slipped him the cup of hot chocolate. "Did the investigators figure out that MacCormack is lying? That the TCI pendants are missing?"

Audrie sighed. "Sid called. He said they found them right where they should be." It didn't surprise me MacCormack would deny our story and replace the missing pendants with fakes to cover up his mistake. He would do whatever it took to remain innocent of taking any action in Saturday's events and shift the blame to us.

"They're fakes." Max almost choked on his gulp of cocoa. "They have to scan them to see they don't have the chips inside."

Rochelle patted Max's back and took the cup from him. "It

doesn't matter. We look bad either way, and the Defiance has all the pendants now."

Max and I looked at each other. Lareina apparently hadn't contacted Rochelle like she had threatened to. Now we were going home, and I would no longer have our physical distance or Lareina's suspicion of the TCI to stop her from telling Rochelle that she had the Optimus pendant.

"They'll check every possibility and figure out the pendants are fake." Audrie glanced at the door. "We just have to give them time to find the truth. You're all innocent."

Rochelle sipped her hot chocolate. "Do you trust them? Don't they all just do whatever MacCormack says?"

"MacCormack has people above him he has to answer to." Audrie brushed Rochelle's hair behind her ear. "And they're all very interested in the role he played in all this. Whatever he's done, he won't get away with it."

"And the Defiance doesn't have all the pendants. There's still one missing." It was my chance to make Rochelle feel better. "The Defiance had four and they took three from the TCI. Griff still needed the Optimus pendant."

Rochelle slid her hand into her pocket. Max nodded, and I knew he wouldn't reveal any more than I already had. He would help me keep Lareina away from Rochelle. But maybe that was the least of our problems.

Audrie sighed and squeezed Rochelle's shoulder. "Alexander is going to take you back to my apartment so you can take a shower and get some rest."

"No, I'm fine," Rochelle protested. "I can rest here in the chair."

"You're going on two days without sleep. Why don't you take Max back to his room before he gets caught sneaking around? Alexander will be there any minute." Audrie stiffened, bracing for a fight with her usually obedient niece. "Please."

Rochelle stepped up to my bed and took my hand. "Is that okay, if I leave for a little while?"

I didn't want to cause a fight between my friend and her aunt, and Rochelle could barely keep her eyes open. "I'll be fine. Go get some sleep."

She leaned down and kissed my forehead. "I'll be back in a few hours."

I expected Audrie to leave with my friends, but after she helped Rochelle wheel Max through the door, she returned and sat down in the chair by my bed. "It's kind of cold in here. Do you want me to get you a blanket, kiddo?"

"No, I'm all right." I couldn't even stand the weight of the sheet on my aching body. "We shouldn't go home if we'll just have to leave again for prison. It'll be harder for everyone." It was my last attempt to avoid rejection and keep Rochelle far away from the final pendant.

"I know, but we can't all stay in my tiny apartment. And I think we all need some new scenery away from MacCormack." She stood and readjusted my sheet so it wasn't tucked in so tight. "Plus, this investigation could take years. You can't all put life on hold, expecting the worst. What if everything turns out all right?"

"What are the chances it will?" I closed my eyes, fearing the answer. "No sugarcoating."

"We're definitely facing some trouble, but I'm not giving up." It was enough to verify the situation wasn't as sunny as she tried to paint it for Rochelle. "Charlie, I need to know now that you've told the TCI everything. If there's anything you haven't told them and they find out about it in the investigation, I won't be able to help you."

My breath hitched. I'd written down Lareina's story. The evidence was in the black binder she had in Maibe. It was too late to do anything about the fake pendants, but this was my opportunity to tell Audrie the truth about the Optimus pendant. She could deal with all of it and I would be free. But the TCI had already failed to protect the pendants in their possession. Lareina and I were all that stood between the Optimus pendant and the Defiance, and we had been successful at hiding it.

"There's nothing else to tell." Just like that, I was back to keeping secrets. I turned away from her, afraid of the consequences that would eventually catch up to me.

# CHAPTER 30

# ROCHELLE

*May 8, 2091*

"You have to come back with us," Keppler pleaded with Alexander from the living room of Audrie's apartment. "I'm not going if you're not going."

I tried not to listen in on their conversation, but I could hear them loud and clear through the thin wall. I sat on the bed in Audrie's room and combed my damp hair.

"It'll only be a couple of days, Charlie." Alexander had informed us at breakfast that he wasn't returning to Maibe with us. Instead, he was catching a train to Philadelphia for another important leaders' meeting. After the chaos that unfolded at the AEI, all the trains within a two-hundred-mile radius had been stopped in response to the Defiance in the area. They were set to start running again after lunch, and Alexander had learned of the new meeting that morning.

"That's too long. I won't even be able to walk onto a plane or train without your help." Keppler was nervous enough about going home without this latest news. Since Keppler was released from the hospital yesterday, he had needed Alexander's help to shower and move from the couch to the bed to the bathroom. Alexander had changed Keppler's bandages, comforted him when he had to do breathing exercises with a spirometer, and promised him he could live at his house if Kinley was still upset.

As I listened to the conversation in the next room, my hand

forced the comb through the stubborn knots in my hair. After everything Keppler had been through, how could Alexander promise to take care of him and then rip it all out from under him when he was clearly miserable and scared?

"Then tell Audrie we should stay here a few more days until your meetings are over." Keppler's voice wavered, just short of breaking.

Unable to take it anymore, I stood and strode into the living room.

"Wouldn't you rather be at home, far away from MacCormack?" Alexander said. He sat on a chair next to the couch where Keppler rested. "You'll be with Rochelle and Max. And if Kinley isn't ready for you to move back in, Emma promised you can stay with her until I get home. Today is her last day of teaching and then she's off for the summer. You know she'll take good care of you."

"I'm not ready to travel. I need a few more days to rest." Keppler had been trying to buy a few more days in New York since I'd broken the news we were going home. I knew he was worried about the way Kinley and the others in Maibe would react to seeing him after he had appeared to run away with the Defiance in December. I didn't know what Kinley would say when Keppler walked through the door with us. Although I could relate to Keppler's anxiety because I didn't want to explain my own mistakes to Kinley, his desperate protests to going home seemed disproportionate to the situation. I considered there might be something he wasn't telling me, but then I reminded myself he wasn't feeling well, and he'd been hurt by so many people he had once believed he could trust.

"Alexander, it's just one meeting." I stood behind the couch, looking down at Keppler's bruised and swollen face. His only defining features were his steel-blue eyes and dark hair that had grown long enough to curl over his ears. His left arm was in a sling to stabilize his dislocated shoulder while it healed. "Can't you skip this one and go to the next one?"

Alexander shook his head. "I'm sorry, guys. I have responsibilities, and if I'm going to win the election for governor in the fall, I have to actually look out for our state's best interests. That means attending these meetings to ensure the others don't put us on the bad end of some deal."

"You're not the only one running for governor." I folded Keppler's blanket down, knowing he didn't like the weight on his chest. "Let one of the other candidates step up and handle this meeting."

"I know it's hard to understand, but I can't miss this one." Alexander stood. "It's important."

Keppler turned his face toward the back of the couch, wincing with every movement.

"You'll be fine." Alexander rested his hand on the top of Keppler's head. "You're in good hands for now. I'll see you on Thursday." He looked at me and sighed. "Can you stay with him? I have to get back to the hotel and arrange things for my trip." Without waiting for an answer, he walked away.

"I'll be right back," I told Keppler and followed Alexander out the front door and into a hallway. "Alexander, wait."

He turned and looked at me. "Rochelle, listen, I really am running late—"

"No, you listen." My harsh tone surprised me. "Keppler is really struggling right now. He needs you to come home with us and help him get settled."

"I wish I could, but our state needs me too, and things are happening fast." He pressed his hand to the back of his neck. "I made a promise to the people of Nebraska—"

"You made a promise to Keppler first. When you signed the

guardianship paper, you said you'd take care of him." I was so angry my chest hurt. "His parents, Griff, the TCI, and MacCormack have all broken that promise, and now you're doing the same thing. He doesn't deserve that."

"I love Charlie like he's my little brother, but I have other responsibilities." Alexander sighed. "It's only a couple of days."

"To him it feels like years." I swiped at my wet hair that stuck to my face. "Is that why you were so quick to sign him over to the TCI? One less responsibility?"

Alexander shook his head. "I can't believe you would say something like that. You know it isn't true."

"Prove it." I stepped between him and the path to exit the building. Keppler had always been there to protect me, and now it was my turn to do the same for him. "Go back in there and tell him you're coming home with us, or you can stay out of our lives. Keppler doesn't need anyone else pretending to care about him, and neither do I."

"I'm sorry, Rochelle." He blinked and took a deep breath, then reached into his pocket and pulled out a set of keys. "Emma's coming to pick you up at the train station, but she won't have enough room for all of you in her car. I'm trusting you with my truck until I get home."

I took the keys and shook my head.

"Be mad at me if you have to. We can talk when I get home." He squeezed my shoulder. "Bye, Rochelle."

I should have hugged him and said a proper goodbye, but instead I stepped aside and watched his back retreat down the hall and through the exit. Taking a few deep breaths to calm myself down, I walked back into Audrie's apartment and crossed the room.

Keppler sat on the couch, legs stretched across the cushions, and shoulders trembling. "He left, didn't he?"

"I'm sorry." I sank into the chair where Alexander had been sitting. "I tried to make him understand."

"It's okay." His head bowed forward. "He has important things to do. I don't want my mistakes to ruin his chance to be governor."

"We don't need him anyway." I held up the keys Alexander had given me. "I'll take care of you. If Kinley won't let you live with us, then I'll move in with Emma and Todd until you're better."

"Promise you won't abandon me once we get home?" His eyes brightened. "Even if your friends, like Lareina, want to hang out and catch up?"

"I'll have plenty of time to catch up with friends when you're feeling better. For now, I need to focus on getting my life together and proving to Kinley and Audrie that I can do something right."

Keppler nodded. "I'm not sure I could prove that about myself if I tried."

I shoved Alexander's keys into my pocket. "I'm tired of adults telling me what's right and smart and responsible. I've spent seventeen years listening to them, and they're hypocrites. Now I'm about to be disowned by my family, and after all these years of studying and getting good grades, my only future is behind bars." Too overwhelmed to get any more words out, I covered my face with my hands and squeezed my eyes shut to stop the tears.

"Don't say that, Aumont. At least not about Kinley and Alexander." He groaned and the couch squeaked. "They're trying to help us, but they don't have all the answers either."

"Then they should stop acting like they can solve all of our problems." The stress of the past year had been too much, and the uncertainty of the weeks to come was more than I could handle. "I just wish, for once, they would be the ones worried about disappointing us, because I'm tired of trying to live up to impossible standards. I'll never be good enough for any of them."

Keppler patted my knee, but he didn't say anything.

"I could have my pilot's license in no time," Max's approaching voice exclaimed. "I'll fly you and Rochelle and Keppler anywhere in the world. Where should we start?"

"If you fly a plane the way you drive a car, I'm not going anywhere with you." Todd didn't give Max a second to interrupt. "I'll drive us, safely on the ground, anywhere we need to go."

I rubbed my hands over my face and took a deep breath to compose myself.

"How do you plan to cross the ocean in a car?" Max, hair wet from his shower, leaned heavily on Todd as he hobbled toward us.

"I don't plan to cross the ocean at all." Todd helped Max to the other chair and lowered him into it. "If I can't drive to a place, I don't need to go there."

Max winked at me. "You have to cross the ocean to take Rochelle to Paris."

"Where are your crutches?" I ignored his comment. "You're supposed to be practicing with them."

Todd shook his head at Max. "He says they hurt his armpits."

"I've been using them all morning." Max shook out his hair with a hand, splashing little droplets of water in every direction. "My leg will be healed before I get used to them anyway."

"Lucky you," Keppler groaned. "It'll be a miracle if I can walk to the bathroom on my own or eat solid food by this time next month."

Although his doctor had determined his jaw wasn't broken, he said it hurt to chew, so he'd been eating mashed-up bananas and scrambled eggs. He excused himself to the next room while the rest of us ate pizza and hamburgers, and blushed every time he had to ask for help doing things a four-year-old could handle on his own.

"Look at it this way." Max leaned forward in his chair. "Once you get used to it, it'll be kind of nice having everyone take care of you. Just pretend you're a little kid or a really rich guy."

Keppler gave Max a disgusted look, and I stood. "I have to finish packing." I ruffled Keppler's hair and rushed to Audrie's room where I fell back on the bed.

My aunt would be back from running errands any minute, and I wanted to be calm in front of her. On one hand, she had promised that all of my problems would be solved if I came to New York with her. In reality, it had only complicated my life more, and I was upset I had given up everything just for her end of the deal to fall through. On the other hand, she had quit her job to stand with me, and I had to respect her for that. Despite everything, my aunt was in a good mood. She had made us breakfast in the morning and smiled as she made arrangements on the phone for a long stay away from her apartment. She was looking forward to returning to Maibe, and I didn't understand why.

"Rochelle, are you okay?" Todd asked from outside the half-open door.

"No." I sat up and slid to the edge of the bed. "Everything I say only makes Keppler more anxious, and I'm saying all kinds of things I don't mean. I yelled at Alexander. I told him to stay out of our lives, and now I want to take it all back, but he's gone."

"I'm sure he knows you didn't mean it." Todd walked to me and sat down.

"I can't pull myself together." A few tears trickled down my cheek, but I didn't care. "There's a new problem every minute, and everything's a mess . . ."

Todd's arms enveloped me and pulled me close to him. "When we get home, everything will calm down."

I leaned into him and closed my eyes. "I wish I could be more like Kinley. She knows how to handle problems, and she's good at everything. Just think about the successful life she'd have right now if she didn't have to deal with my messes. She shouldn't have come back for Kat and me."

"You know Kinley better than that. She never would have abandoned you." Todd paused. "She's missed you so much over the last four months, she won't even care why you got sent home. She'll just be happy to see you."

I sighed. "You're right." I sat up and dried my eyes with my sleeve. "We're going home and that's a good thing. Once I hug Kinley, everything will be okay."

"That's better. Now we just have to get through the flight." Todd smiled but his face tightened with worry.

"You're scared of flying to Nebraska, aren't you?" I asked. He'd been avoiding all subjects concerning flying, planes, and Max's new obsession with becoming a pilot ever since Audrie told us how we'd be getting home.

He nodded. "More accurately, I'm scared of crashing. How are the rest of you not panicking about that?"

I looped my arm through Todd's and took his hand. "According to Audrie, Sid flies all the time. He knows what he's doing. But if it helps, I'll hold your hand the entire time we're in the air."

He squeezed my hand. "That's the only part of the flight I'm looking forward to."

"I'll be a great pilot." Max's voice carried in from the other room. "I'll be able to fly planes upside down and everything."

Keppler laughed. "There's no way they're going to give you a license."

I felt myself smile. If Max could make Keppler laugh, there was still hope for all of us. "I'm just going to stay in here for a while, finish packing, and pull myself together. Can you take care of those two for me until Audrie gets back?"

"Of course." Todd stood and kissed the top of my head. "I promise everything will be okay."

After he left, I sat on the bed for several minutes. Refusing to give in to the exhaustion, I stood and walked to my pile of clothes that were discarded on a chair in the corner. I hadn't had time to think about laundry, but it didn't matter. I would have plenty of time for that when I got home. Picking up the shirts one by one, I folded them and flattened them into my already overstuffed bag. When I got to my jeans at the bottom of the pile, something bounced on the carpet, barely making a sound.

I leaned down and picked up the pendant I'd taken from Max's room and ran my fingers over the word "Optimus" written across the bottom. It was the fake version of what Keppler had identified as the missing pendant. Could I make it up to the TCI by using it to trick Molly somehow?

No. Audrie wasn't an agent anymore, and I never should have trusted the rest of the TCI. If there was a solution to be found, I would find it by myself. The door to the apartment slammed, and I rushed to my bag. I dropped the fake pendant into the front pocket with my hummingbird bracelet and zipped it shut just as Audrie entered the room.

"Hey, kiddo." She carried a grocery bag in her hand. "Why aren't you out there with everyone else?"

"I wanted to finish packing." I patted my bag. "I'm ready to go home."

"Me too. I can't wait to get out of here." Audrie tossed the bag onto the bed, and we watched boxes of granola bars and bags of cookies spill out. She had promised Max she would buy snacks for the trip. "I'm a little nervous though."

"You are?" I sat down and neatly stacked everything back in the bag. "Why?"

My aunt smiled, but her forehead wrinkled the way Kinley's always did when she was worried. "I didn't do a very good job of taking care of you and Charlie like I promised. And I know I've made a lot of mistakes I'm going to have to explain to Kinley and Kat. I'm not sure where to start."

"Start at the beginning. I'll help you," I said. "She'll understand the things that went wrong weren't your fault."

"I hope so." Audrie slid back and folded her legs under her. "But if she doesn't understand, I want you to know it's okay. If she doesn't want me to stay with you guys in Maibe, I'll find a hotel nearby. I don't want you to fight with her about that."

"I won't," I said. I knew Audrie wanted to make amends with Kat and Kinley. To be a family. "I'm sorry I gave Molly the passcodes. I swear I didn't know them until I talked it over with Todd, and I realized the bracelet—"

"It's okay. I didn't think of those nicknames either. That was clever of Auggie, like hiding it in plain sight." She patted my hand.

"I'm sorry about your job too." I looked down at my feet.

"Don't be. I was wrong about what I wanted, and I wish I would have figured that out a long time ago." She wrapped her arm around me and pulled me closer. "We have some tough stuff to face, but we'll get through it together."

I nodded. She and Todd were right. It would all turn out okay in the end. Still, my stomach and chest hurt. I knew home wouldn't be the place I remembered, but I didn't have the imagination to envision just how bad it could be.

# CHAPTER 31

# CHARLIE

*May 8, 2091*

After hours of travel, first on a plane and then on a train, my body was so stiff I could barely move. It took both Todd and Rochelle to pull me to my feet and maneuver me into the aisle of the train. I shuffled my feet forward, holding my breath against each bolt of pain that shot simultaneously up my leg and across my chest. My friends, sympathetic to my discomfort, moved at my pace, ignoring the stares of horrified passengers seeing my bruised, swollen face as I passed.

"Ready?" Rochelle asked when we finally reached the door.

I took a deep breath and nodded.

We followed Max, who maneuvered his way onto the platform using his crutches. Sid and Audrie were behind us. Although they didn't show it, I imagined they shared some of my anxiety since they would have to explain our predicament to Kinley, and Max's aunt and uncle. They had promised we would be safe, and we were proof they hadn't kept that promise.

Leaning heavily on Rochelle, I stepped off the train and back into Maibe. Since I'd left, all I wanted was to return to the house with a library and the family that loved me. But I was afraid I had proven myself to be the rotten person I thought I'd left behind.

"She's over there." Rochelle pointed to Emma, who was waving from a few feet down the platform. We lumbered toward her as she ran in our direction, meeting us halfway. Todd hugged her, then excused himself to help Audrie get our bags.

Emma studied Rochelle and me. She was smiling, but her face was tight with worry. "Charlie, what happened to you?"

I turned to Rochelle. She had been the one to call home, so I figured she had prepared Emma and Kinley for my very visible injuries.

"It was all so hard to explain over the phone." Rochelle glanced around us. "Where's Kinley?"

"She wanted to come, but she's still not feeling well." Emma fidgeted with her keys. "I told her I would bring you guys to her."

Rochelle's shoulder slumped under my arm. "She didn't tell me she was sick. She just said she had a headache."

Emma nodded. "Her headaches have been worse than usual over the last few weeks and unbearable since yesterday. She doesn't want me to tell you this, but she got the grade back for the big test she had on Friday, and she didn't score high enough to pass to the next level of her program."

"That can't be right." Rochelle's words were breathless, as if the air had been knocked out of her. "Kinley doesn't fail tests. Kinley doesn't fail at anything. She must be really sick."

Emma wrapped one arm around Rochelle. "I don't want you to worry. I just want you to be really gentle with her. Help me convince her to go see a doctor."

"Will she be okay?" My earlier worries evaporated and concern for Kinley gripped my heart.

"She will be now that you two are home. She's missed you so much." Emma reached for me. "Here, Rochelle, let me help you." Rochelle shifted my arm from her shoulder to Emma's, who wrapped her arm around me. "Don't worry, sweetie. If Kinley needs a few days to rest, I'll take care of you until she's feeling better."

"Hey, Rochelle." Max waddled over to us on his crutches. "Sid was wondering if he can drive me home in Alexander's truck. We're earlier than we expected, and my family isn't here yet."

"Yeah, of course." Rochelle reached into her pocket and pulled out the keys.

Max took the keys, and leaning on one crutch, enveloped Rochelle in a hug. "I'll call you tomorrow, okay? Kinley's going to be so happy to see you."

She just nodded. Neither of us had the strength to explain.

"Relax and let everyone take care of you, *hermano*." Max gave me the best one-armed hug he could manage. "It'll be weird not having you as a roommate, but I'll come visit as soon as my family will let me leave the house."

I nodded and watched Max propel himself toward Sid. By then my legs were wobbly from standing for too long, and the rest of my body ached even when I remained completely still. Finally, Audrie and Todd approached with the bags, and we all made our way to Emma's car.

"Did Kinley tell you she was sick when you talked to her yesterday?" Rochelle sat in the back seat between Todd and me.

"No." Audrie turned in her seat so she could see us. "She said she couldn't talk long, and she sounded a little tired. I gave her our travel schedule and told her I could explain everything else in person."

That meant Kinley had no way of knowing she was about to be bombarded with a whole new set of problems she never could have anticipated.

"Emma said her headaches have been worse." Rochelle rubbed her eye, and Todd gripped her free hand. She had been so strong through the constant turmoil of the past month, but she would be devastated if Kinley got worse.

Audrie reached back and patted Rochelle's knee. "Try not to worry until we talk to Kinley and figure out what's going on."

Memories of Kinley and Audrie arguing flashed through my head, and I wondered whether it was a good idea to bring her with us. Then again, maybe we needed her help.

Pushing all of that aside, I focused my attention on the familiar scenery out the window. The late-afternoon sky was covered by thick, dark clouds, but it wasn't raining. Everything in Maibe was as I remembered it, from the houses to the Main Street businesses. Even the Aumonts' house looked the same, with the big tree in the front yard and the wide path leading up to the glass doors of the dining room. But the sense of comfort and safety I'd usually felt had been replaced by anxiety and uncertainty.

"Can we go in first?" Rochelle jumped out of the car the minute Emma parked in the driveway.

"Go ahead, kiddo." Audrie pushed her door open. "I need a minute to talk to Emma. Todd, can you help with the bags?"

Rochelle rushed around the car and helped me to my feet, positioning my arm around her shoulders so she could support the weight I couldn't. As anxious as she'd been about coming home in the days leading up to our trip, she was equally eager to get inside. Forgetting about my injuries, she pulled me toward the back door so fast my muscles throbbed, but I didn't protest because I knew the queasy feeling in my stomach wouldn't stop until I saw Kinley.

When we reached the screen door, Rochelle pulled it open, pushed the storm door in, and helped me up the steps into the laundry room. In the usually bright, tidy kitchen, the shade was pulled, blocking out even the dim light from outside. The table was scattered with Kinley's books and notes, cups and coffee mugs cluttered the counter around the sink, and the radio muttered something about a special news report.

"Rochelle, is that you?" Kinley trudged into the room, holding her forehead in one hand. "There was something on the news about a train derailment, and I was so afraid you wouldn't make it home." She hurried to us, embracing Rochelle with one arm, and cupping my face with her free hand. "Charlie, they didn't tell me you were in such rough shape." Tears welled in the corners of her eyes. "I'm so sorry I couldn't keep you safe." Her eyes were sunken and outlined by dark circles. Her hair wasn't braided as usual but hanging loose and tangled down her back.

My breath hitched and I couldn't vocalize a reply. I had been prepared for Kinley to be angry and throw me out. Now I wished I were the one crying instead of her, but everything was out of my control.

"I have to tell you guys something. Promise you won't be disappointed?" She blinked away tears and waited for us to nod. "I've decided to quit my program. I don't want to be a doctor anymore."

"It's okay. I'm not disappointed." Rochelle's voice shook as she turned to me. She had wished earlier that the adults would be the ones worried about disappointing her, and now that it had come true, she wasn't happy about it.

Kinley took a step back and clutched her head in both hands. Her knees buckled, and Rochelle lunged forward to catch her. That left me stumbling backward, but a hand caught my elbow, steadying me before I lost my balance.

Audrie rushed past me and pulled a chair across the floor to Kinley.

"Here, Charlie." Todd slid the nearest chair back from the table with his foot and helped me lower myself into it. I hadn't even heard the others come in.

"Emma told us you've been having bad headaches." Audrie

knelt next to her niece's chair, speaking in a soothing voice as if Kinley were a three-year-old instead of an adult. "Can you tell me what hurts?"

"My head never stops throbbing," Kinley whimpered. "I always have headaches, but they've never hurt this bad before."

"What does that mean?" Rochelle sat on the floor next to Kinley's chair, clutching her cousin's hand, and choking back sobs.

"I don't know. Maybe I just need more sleep." Kinley's serious tone indicated she had imagined some scary possibilities.

"I'm sure that's probably all it is." Audrie's forehead wrinkled with worry, and she reached a shaking hand toward Kinley. "But maybe we should take you to the emergency room and get you checked out just in case."

"I can't leave now. Rochelle just got here." Kinley stroked her cousin's hair, failing to comfort her. "And I have to take care of Charlie."

"Rochelle can come with us, and Charlie will stay with Emma until we get back." Audrie slid her hands under Rochelle's elbows and pulled her to her feet. "Come on, Rochelle. Let's not jump to conclusions until the doctor tells us why her head is hurting."

I watched the people in the kitchen in a surreal, detached way, as if the events around me were a scene from a movie. Kinley stood, face pinched with pain, and reached for Rochelle. Audrie kept a hand on each of their shoulders, trying to comfort them with short, calming phrases as if they were too young to understand anything more complicated. For the first time it occurred to me that maybe Audrie still saw them as those little girls she had walked away from all those years ago when they needed her.

"You can take my car. Don't worry, I'll stay right here with Charlie until you guys get back," Emma said. She grabbed a napkin from the holder on the table and handed it to Rochelle, who was sobbing uncontrollably.

Audrie wrapped a supportive arm around Kinley and guided her to the door. Rochelle trailed behind, holding Kinley's hand and pressing the napkin to her face. With Emma, the four of them vanished through the door, leaving Todd and me in the kitchen.

Todd took a step toward the door as if he would follow them, then turned back to me and sank into the nearest chair. "I've never seen Rochelle cry like that before. Not even when we were little kids and she scraped her knees or fell off the monkey bars."

"It's been a bad week." I didn't like seeing Rochelle so upset, but she had every right to be. "If Kinley doesn't get better, Rochelle will blame herself. She's doing that already."

"What do you mean if Kinley doesn't get better?" Todd's voice rose in unusual annoyance. "She has headaches all the time."

"I lived here for almost a year, and I've never seen her have a headache like that." My voice broke and I cleared my throat. Kinley always had a plan. She always knew what to do, but this time she was as uncertain as the rest of us. "Have you?"

Todd shook his head and looked down at the floor.

"Returning to the breaking news of the train derailment outside Philadelphia," the radio droned in the silence. "The Defiance is now taking responsibility for setting up explosives on the railroad bridge. The train was bound from western New York, and we're just getting information that several state leaders were on board en route to a special meeting to discuss the next steps in dealing with the Defiance."

Todd looked at me, then sprang out of his chair and turned the volume all the way up.

"We can't yet report on the extent of the injuries or fatalities from this attack. All trains across the country have been halted until further safety assessments can be conducted—"

Todd snapped off the radio and turned to me, face drained of color. "Wasn't Alexander going to Philadelphia today?"

I couldn't breathe, so I nodded. The screen door slammed, and we both jumped.

"You two look like you've seen a ghost," Emma said. "What's wrong?"

"Emma." Todd took a step toward us, eyes wide like a little boy about to claim there were monsters under his bed. "There was a train accident on the news just now. We think it might be the same train Alexander was taking to Philadelphia."

"A lot of trains go to Philadelphia every day." She took a deep breath. "Let's not panic yet. Come on, Charlie. Let's get you somewhere more comfortable."

I let her help me into the living room where Todd moved books off the couch and piled all the pillows on one side. Emma eased me back against the pillows and propped my feet up on another pillow she took from the love seat. Todd switched on every light in the room and turned the TV to a news station.

An image of a toppled train, some of the cars scattered in a field, some dangling off a bridge, and others half submerged in a river filled the screen. One end of the bridge had completely collapsed into the water.

"This is the first Defiance attack to happen so far north, and the country is bracing for more," the newscaster reported. "All trains have been halted for at least the next two days while authorities work to determine the safety of thousands of miles of track. At this time, we have five confirmed fatalities with hundreds expected."

"Let's not listen to that until they've separated what they think they know from what actually happened," Emma said as she covered me with a light blanket. "I'm sure Alexander will call soon, and then we'll know what we can do to help him. When Kinley gets home, we'll know what we can do to help her. For now, we just have to focus on the things we can control."

Todd nodded and switched off the TV. "If Rochelle didn't come home, I would have gone to Philadelphia with Alexander."

"But you came home and you're safe." Emma turned and pulled him into a tight hug. She was facing the very real possibility of losing Kinley and Alexander, and yet she was calm and comforting us. "When Sid brings Alexander's truck over, I need you to pick up Lily from volleyball camp. I'll make us something to eat, and hopefully we'll have some good news by then."

Todd rubbed his hands over his face and nodded. "Charlie needs soft food. His jaw is still sore."

"I'm sure I can figure something out. I'll be in the kitchen if you guys need me. Say a prayer for Alexander and Kinley." She squeezed Todd's arm and kissed the top of my head, then she was gone.

"Maybe Alexander was in the part of the train that's still on the tracks." I tried not to move. Whatever Emma had done with the pillows had put me in a position that it didn't hurt to breathe. "Maybe Kinley was just so worried about Rochelle it made her headaches worse than usual."

"I hope so." He glanced at the black TV screen. "But that video on the news looked pretty bad, and Kinley could barely stand up. Rochelle said she argued with Alexander before he left Audrie's apartment, and she felt really bad about it. If he doesn't come home, she's not going to be able to handle it."

He was right. The situation appeared overwhelmingly hopeless. My earlier fears of being rejected by my family were suddenly small and manageable. The possibility that Alexander hadn't survived the derailment and Kinley was seriously ill were the likely nightmares.

"I don't think I can handle it either." Without Kinley and Alexander, I had no guardians and no guarantee of a home. I just wanted everything to be the way it was before I left. "Why couldn't he have just come home with us?" Without Alexander to fight for his proposal to give street kids an alternative to the Defiance, what hope was there to stop the war? We would all be under Defiance control by September.

"I don't know. This morning I thought the plane ride would be the worst part of the day." Todd sank into a nearby chair and gave me a sympathetic look. "I think Emma's right. For now, say a prayer and then try to get some rest. I'm sure we'll know more by the time you wake up, and things won't seem so bad."

I didn't know much about praying, but there was no one left to help me. Unsure of how to start, I closed my eyes and wrote a letter in my head.

*Dear God,*

*If you can hear me, please bring Alexander home safely and heal Kinley. I need both of them. If you help me this one time, I'll be a good person from now on. I'll never hurt anyone again. I'll even go to church with the Aumonts. I know I don't deserve your help, but Kinley and Alexander do. Please don't punish them for the bad things I've done. It's okay if they throw me out or if the TCI sends me to prison. All that matters is that my family is safe and together.*

Exhausted, I drifted toward sleep, holding on to the hope that by some miracle when I woke up Alexander would be home, Kinley would be sitting beside me, and Kat would be making breakfast. The TCI would drop their investigation, Rochelle and Max would be laughing in the next room, and this whole nightmare would fade behind us. I didn't want to lose hope, but I knew, whether my prayer was answered or not, everything was about to change.

# ACKNOWLEDGMENTS

A special thanks to Terri Leidich and everyone at BQB Publishing for their support in bringing my vision to life; to Andrea Vande Vorde for the clarity and support during the editing process; and to my family, friends, and students who cheer me on and inspire me to keep writing. I couldn't do this without all of you.

# ABOUT THE AUTHOR

**Vanessa Lafleur** is a high school English teacher and speech coach. She lives in Nebraska where she enjoys spending summer days outside and writing during her free time. Vanessa loves discussing literature with her students and helping them discover their writing talents. When she isn't teaching, she spends her time reading, gardening, taking graduate classes, and counting down the days to the next speech season. *Nothing Happens by Chance* is the fourth book in the *Hope for the Best* series. Find out more about Vanessa Lafleur at vanessalafleur.com, and follow her on Facebook @vanessalafleurauthor and Instagram @vlafleurauthor.

# OTHER BOOKS IN THE HOPE FOR THE BEST SERIES

Seventeen-year-old Lareina has no family, no home, and no last name. What she does have is an oddly shaped pendant and Detective Russ Galloway who would follow her across the country to take it from her.

Through her own resilience and wit, Lareina has survived her teenage years in a chaotic and crumbling world by stealing what she needs. Hoping to escape the detective and discover the truth about her pendant, Lareina flees the city.

On her journey she meets Nick and Aaron who remind her how much she has missed feeling a connection to other people. Together they learn survival is impossible unless they can learn to trust each other. With every mile they travel, Lareina races to escape the past and discover the truth.

The brand burned into Charlie's arm is a constant reminder that family doesn't exist, people only care about their own selfish interests, and a handful of pendants, if united, could lead to negative consequences for the entire world. All he wants is to escape his perilous past and the people who want him dead. By accident, he arrives in the small town of Maibe, Nebraska where he has the chance to change his life and start over.

Rochelle is trying to pick up the pieces and move forward after a year filled with loss and illness. She just wants to take care of her family, prevent her home from becoming a ghost town, and save the world if she has time. When an old friend shares secret information about pendants that could save millions of lives, she finds herself and everyone she loves plunged into a world more dangerous than she could ever imagine.

As it becomes clear that nothing happens by chance, Charlie and Rochelle must face the trauma of their pasts and work together to ensure tomorrow will be better for everyone.

Who can you trust when everyone is hiding something? After Charlie's worst fears of being discovered by the Defiance become a reality, he is forced to choose between protecting his family and being pulled back into the treachery he hoped he had escaped.

For Rochelle, the stakes are higher than ever and the pressure to finish what her dad started pulls her away from her family and friends.

In book three of the *Hope for the Best* series, Charlie and Rochelle must each prepare for the worst and accept the consequences of their actions before they lose everyone they love forever.